# VICTORIA'S
# SECRET

A NOVEL

## JASON POOLE

PUBLISHER'S NOTE:
This book is a work of fiction.
Names, characters, businesses, organizations, places,
events and incidents are the product of the author's imagination or are used fictionally.
Any resemblance of actual persons, living or dead, events, or locales is entirely coincidental.

Library of Congress Control Number: 2008923074

ISBN: 0-9794931-4-5

ISBN 13: 978-0-9794931-4-0

Cover Design: Davida Baldwin www.oddballdsgn.com
Editor: Carla Dean
Graphics: Davida Baldwin
Typesetting: Carla Dean
www.thecartelpublications.com

First Edition

**Printed in the United States of America**

# DEDICATION

This novel is dedicated to my newborn son "Elijah", his brother Lil Jason and my Dearest Comrade James "Fry Fowler"... whatever you do in life, do it well and Never Give-Up!!!

# ACKNOWLEDGEMENTS

I'd like to thank God and all those who supported me and my work. There are too many of you to name. You know who you are, and where you belong. Continue to support me and I promise to always deliver you Classic Novels...

To T. Styles and the entire Cartel staff. Thank you so much for Being "Real" and Supportive. Now's the Time to make an impact on The BookGame.

To the "Haters" Thank You so much for hating on my work. Its people like you who make me work harder with the strength to *"Never Give Up"*!!!

*What Up Babies,*

As you know in every novel we publish we'll include a letter to our fans. We do this not only for you to get a feel for what we're going through during the time we publish *each* story, but also to express what our readers mean to our company by writing to you directly.

I am extremely blessed and thankful for the success of *Shyt List* by Reign and *Pitbulls In A Skirt* by Mikal Malone and I look forward to the continued success of *Victoria's Secret* by Jason and *Poison* by K.D. Harris.

To all my readers and fans, who ask me what it takes to become successful as a writer I'd say this. *Focus on the work and the rest will follow.* Understand that the universe will bring you whatever your heart focuses on whether good or bad. If you continue to allow negative energy into your life, why are you surprised when it's still around? Learn the power of your mind and don't allow hate to consume you. If faced with it, walk away. Your life is what you make it! So the only question remains is, what will you do?

With that said, this letter is very special to me. The reason being, I have the pleasure of publishing a novel by the *great* veteran author Jason Poole. It is no secret that Jason, who has received GREAT success in his literary career, could've gone with any other publisher. His books have made the Essence Best Sellers list and his has fans adore him. And I'm confident that his fans both old and new will love the tale he's weaved within the pages of Victoria's Secret.

Lastly, as you know in every novel we publish, we pay homage to an author who has paved the way, or one we adore simply for his or her literary journey. So it is with great pleasure that we pay homage to:

# "KWAME TEAGUE"

Kwame is a great literary author. The *Dutch* series in undoubtedly one of the greatest works of our time. Kwame thanks for setting standards and we love what you do.

Lastly I would be remiss if I didn't thank my Cartel Pep Squad. We love these ladies because they do a stand up job of spreading the word around about our tales!

## "THE CARTEL PUBLICATIONS PEP SQUAD"

*Jessica aka "Lyric" (Squad Captain), Ms. Toya Daniels, Erica Taylor, Shawntress, Kim "Bookbabe" Gamble, Victoria "Tori" Johnson,
Lisa aka JSQueen625, Kariymah.*

Lastly I'd like to thank *The Cartel Street Team*. These guys are out there hitting up book stores and spreading the word around about our company on the streets!

And it is with great pride that I announce that the Street Team is headed up by Pep Squad member *Lisa aka JSQueen*. Lisa is the new Director of our Street Team and is instrumental in making sure the captains and their members remain energetic about our books. Want to become a street team member? Visit our website for details and join our family!

Until I hug you later......

Yours truly,

T.Styles, President & CEO, The Cartel Publications
www.thecartelpublications.com
tstyles@thecartelpublications.com

# PREFACE

I'd be lying if I told ya'll I didn't do anything to deserve this shit, but when you're living a certain lifestyle some things just go unsaid. Damn, look at me laying here all helpless and what not. I can't even move, let alone think straight. The last thing I can remember is that my life had just started to take a turn for the better. Everything was going perfect...too perfect to be exact. Then, all of a sudden, out of nowhere this shit happens. I don't even know where the hell I'm at. All I know is my profession is what got me here.

Now hold up, I know what you're thinking. Don't go pre-judging me. I'm not the one to blame here. I'm just a victim like everyone else, but I'm not trying to justify my actions either. First, please listen and analyze the facts before you go jumping to conclusions. I'm more than certain you'll understand. By the way, if you don't know by now, let me make it clear who I am and why I'm introducing myself to you. My name is Victoria, and these are my secrets.

So sit back, be quiet, and keep this shit between you and me.

# CHAPTER 1

## COMES AROUND, GOES AROUND

As he dodged in and out of traffic, the pearl white Mercedes-Benz AMG 600 looked like the NASA space shuttle while it forced its way up Pennsylvania Avenue at top speed. Babyface's adrenaline was pumping so hard that he didn't even notice he had ran two red lights in the process of trying to get to DC General Hospital. All types of thoughts raced through his mind. Something was wrong; something had happened; and he was determined to find out the answers to the questions what, who, and why. Just last night, everything was perfect. His whole world was like a gift from God. He'd been through so much drama at such a young age that he knew life itself had so much to offer...not just for him, but also for the love of his life, Victoria.

He didn't even bother putting on his hazard lights as he pulled the Benz into the emergency ramp reserved for ambulances only. As Babyface got out of his car and entered the emergency room, an elderly looking security guard dressed in a brown uniform, which made him think of the character from the hit TV series *Martin*, yelled out in the lobby, "Whoever is driving the white Mercedes is in violation of Code Section II of this hospital's rules! I would advise you to move it now, or else it will be towed!"

Babyface was in too much of a hurry to go back and park it. He loved his Benz, but he loved Victoria more. So, having his car towed would be the least of his worries. Instead of moving it, he ignored the security guard's warning and proceeded to the receptionist desk. Behind the counter sat a young, chubby, white girl

1

# VICTORIA'S SECRET

who looked like she had too many Twinkies and cupcakes in her lifetime. As she talked on the phone, Babyface eavesdropped for a second before interrupting.

"Excuse me, miss."

The receptionist put up her finger as if to say 'hold on', but Babyface wasn't going for it. From the way the conversation was going, he knew it was not a business call, but a personal one. Anger immediately overcame him, and his tone of voice changed from soft to hard, smooth to rough.

"Look here, you going to sit back on your fat, lazy ass and gossip all fuckin' day?"

The receptionist quickly hung up the phone and stood up in an attempt to hold her ground. "Now look, sir, you don't have to be rude. Can't you see that I was in the middle of a conversation?"

"Yeah, I see," said Babyface, "but I also can see that your conversation had nothing to do with your job. In all honesty, I just may have saved your job. What if I was your boss and overheard you gossiping on the phone to your girlfriend? You'd be standing in the nearest unemployment line."

Left speechless and defenseless, the receptionist evaluated his answer. This was one of many traits that made Babyface a "Don" in the pimp game, to leave a broad dumbfounded, and once he noticed he succeeded, he'd then take on an even smoother approach and move in for the kill.

Babyface looked her deep in the eyes, giving her a chance to examine his smooth caramel complexion with jet black curly hair, thick eyebrows, and neatly trimmed moustache. It wasn't by choice that one would give him the name "Babyface" because of his young looking features. Yet, in all honesty, he really did look like the singer Babyface.

"Now, look here, sweetheart. I'm sorry if I've offended you in any way. You're a very beautiful girl and I didn't intend to hurt your feelings, but I had to find some way to get your undivided attention. Please understand that I'm very upset right now and in a state of oblivion. Something terrible has happened to my fiancée.

She was admitted here last night, and I'm just now finding out about it."

The girl blushed slightly at Babyface's plea for forgiveness. Also, the compliment at being called a beautiful girl coming from a man as handsome as himself made her more available to his needs than anyone else that had ever approached her desk.

"I do understand, sir. Now what's your fiancée's name?" she said as she tried to hide the hardness of her nipples.

"Her name is Victoria Gray."

"Hold on for a second." She looked over the roster for all those admitted last night, and after reading that diagnostics for Victoria Gray, she look down at the floor with a sad expression. You could tell she wanted to hold something back, or at least not be the one to bear him the news.

Babyface sensed something was wrong. "Is she here?"

"Yes, sir, she was admitted in the intensive care unit last night. She's on the fourth floor in room 419. I'll call up there and tell the head nurse you're on your way up. She'll give you the full details of what is happening with your fiancée."

Babyface didn't even bother to thank her as he dashed off to the nearest elevator. As the elevator moved its way up to the fourth floor, the butterflies began to build even more. He was a nervous wreck. He couldn't imagine what had happened. He began to talk to himself. "Intensive care? Who the fuck violated like that? I told Vickie she didn't have to go out last night. Only if she wasn't so damn naive, this probably would have never happened."

For a moment, he contemplated on praying to God, asking Him to spare her life. But then his reality kicked in. Babyface didn't believe in God. To him, if there was a God, he always felt God neglected him and his whole life. Therefore, it would be useless to ask that He accept his prayers now.

*Bing!* The elevator door opened, and for the first time in his life, Babyface was overcome with fear. He feared the worst; he feared for Victoria, the only person he had ever loved in this world. The complete silence of the floor made the beeps from the various life-support machines sound louder than a taxi's horn in rush hour traffic. He wanted to go to sleep and wake up just to say he was having a bad dream, but he couldn't. This was real. He'd been through the worst of things in his life, and faced every crisis fearless, independent, and upright, but for some odd reason, this time he couldn't. This time was different. This was true love.

"Excuse me, sir. May I help you?" asked the elderly white nurse in the softest tone of voice.

"Ahh, yes, ma'am. My fiancée was admitted to this unit last night."

"Oh, you must be the young fella the receptionist just called about."

"I believe I am."

"Let me make sure I'm correct. Gray is your fiancée, right?"

"Yes, ma'am."

"Okay. Well, I'm her nurse. My name is Ms. Winters. Now before you go in, I wanna give you a full brief of what's going on with your fiancée, okay?"

"Do I need to sit down, Ms. Winters?" asked Babyface.

"I believe so, sir. Now before you go in, I want to advise that you don't make any loud outbursts. She needs to be as settled as possible."

"Why is that, Ms. Winters?"

"Well, your fiancée is in a very deep coma. She has external bleeding in the skull and her throat has been cut seven inches. She has lost almost ten pints of blood, and her membrane is constantly swelling. To be honest with you, sir, your fiancée is barely making it. All we can do for her is to hope the swelling stops."

"So you're telling me no doctor can stop the swelling?"

"Well see, it's very complicated. If they do surgery on her brain, most likely she'll die because the vessels aren't functioning. Right now, she's only living on the blood flowing from her heart."

The information Ms. Winters provided was too painful for Babyface to bear. For the first time in almost twelve years since juvenile detention, tears streamed down his face like a waterfall.

Nurse Winters placed her wrinkled, soft hand on top of Babyface's manicured hands, and in a soft, subtle, sincere voice, she began consoling the disturbed young man. From her experience, one would note she'd been doing this type of work for a very long time.

"Now, sir, what she needs from you is to be strong. Although it may seem like there's little hope, we still have faith in God. Put your trust in the Lord. The Lord is merciful."

He wasn't for all this "put your trust in the Lord" stuff, and he didn't believe in God. If He existed, then why in the fuck did He create this cruel ass world? Babyface was a warrior, and the world had made him like that. He then stood up fearless, independent, and upright, and wiped his tears away. He almost felt embarrassed to let someone see him cry. Crying wasn't for him. He was a pimp and he PIMPED HARD!

"Okay, thank you, Ms. Winters. Can I go in to see her now?"

"Yes, you can, but before you go in, let me give you her belongings."

The nurse returned and handed Babyface a plastic bag which contained what little items Victoria had left. He could tell by the size of the bag that most likely the paramedics that found Victoria had stolen her valuable jewelry, as well as her full-length, snow white, chinchilla fur coat. He solemnly took hold of the bag as the nurse escorted him down the hall to Victoria's room. Once outside the room, he stopped for a second to take a deep breath before entering. Then, as he proceeded to open the door, the nurse interrupted to tell him one last thing.

"Oh, sir, one more thing."

"What's that, Ms. Winters?"

"I forgot to tell you that two detectives were here earlier, and since there wasn't anyone here to claim Ms. Gray, I had to turn her driver's license over to them. Most likely they'll be coming back to check up on her. When they were here, they did go in, but for the life of me, I don't know why. After all, she is in a coma and unable to answer any questions."

"Well, Ms. Winters, you know how police are. They probably

had to go see for themselves."

"Yeah, those damn people make me sick. They don't care anything about the victim. All they want is some type of information."

It was kind of funny to Babyface to hear this sweet old lady talk in that fashion. In fact, it eased his tension just a bit. Babyface forced a light smile and thanked Ms. Winters. She then proceeded down the hall to attend to another patient. As he walked in, the sight of Victoria hooked up to so many tubes and IVs was unbearable, along with the annoying sound of the life-support system that constantly beeped in rapid rhythm, letting him know that she was still alive but barely making it. As he sat down next to her, he began to talk in a light whisper, hoping and wishing she would hear his voice and suddenly snap out of her coma.

"Hey, baby. Damn, what happened to you? How did I let this happen to you? Baby girl, I'm sorry for failing you. I should have been there with you, and then none of this would have happened. Vickie, you can't die on me. You're all I have in this world. You and me, remember? Pull through for Daddy. You're a warrior. I know you can do it. Tomorrow's my birthday, remember? I know you want to be there with me to celebrate. We still gonna do our thang just like old times, but baby girl, I need you to pull through for me like you always do. Don't fail me now."

As he continued to talk, he could see that his attempts at waking his sleeping beauty were of no avail. He leaned back in his chair, took a deep breath, and closely observed the room. As he looked around, he noticed he had placed her belongings on the floor next to him. Babyface wondered for a second if Victoria had pulled any tricks last night for old time's sake. Also, he wondered if she had any clue as to what happened to her and her belongings.

He opened the bag to pull out her blood-stained Gucci blouse with matching skirt. As he checked the pockets, he knew most likely nothing would be in them. As he folded her clothes and placed them back in the bag, he noticed her Gucci pocketbook was open, yet it looked like something was still inside. He picked it up, turning it upside down and dumping its contents onto the floor.

Mascara, condoms, and other knick-knacks that most women carry in their purses fell out. Giving it one last hard shake, something heavy fell out and hit the floor with a thud. To him, it looked like a small book, maybe a Bible or thick ass address pad. At the very thought of addresses, he quickly picked it up, hoping to find something that could help him understand what had happened.

*Damn, this is a thick ass address book,* he said to himself. Babyface opened it, and thanks to his curiosity, he was faced with the shock of his life. It was Victoria's personal diary, something she kept from Babyface. It was her true life, her story, a diary of a hoe. He picked it up and began to read, but before he flipped to the first page, he leaned over to Victoria, held her hand in his palms, and gently planted a kiss upon her forehead.

"Whatever's in this diary, I swear I will never hold it against you. I love you, baby girl."

He then began his journey into a world of pain, hate, and love…the story of Victoria, his best hoe, the baddest bitch on the East Coast, a pimp's dream hoe.

# CHAPTER 2

## DADDY'S LITTLE GIRL

*Ever since I could remember, my whole life has been a tragedy. My only joy was taken away from me at the tender age of nine, when I was too young to understand, but yet old enough to remember.*

**O**ctober 30th: Victoria had just come home from one of the happiest days she ever had in 4th grade. It was the day she entered into a lifestyle that would one day be her most valuable profession.

In class, Victoria was one of the most bright and prettiest girls. All the teachers loved her charm, and the boys loved her aggressive style. At nine years old, most kids wouldn't even worry about having their hair neatly done and clothes perfectly matched. However, every night before bed, Victoria made sure her mother, Diane, combed her hair and plaited it in two long ponytails. She also made sure Diane picked the perfect outfit for the next day of school. She would arrange which color barrettes she would wear to match her outfit, as well. Diane had no problem with assisting her daughter's every need. In fact, Diane catered to Victoria. Not because of a mother's love, but mostly because Victoria knew things about her mother that her Daddy didn't.

At recess time, all the kids went outside on the playground after eating lunch. Victoria and her friends Linda and Tanya were playing jump rope and having the time of their lives, when all of a sudden, the baddest boy in school, Derrick, jumped in the middle of the rope right when Victoria was about to leap in.

"Boy, will you get outta the way wit ya ugly self," said Vickie.

"Shut up, girl. Who you callin' an ugly?" said Derrick.

Instantly, she got up in his face as his buddies egged him on. "Oooh, Derrick, she's all up in your grill."

"I'm calling you ugly wit ya big lip self," she replied.

"Girl, I'll smack you."

"Yeah, and I'll kick your butt."

"Oooh, Derrick, what you gonna do?" said one of his buddies.

Derrick didn't want to fight Victoria. He secretly liked her, and really wanted to kiss her. That had been his fantasy ever since she was enrolled in his school. Derrick had a secret crush on her, but it was not much of a secret to Victoria. After all, she was the prettiest girl in class, with her light-skinned features and golden brown hair.

"Boy, just get out my face."

"Make me get out your face."

Derrick then pushed her and ran around the side of the school. Immediately, Victoria took chase after him, while the other kids laughed. Linda and Tanya were scared of Derrick, so instead of helping Victoria chase him, they just yelled out, "Get him, girl!"

As Derrick reached the side of the school, he looked around to make sure there were no teachers or other kids in sight. As Victoria caught up with him, she proceeded to push him back.

"Girl, what's wrong wit you?"

"Why you push me, Derrick?"

"'Cause."

"'Cause what?"

"'Cause I like you."

"Boy, you stupid. I don't like your ugly butt."

"Why?"

"'Cause I don't, that's why."

Derrick reached into his pocket, pulled out a piece of bubble gum, and began to unwrap it. Victoria wanted some bad, but didn't know how to ask.

"Why you looking at me all crazy like that, girl?"

"'Cause I want a piece of bubble gum."

"Sorry, this is my last one. Plus, you don't like my ugly butt, remember?"

Instantly, Victoria worked her charm. "Boy, I was just playing with you."

"Well then, why don't you be my girlfriend?"

"Do you have bubble gum all the time?"

"No, not all the time."

"Well, that's why I'm not your girlfriend. You gotta have it all the time."

"Well, I got this one piece left."

"Let me have it, Derrick."

"No."

"Please."

"No."

"Okay…what if I give you a kiss? Can I have it then?"

Derrick smiled at the thought of kissing Victoria. To him, that was better than her being his girlfriend. After all, he wouldn't have to admit to his friends that he liked Victoria.

"Okay, give me a kiss then."

Derrick puckered his big lips and closed his eyes, only to receive a light smack.

"Girl, what's wrong with you? Why did you hit me?"

"Derrick, I'm not kissing you until you give me the bubble gum first."

"Shucks, girl, all you had to do was say so. You ain't have to smack me. "

"I'm sorry, said Victoria as she held out her hand to receive the gum."

"Here. Now, where's my kiss?"

Victoria looked around to make sure no one was looking.

"Okay, close your eyes."

Derrick closed his eyes once again and poked his lips out, only to receive a small peck. As he stood there waiting for more, Victoria took advantage of the opportunity to go back to jumping rope with her girlfriends. After a few seconds, Derrick opened his eyes in disappointment to see Victoria running back to the playground.

*Man, she tricked me,* he said to himself.

═══════════

After reading the first two pages of her diary, Babyface couldn't help but laugh at the fact that Victoria, his best hoe, turned her first trick at the age of nine. He placed his hand on top of hers and whispered in her ear, "I see why you were the best hoe in the game, baby girl. You knew what you was doing from the very start, huh?"

As he was still talking to his sleeping beauty, Ms. Winters quietly entered the room. Babyface removed his hand from Victoria's and asked, "Is something wrong?"

"Oh no, baby. You go right ahead and continue consoling her. I'm just here to check her IV, and then I'm going. How 'bout you? Are you okay?"

"Yes, ma'am."

"Do you want some of this nasty hospital food?"

"No, thank you, Ms. Winters. I'm cool."

"Okay, then I'll be back later to check on her again."

"Okay," said Babyface.

After she left the room, Babyface buried his head back into Victoria's diary and continued to read.

═══════════

Coming home from school and seeing Randy, the neighborhood drug dealer, sitting in her living room was no surprise to Victoria. In fact, it became a regular thing while Victoria's father, Toney, was at work down at the Exxon gas station fixing on somebody's battered car. It was so normal that whenever Victoria came home, she would acknowledge Randy by saying hello, and then proceed to her room without saying a word to her mother. Before she would disappear, though, Randy always had a piece of candy for her.

This was her and her mother's little secret. Victoria never talked about it to no one, and for that, Diane spoiled Victoria rotten, giving her what she wanted when she wanted it.

Once inside her room, she would throw away the candy Randy gave her and turn on the cartoons. Victoria never came out of her room while Randy was there. Sometimes, she would have to urinate in a cup just so she wouldn't have to interrupt whatever they were doing.

On this particular evening, something was going on out there that didn't seem right to Victoria. Most of the times when Randy was there, she would hear them laughing, and on some occasions, she'd hear soft moans and groans. But today, she heard something that sounded like a loud cry. As she turned down the television and put her ear to the door, she could hear her mother trying to muffle her cries.

Victoria was curious and couldn't take it anymore, so she quietly cracked her door to see what was going on in the living room. As she peeped out, Victoria saw something she could never understand. Her mother was in a doggy-style position with her head sunk deep in the sofa pillow, screaming out as if she was in pain. She couldn't help but notice Randy pumping at least ten full inches of raw meat into her mother's asshole. At the sight of this gruesome act, she hurried and shut her door, burying her face in her own pillow to hide the disgusting hate she had for her mother.

Sometimes she thought about telling her father. But then, she feared her parents would split, or else somebody would get hurt behind her mother's devious acts.

After Randy left, Diane called Victoria out of her room for dinner.

Victoria opened her bedroom door. "I'm not hungry."

Diane sensed something was wrong. "Why aren't you hungry?"

"'Cause I'm not."

"What's wrong?"

"Nuthin'," Victoria snapped.

Diane got angry as she sipped on her glass of Hennessey. "Okay, starve then. Act just like your stupid-ass father...stubborn as shit."

With that, Victoria closed her door, cut the lights off, climbed into bed, and pretended to be sleep just so she wouldn't be annoyed by her mother's drunkenness. She hated being home alone with Diane.

———

Babyface stopped reading for a short second to watch Victoria's life-support machine beep. He then looked over at her. "Damn, baby girl, moms was a hoe, too, huh? I see why you turned out like this. That shit runs in your blood. Pops must wasn't doing something right." He lightly laughed at her mother's infidelity. This was nothing new to him. After all, he was a pimp, and it was his duty to understand a woman's desire.

———

Later on that night, Victoria's father came home only to find his wife in a drunken rage. As soon as he walked in the door, the fighting began.

"Now where the fuck you been at, nigga?" Diane asked in a slurred voice.

"I was at work, but I see you been drinking."

"Fuck you, Toney! I hope your broke ass brought some money home. We got bills, you no-good motherfucker."

Toney was tired from working all day, and wasn't in the mood for fighting, not tonight. All he wanted was to eat his dinner and go to bed.

"Look, Diane, I ain't for no fighting tonight. Now where's my dinner, woman?"

"Fuck you, nigga! Make it yourself!"

"C-mon now, Diane, why the fuck you gotta get drunk all the time?"

Toney then went back to Victoria's room and peeped in on her to make sure she was asleep. She was his baby girl, and the only thing that mattered to him was her. He worked hard so he could save up enough money to put her through college. He didn't want his baby girl growing up having to fuck with different niggas just to get by. He wanted something better for her. He didn't want her having to live in the projects like this shit-hole apartment they lived in on Clifton Terrace. All his life he lived in Washington DC's slums. He didn't want Victoria to turn out like her mother, either, for he knew when he first met her that Diane was no good. She was the neighborhood freak, but like always, a nigga gets the best pussy he ever had in life along with some mind-blowing head and he forgets everything in her past and falls in love, thinking he can change a bitch into the woman of his dreams.

When he met Diane, she was already two-months pregnant by some other nigga. By the time he found out, it was too late for her to get an abortion. Toney loved Diane, but he couldn't bear the fact of marrying her and raising a child that was not his.

At that point in Diane's life, she needed Toney. He was the only man to ever love her. Although she never really loved him, she knew if she played the housewife role, he would be satisfied, and to add, Toney was easily manipulated by her persuasiveness.

When Toney proposed to Diane, he gave her a choice that would ultimately change the way she felt about him. Whatever love she had for him instantly turned into hate, and this is what drove her to heavy drinking. Toney gave her the choice of putting up her firstborn for adoption or being happily married to a man who would provide for her every need. After months of deciding, Diane had no other choice. For one, she was poor. For two, she didn't even know the real father of the child. And three, she had a hidden cocaine addiction that needed to be supported by a constant cash flow. Diane snorted at least two grams of coke a day. Therefore, there was no way she would be able to provide for an infant child in this cruel ass world. Even though she wanted her firstborn, she knew if she made the decision to keep it, she would lose Toney. So instead, she chose to live in hate than to live with struggle. Three years later, Diane was pregnant again, but this time it was her husband's child…the child he had prayed for…a beautiful little girl, Victoria.

After looking in on Victoria, Toney went back into the living room and poured himself a drink.

"Nigga, don't be drinking up my shit. You ain't pay for it."

"Oh yeah? Well, if I didn't, who did?" asked Toney.

"None of your fucking business, nigga!"

"Goddamn, Diane, why the fuck you gotta keep talking to me like that? I do everything in my power to keep my house in order, and there you go always getting drunk and shit, trippin' all the time about nuthin'."

"Fuck you, nigga! You don't do shit but go to work wit the rest of them low-life ass niggas, and then come home wit your dirty, greasy ass smelling like the zoo. You come in here and sit down, thinking somebody supposed to cater to your ass."

"I pay the bills around this muthafucker, don't I?"

Toney's remark left Diane dumbfounded. "Fuck you, Toney! You fucked my life up!"

"How I fuck your life up? I saved your life, if anything."

"Bitch nigga, you ain't save my life. You made me give up my firstborn for your sorry ass. That was the biggest mistake of my life."

"C-mon, Diane, every time you get drunk, you wanna bring this bullshit up. If that's the case, why you ain't stay with the nigga who got you pregnant? Oh, I forgot. You was so much of a hoe you didn't know who he was."

"Fuck you, bitch nigga. I know who my child's father was."

By this time, Toney had drunk so many shots of Hennessey that he, too, was in a drunken rage. "Yeah, well, maybe he ain't know

**15**

if it was his child since you was out fuckin' the whole entire DC."

"Oh yeah, nigga. Well, answer this. How the fuck do you know if Victoria is your child?

Instantly, Toney got up. "So what you saying, Diane?"

"Muthafucka, I'm saying don't sweat yourself. You just might be taking care of another nigga's child."

With all the commotion going on, Victoria woke up and put her ear to the door. She couldn't believe the words coming from her mother's mouth. If Toney wasn't her father, then who was?

"Bitch, I'll kill your drunk ass!"

"Nigga, you ain't gonna do shit! You's a punk...always was and always will be. Matter of fact, you can't fuck a lick, either."

"So what, you getting it from somewhere else? You suckin' on somebody else's dick?"

"I might as well, 'cause yours don't taste like nuthin', you dirty dick ass nigga!"

"Fuck you, Diane!"

"Nah, nigga. How about Randy fuck me, just like he did earlier when you was at work. Yeah, nigga, Randy got a big-ass dick. He fucked me in my ass right here in this living room while your so-called daughter was in her room watching television."

Quickly, Toney got up and grabbed Diane's neck, choking her with all his might. Diane's fingernails sank deep into his eyeballs as he tried to choke the life from her.

"Ahhh, bitch! I'ma kill you!"

Toney released his grip, and as she dashed in the kitchen for a knife, he went into the bedroom to retrieve his revolver. Through the commotion, Victoria cracked open her door, fearing something bad was going to happen. As Toney emerged from the room with his loaded .38, Diane was coming out of the kitchen with the biggest butcher knife she could find. As they faced each other in the middle of the living room, it looked like a Mexican standoff. Diane pulled the knife up in a striking position, while Toney pointed his revolver at her.

"Put the knife down, bitch!"

"Fuck you, nigga! You ain't gonna shoot nuthin'. You's a bitch ass nigga!"

"Put it down, Diane!"

"Fuck you, Toney!"

"Bitch, I swear to God if you don't put that knife down, I'ma blow your fuckin' brains out!"

Diane never took Toney serious, so why should she now? With that, she plunged forward, and at the same time, he was pulling the trigger, Victoria was running out of her room.

"Noooo, Daddy, noooo!"

It was too late. Toney's bullet ripped straight through Diane's skull. As Diane lay dead in the middle of the floor with her brain matter plastered on the wall, Victoria looked directly into her father's eyes. "Why, Daddy? Why?"

The question couldn't be answered. Victoria was too young to understand. So instead, Toney looked his daughter in her eyes and placed the revolver in his mouth.

"I'm sorry, Victoria. I love you," were his last muffled words before he pulled the trigger.

---

Babyface looked at Victoria, who was still in her coma. "Damn, baby girl, you witnessed that crazy ass shit? How you manage to main'tain your sanity after all that? When I first met you, you did say it was hell for you growing up, but never could I imagine you going through all this."

He got up and planted another kiss on her forehead.

"You're a warrior, baby girl. I know this for sure. Now, c-mon and wake up for Daddy. I need you, just like you need me."

# CHAPTER 3

## BABY GIRL'S LOSS

After the tragic loss of her parents, child protective services admitted Victoria into her first group home, since her parents' extended family wouldn't accept her. The neglect from her so-called grandmother on her father's side made Victoria feel like what her mother said about her being another man's child was true. And the neglect from her aunt Sheila on her mother's side, who claimed it would be too expensive to bring another child in her home, made Victoria think no one in the world ever loved her besides her father.

The House of Love group home sat at the top of 16th and Park Road NW, not too far from Clifton Terrace where Victoria used to live. After hours of counseling from Ms. Nancy, the group home's supervisor, Victoria was escorted upstairs to her newfound home. Once inside the dorm, Ms. Nancy proceeded to introduce Victoria to the other girls who would be sharing her room.

"Okay, everybody, this is Victoria, and she will be staying with us for a while. Penny, I want you to show her around, explain all the rules, and be downstairs for dinner by six-thirty."

"Alright, Ms. Nancy," Penny replied.

Before Ms. Nancy left the room a loud, husky voice came from a girl hidden behind a partition in the back. "I hope she ain't sleeping down here by me."

"Now, Liddia, I run this place, and I say whatever bed is open she can choose. I don't want any trouble out of you tonight. You're already on T.V. restriction," said Ms. Nancy.

Liddia smacked her lips being sassy, but didn't say anything in response.

After Ms. Nancy left, Penny introduced herself. "Hi, Victoria, my name is Penny."

"Her name ain't Penny. Don't listen to her; she's crazy," the husky voice said.

"Whatever, Liddia," Penny replied.

Liddia was the biggest, oldest, and baddest girl at the House of Love. She taunted everybody new until she got comfortable getting to know them. "Girl, you know you crazy. You be hollering in your sleep and talking to yourself."

Penny was so embarrassed and offended at Liddia's remarks, she wanted to run and punch her in the face, but she knew she was not match for Liddia. "Yeah, whatever, Liddia," Penny simply responded.

"Yeah, I thought so, with your crazy self."

Penny just rolled her eyes and smacked her lips.

After introducing Victoria to the other girls, Penny then took her to the back of the room and introduced her to Liddia. As they walked down the aisle to Liddia's bed, Victoria caught butterflies, being somewhat scared of the girl with the husky voice and rude manners. She wondered what Liddia looked like, if she was as big as her mouth, and more importantly, if Liddia would accept her. As they got closer to her bunk, Victoria took a deep breath and put on her toughest game face, hiding all of her fears. Whoever this girl was, Victoria was prepared to stand up to her.

As they approached Liddia's bed, her back was turned away from them. Victoria then stuck out her hand, and in a friendly, soft, subtle voice, she attempted to introduce herself.

"Hi, my name is Victoria. I'm nine years old and in the fourth grade."

"Shut up! You probably crazy, too!" Liddia spat before turning around to face Victoria.

Victoria couldn't believe her eyes. Liddia was pretty, tall, caramel complexion, hazel eyes, and long, jet black hair. Victoria wondered how someone so pretty on the outside could be so ugly on the inside. Victoria immediately stood up to Liddia.

"If I'm crazy, then you must be crazy too, because if you weren't, you wouldn't be here."

With that, everybody in the room started laughing. They couldn't believe this little light-skinned girl was standing up to Liddia. Instantly, Victoria became their hero.

Liddia jumped off the bed and got up in Victoria's face. "Little girl, I'll smack the shit out of you. Get smart with me again."

"I wish you would put your hands on me. I ain't scared of you."

As Liddia was raising her hand to hit her, Victoria peeped Liddia's curling iron that was lying on the bed, and at the same time Liddia smacked her, she instantly picked up the curling iron and gave Liddia the shock of her life. Victoria was so upset that she couldn't stop swinging. She was visualizing Liddia as her mother. This is what she wanted to do to Diane for cheating on her father.

As the fight pursued Ms. Nancy heard the commotion and the egging on from the other girls and hurried upstairs to break up the fight. She couldn't believe someone had the guts to fight Liddia back. Although inside Ms. Nancy was proud of Victoria, she still had to go by house rules and punish both girls accordingly. From what just happened, though, she knew she was going to have a problem with Victoria.

———————————

Babyface put down the diary and smiled at Victoria. He once again kissed her forehead. "That's right, baby girl, never back down from no one." He then began to wonder if that was one of the reasons why she was laying in a coma now, because she hadn't backed down from a trick. He vowed to Victoria that whoever was responsible for causing her injuries would not live to tell about it.

He then picked up the diary and continued to read. Victoria's story was getting very interesting. Her childhood at the group home reminded him and how it was for him growing up in a juvenile detention center. He was proud of Victoria. She came up hard like he did, and this is why she was his best hoe.

---

After a few years at the group home, the girls had established themselves a friendship, especially Victoria, Liddia, and Penny. They became inseparable. Although Victoria was feisty and had the heart of a lioness, which made Liddia respect her even more, Liddia still remained the leader, mostly because she was a few years older than the others. Penny was still the quiet follower, even though she secretly admired Victoria the most. She openly admired Liddia only to gratify her ego.

Penny was self conscious. She was pretty, but in her own silent way. Compared to Victoria and Liddia, Penny always thought she was ugly and fat. Penny was a little overweight for her age, had short hair, and was dark skinned, with a long burn mark on the left side of her face, courtesy of her abusive mother who threw a hot iron at her for coming home late from school. Although Victoria would always tell her that she was pretty, Penny still thought of herself as nothing...worthless...worth nothing more than a Penny.

On the weekends, the girls were paid a twenty-dollar allowance for doing their chores. Since Penny was the master thief, instead of spending money on clothes that Penny could easily get for them with her "five-finger" discount, the three of them would sometimes go to the movies or to their favorite hangout spot down at the Golden Dome arcade located on 14th Street in the heart of downtown Washington D.C. The Golden Dome is where all the hip teenagers hung out at, and was considered heaven on earth for troubled teens, runaways, and soon-to-be drug dealers, pimps, and prostitutes.

Also, 14th Street became the pussy Mecca for Washington D.C. after eight o'clock in the evening. One of the most talked about hoe strolls in the United States of America, mostly because it was located right down the street from the prestigious White

House, 14th Street attracted all hoes of life, from pimps to politicians from petty thieves to neighborhood kingpins. But for Victoria, Penny, and Liddia, 14th Street is where they went to admire the hoes. They admired their style of dress and their beauty. Some even looked good enough to be cover models for Essence Magazine.

While they admired hoes, they resented the pimps. They hated to see pimps jump out of their big cars, wearing their suits, smacking their hoes just because she stopped walking to rest her feet.

Out of all the whores on 14th Street, there was one hoe that Victoria admired the most, Precious. She was tall, dark skinned, very pretty with long black hair, and stood out from the rest, as she sort of resembled the gorgeous cover model Naomi Campbell. When Precious walked down the hoe stroll, all traffic stopped. She was the Queen of 14th Street, and she wore her crown well.

Precious was Victoria's hero. Precious didn't take shit from nobody. Once, Victoria saw Precious beat up two hoes at the same time, and she still came out unscratched. Even though Victoria didn't like the fact that Precious sold her body for money, she still had to admit to herself she did it well.

# CHAPTER 4

## LOST & FOUND

*My 12<sup>th</sup> birthday was the first outside visit I had ever since I've been admitted to the House of Love. Other than Penny and Liddia, the only other family I knew was Ms. Nancy. So, naturally, it wasn't just a shock to hear that I had a visitor. I also was scared, and curiosity itself almost killed me...*

As Victoria was doing Penny's hair, Liddia came running upstairs to their dorm, with a frightened look on her face. She tried to catch her breath and explain what she just witnessed.

"Ah, y'all. Ah, y'all, hold on a sec." Liddia then took a deep breath.

"Damn, bitch, what's wrong? You act like you just saw a ghost," said Victoria.

"Calm down, Liddia. You're scarring me," said Penny. Now what's going on?"

"Ah, y'all, I was just downstairs with Ms. Nancy and this lady just came in talking about she was here in regards to Victoria Grey."

"Who?!" said Victoria and Penny at the same time.

"You," answered Liddia, as she pointed her finger at Victoria.

"Are you sure you heard Victoria's name and not somebody else's name?" asked Penny in her soft, whiney voice.

"Yeah, I'm sure. I know what the fuck I heard."

Penny turned to Victoria. "Who could that be, Victoria?"

"I don't know. Y'all are the only family I got, unless it's one of my teachers from school."

"Nah, she doesn't look like a teacher. Maybe she's from Child Protective Services," Liddia said.

"Why would they be coming to see Victoria after all this time?" Penny asked. "Shit, we've been here longer than Victoria, and ain't nobody from Child Protective Services come and see us."

"What she look like?" asked Victoria.

"She's kind of skinny, light-skinned, and she's wearing some type of work uniform. To be honest, she looks like a retired crack head," Liddia comments.

Penny turns to Victoria, with a look of curiosity. "Who in the world could it be? Do you know anybody that fits that description?"

Victoria hunched her shoulders. "Not really."

While the girls were talking, Ms. Nancy came upstairs. As the girls studied Ms. Nancy's facial expression, they could tell she was upset.

"Well, Victoria, somebody's downstairs to pick you up."

"Who? Why? Ms. Nancy, I don't want to go nowhere."

"I'm sorry, Victoria. I tried my best to keep you here, but it's out of my hands. She has a court order to take full custody of you."

"Noooo!" cried Penny. "Noooo! You can't leave us, Victoria. Please, Ms. Nancy, do something."

As Ms. Nancy looked up at the girls, this was the first time they'd ever seen her cry. Ms. Nancy was devastated. After all those years of taking care of Victoria, she felt as though she had given birth to her. "Penny, I feel the same way you do, baby, but like I said it's out of my hands."

"Fuck that!" said Liddia. "She ain't going anywhere!"

"Now, Liddia, I know you're mad, but you're not going to use that type of language around here. Victoria, pack your things and come downstairs."

Victoria then got on her knees, tears gushing out of her eyes like the Nile River. "Ms. Nancy, out of all the years I've been here,

I never asked you for anything. P-L-E-A-S-E, Ms. Nancy, do something. Don't let them take me away from the only people in this world that I love, please."

"Victoria, I'm sorry, baby, but your aunt Shelia has been to a rehab and turned her life around. She has a job with the Transit Department, and has an extra room at her new apartment. Victoria, she went to court and got full custody of you."

"What? Sheila? Why would she come after all these years? I don't know her anymore. She died when my mother died. I don't want to go nowhere with her. Ms. Nancy, I'm begging you. Please, don't let her take me."

Ms. Nancy couldn't take it anymore, and broke down crying like the others. As she held Victoria in her arms, she assured her if there was anything she ever needed she and the House of Love would always be there for her.

"What am I going to do without you?" Penny cried, while holding on to Victoria so tight that it would take a chainsaw to loosen the grip. "How am I going to survive?"

"I love you," Victoria said through her tears, "and you're my sister. No matter what we still gonna be sisters, always and forever. Nobody can take that away."

Liddia then jumped up in rage. "Fuck that! I'm going downstairs to beat that bitch's ass!"

While Ms. Nancy pulled Liddia to the back room to restrain her, Penny went downstairs to confront Sheila. "Please don't take my sister away from me," she cried.

Shelia was tough from the streets; therefore she was not moved by Penny's tears. "Look here, little girl. Victoria ain't no kin to you or anybody else in this house, but me. I'm taking her home with her real family, so get over it will you."

The rawness and reality of Sheila's words crushed Penny so much that she no longer cried. Penny just slouched down the wall in amazement and looked at Sheila in shock. She was taking something away from Penny that she longed for all her life, a loving family. Penny was devastated, and it would be a long time before she'd ever trust or love anyone like the way she did Victoria.

——————

Babyface stopped reading for a moment, sat back, and reminisced about Penny. He never knew these things about her; he never knew how disturbed she was. "Damn, baby girl, Aunt Sheila was raw. She ain't have to do that to Penny. Now I see why she was like she was. Damn, boo, you went through some tough shit and still survived. You're a warrior, the realest bitch I know. That's why you got to wake up, baby girl. It's over now. We can live how we want now, do our thang. Our dream has come true, but a nigga can't do it without you. Now, c-mon, girl, and get your ass up out of that coma."

# CHAPTER 5

## I'M A SURVIVOR

Four years later, Sheila was doing well, and her relationship with Victoria was getting a littler better, aside from the fact that she prohibited Victoria from seeing Liddia and Penny. Sheila felt Penny and Liddia were bad influences and would most likely end up on drugs or stuck on welfare with a house full of children.

Sheila did the best she could with taking care of Victoria on the money she made on her job, and anxiously awaited the release of her boyfriend from prison. "As soon as Rico gets home, we're getting married," she would often say.

The mere mention of Rico's name made Victoria's stomach turn. Aunt Sheila's dope fiend boyfriend, Rico, who was sentenced to four years in Lorton Maximum Security Prison for armed robbery soon after Sheila took in Victoria, was a pervert. When Victoria first moved in, Rico would always stare at her and make lewd comments.

By the time Rico was released, Victoria had blossomed into a curvaceous sixteen year old. Around Ballou Senior High School, she was considered a dime piece, and had every hustler in southeast trying to get her. Victoria knew she looked good, with titties like a stripper and the ass of a porn star. However, Victoria paid them no mind; she was too much into her schoolwork. At sixteen, she was still a virgin, and besides that, Aunt Sheila enforced strict rules.

In school, Victoria kept to herself. She didn't have many friends, just a few associates. Out of all her associates, she developed a friendship with the most well-known guy in school, Wayne

Wayne, who was a true thug in every sense of the word. Everybody in school feared him, and it was rumored that Wayne Wayne was killing people at the age of ten, when he shot his stepfather in the head for beating up his mother. Victoria never knew those rumors to be true, mostly because Wayne Wayne was extremely polite to her, He liked Victoria and she knew it, but Victoria didn't like him the way he liked her. She viewed him more as a big brother.

One day, as Victoria walked into the apartment after school, she heard noises coming from the back room, which reminded her of when her mother Diane used to have Randy over. As she began to fix herself something to eat, Sheila emerged from her room looking a shitty mess, her hair all wild and clothes halfway on.

"Oh, there you are. How long you been here?" her aunt asked, while trying to stabilize her breathing.

"I just came in."

"Whew, what time is it?"

"Almost 4 o'clock," Victoria answered.

"Damn, I got to get ready for work."

As soon as Sheila said this, Rico came out of the room wearing a pair of jeans and bare-chested, showing off his fresh out-of-the-joint chiseled body.

"Oh, I forgot to tell you that Rico was released today."

"Who's that? Is that you, Victoria?"

"Yes, Rico," Victoria replied dryly, lacking enthusiasm at his presence. "Welcome home."

"Damn, girl, you sound like you ain't happy I'm home. Come here and give your uncle a hug."

Sheila looked at Victoria. "Don't be rude, girl. Give him a hug."

Reluctantly, Victoria got up to give Rico a hug, and at the sight of her perfectly shaped body, Rico's eyes widened.

Victoria broke free of his strong hold as she felt the big bulge in his pants.

"Look, I gotta go to work," said Sheila. "I'll be back around ten o'clock tonight."

Immediately, Victoria asked if she could go over her friend's house, not wanting to be left alone in the apartment with Rico.

"What friend?" Sheila asked.

"Umm, Tracy."

"Who's Tracy? I never met her."

"She is a friend from school," Victoria explained.

"Now, Victoria, you know I can't let you go over nobody's house I haven't met yet. Besides, you need to stay home and study."

"I don't need to study. I get A's and B's."

"Well, in that case, you need to study some more so you can get *straight* A's," her aunt replied.

Victoria stormed off to her room and closed the door.

As Victoria lay flat on her stomach on her bed watching television, and after her aunt had left for work, Rico entered her room.

"What's up, Vic?"

Victoria didn't want to disrespect Rico, even though he caught her off guard. "Nothing, Rico, I'm just watching TV."

"Why can't you watch TV in Sheila's room?" he asked.

Instantly, Victoria felt a bad vibe. "Because I don't want to, and can you please leave my room now?"

Ignoring her request, Rico sat down on the edge of her bed. "Come on, Vic. You and I both know you really want it. Stop faking, girl. I bet that pussy is dripping wet right now."

Victoria quickly jumped off the bed with her fists clenched. "Rico, leave my room!" Rico moved closer. "Rico, get the fuck out of my room!"

"Now that's the way I like it. Get feisty," he said, as he tried to fondle Victoria's breast.

She swatted his hand away. "Nigga, get the fuck off me!"

"Come on, Vic. You know you want this dick," he said, as he grabbed her by the waist and palmed her perfectly round ass.

"Get the fuck off me, you freak ass nigga! I'm telling my aunt Sheila on your bitch ass," she screamed while trying to pry from out of his strong grip. It was useless, though. Rico was fresh out the joint and strong as an ox.

"Go 'head and tell her. Who you think she's gonna believe, me or you? Now, come here and give me some of that pussy," said Rico as he tried to force her onto the bed.

Victoria had to think quickly. Rico was strong, way too strong to fight. So instead of putting up a fight, she used her charm. As Rico threw her on the bed, she held back her tears and began to work it.

"Okay, Rico. Is this what you really want?" She flashed him her perky titties. Rico's hard-on began to stiffen even more from the sight of Victoria's breast and the sultriness in her voice. "You really want this pussy, huh, Rico?"

"Yeah, Vic, I knew you'd give in. I knew you was a freak bitch."

"That's right, Rico. I'ma be your freak bitch. I'ma suck the shit out of that dick, and then I want you to fuck this pussy good, but first, you got to slow down. Don't be so rough."

After hearing Victoria talk, Rico was anxious. Yet, he calmed himself down to meet this young freak's demand.

"Okay, what do you want me to do?" he asked in a submissive voice.

"I want you to get on your knees and eat this pussy first."

Rico graciously obliged. As he got on his knees, Victoria took a deep breath, reached over to her nightstand, and grabbed hold of her lamp so tight that it would have taken a chainsaw to pry it loose from her grip. Within a millisecond, she swung the lamp and split Rico's head wide open.

"Ahhh, bitch, I'ma kill you!" he yelled as he fell backward onto the floor.

Victoria stood overtop Rico, and while holding the lamp with two hands, she said, "Not if I kill you first, bitch ass nigga." Then she smashed his skull once more. As he began to regain consciousness, she grabbed her jacket and shoes and ran for dear life.

Victoria fled from the apartment, but had no clue as to where she would go. The only thing on her mind was getting away from

Rico. As she franticly looked back, hoping not to see Rico chasing behind, a familiar car pulled up next to her and rolled down its heavily tinted windows. The black Acura couldn't have pulled up at any better time. Even if she didn't know the owner, she still would have gotten inside.

"Hey, Vic, where you running to?" Wayne Wayne asked.

"Boy, I'm sure glad to see you."

"Where you going, Vic?"

"Umm…umm…I don't know, Wayne. Just pull off."

"Damn, girl, you alright?" Wayne Wayne asked, concern in his eyes. "You acting like you just done something."

"Nah, Wayne, everything's alright. I'm just blown right now. My uncle is trippin'."

"What happened?"

"Nothing, Wayne. I ain't even tryna talk about it. You okay?" Victoria asked him, trying to take the focus off of her.

"Yeah, I'm just a little fucked up in the head. Where you tryna go?"

"I guess I can hang with you for a while, if that's okay."

"Alright then, boo. You wanna hang out with me; it's cool, and since I see you going through a lil' crisis, I got something that'll cheer you up." He smiled as he held up a fresh twenty sack of DC's finest Hydro.

"Shit, Wayne, I might as well try it. My day couldn't have been worst."

Although Victoria had nowhere to go, she figured she'd hang out with Wayne Wayne for a while just to get her thoughts together and figure out what to do next. One thing for sure, she made up her mind she would never go back to Sheila's house again.

———

Babyface sat back after reading about what Victoria had been through. He couldn't help but think about his old comrade, Wayne Wayne. They both met at Oakhill Youth Center, where Wayne was doing time for attempted murder and Babyface graduated from foster home to juvenile jail for assaulting his foster parents. While at Oakhill, Babyface saved Wayne's life when some niggas there from southwest was putting down the most vicious hit on him. That day, Wayne Wayne promised to take care of Babyface once he was released.

———

Wayne Wayne rolled up the blunt and passed it to Victoria as he pulled his Acura into an alley behind Third Street.

When Victoria took her first pull, she damn near choked to death. "Damn, Wayne, this shit is too strong."

Wayne simply laughed. "Girl, relax," he said as reached over and reclined Victoria's seat as far as it could go. "There you go, girl. Now, sit back, relax, and pull real slow."

The more Victoria pulled the higher she got, and for the first time in her life, she felt relieved of all her worries in the world. The feeling was so good she wished she could stay like that forever.

As Wayne took his turn hitting the blunt, he looked over at Victoria's smooth, thick thighs that were visible with the skirt she was wearing. From the way her seat was reclined, he could see clear up to her pink panties. Noticing the fatness of her pussy, Wayne's dick instantly got hard. He always wanted Victoria. As the weed began to take effect, Wayne's whole demeanor changed from gentleman to aggressor.

"Hey, Vic, I gotta tell you something."

"What's up, Wayne?" she asked.

"You know all this time I been tryna get at you, but you be on some ol' 'sister brother' bullshit."

Man, come on, Wayne, I don't even look at you like that."

"That's why I'm saying, Vic, you need to start."

"Wayne, I'm just not feeling you like that," Victoria replied. "We're friends."

At that moment, Victoria saw another side of Wayne he had

never used with her. "Fuck that friend shit! I'm tryna get some pussy!"

Victoria attempted to get up, but he held her back with one hand on her chest. "Look, Wayne, I been through a whole lot today. Don't start trippin' on me now. Matter of fact, I'm gone."

"You ain't going nowhere until you give me some pussy!"

At that moment, Victoria felt the most excruciating pain as his fist connected with her jaw. He hit her once more in the eye before grabbing his gun, placing it to her head, and ripping her clothes at the same time.

*Oh my God, this nigga is going to try and take my virginity.*

While Victoria tried to put up a struggle, Wayne pulled off Victoria's skirt and tried to insert his penis as she squirmed from side to side. Every time she moved, he would punch her even harder.

Fearful, Victoria screamed for help as the blood gushed from her mouth and nose. "STOP! HELP! RAPE! RAPE!" she screamed, hoping someone would hear.

As she yelled, he continued to beat her until she was unconscious, then he inserted his penis into her tight, virgin womb and pounded her pussy relentlessly.

However, during the assault, he was alarmed by a knock on his window. Instantly, Wayne got up from off of Victoria to see Babyface standing there.

"What's up, my nigga? Get in," Wayne said as he unlocked the doors.

Babyface looked at the beaten girl who was finally gaining consciousness. "Man, what the fuck you back here doing? Ah, slim, don't tell me you doing what I think you doing."

"Man, shut the fuck up and get in."

"Nah, Wayne, you lunchin' out. Slim, let that girl go before you catch a case."

Now fully conscious, Victoria started kicking and screaming, "Get off me! Get off me! HELP! HELP!"

"Shut up, bitch," Wayne spat, hitting her again.

"Wayne, stop! What the fuck is up wit you? You on some different shit."

Wayne glared at Babyface. "Fuck you, Face. Fuck you and that bitch."

As Wayne tried to hit Victoria again, Babyface blocked his punch and began to struggle with Wayne.

"Nigga, I'ma kill you," Wayne said as he reached for his 9mm.

As the two men struggled for the gun, Victoria got out the car and ran a short distance. When Wayne managed to get his hand on the grip, Babyface was left with no other choice but to strike Wayne with his most powerful left hook, which dazed Wayne. Babyface then grabbed the gun out of his hand and pointed it directly in Wayne's face. Still, Wayne wasn't giving up.

"Nigga, you ain't no killer," he said, while lunging at Babyface.

Proving him wrong, Babyface pulled the trigger one time, blowing Wayne's brain all over the dashboard of his brand new Acura.

Standing only two feet away, Victoria witnessed her second murder. This time, though, she felt it was a justified killing. Wayne took something from her, and in return, he got what was coming to him. Instantly, she had admiration for Babyface. He was the only person to show genuine concern for her, besides her father Toney. He had actually killed a man for her.

After taking off his brand new Coogi sweater that Wayne had sent him to come home in after his release, Babyface handed it to Victoria so she could cover her nakedness. Then he went back to Wayne's car and checked his pockets for cash, finding seven hundred dollars.

Once he wiped their fingerprints from the car, he turned to her and said, "Come on. Hurry up before somebody sees us."

# CHAPTER 6

## CHANGE IS GONNA COME

As Babyface and Victoria rode the bus in silence, many thoughts ran though his mind. *Damn, what the fuck did I just do? Why the fuck did I have to walk up on some shit like that?* He hated the fact that he'd just killed a dear friend; it crushed him.

*And who the fuck is this little bitch? Why was she with him in the first place? She's probably some lil' freak bitch anyway. She's pretty, but what the fuck was she doing sitting in the alley with Wayne? And why did she tell me that she has nowhere to go? I hope she don't think I'ma take her home with me, 'cause I don't even have a home. Plus, my name ain't Captain Save-a-hoe. All I got is seven hundred and fifty dollars to my name. How the fuck I'ma survive off that, and to add, where am I taking this bitch?*

Babyface broke out of his train of thought when the bus driver yelled over the intercom, "This is the last stop. Next bus doesn't arrive until six o'clock tomorrow morning," before he dropped the remaining passengers in front of Iverson Mall.

After they got off, Babyface reached in his pocket and peeled off three hundred dollars, shoving it in Victoria's direction. "Here, take this."

"What's this for?" Victoria asked.

"I don't know. You figure it out. Go back home."

"I can't," Victoria cried.

"Please don't do this to me. I told you I don't have nowhere to go either. All I got in this world is seven hundred and fifty dollars. How the fuck I'ma take care both of us on that, huh?"

"Look, you got me now," Victoria pleaded. "We can make it

together. Whatever you want me to do, I'll do it. I owe you. I have nowhere to go, just like you." Victoria then took the time to give him the condensed story of her life, including the sexual advances of Rico. "So, you see, I can't go back."

Babyface looked at Victoria's battered face, with her swollen eyes and split lip, and felt sorry for the lost girl. He knew she was lost, but yet and still, he was unsure of how he could help.

He looked at her for a moment, and as the words came out of his mouth, he couldn't believe what he was saying. "I guess I'm stuck with you, huh?"

Victoria smiled, hugged Babyface, and then took a step back so she could take a good look at her prince. He was extremely handsome with dark brown, milky skin, thick eyebrows, and curly hair. He wore his hair tapered low on the sides, and he was in very good shape. His body was hard as a rock, but his touch was smooth as butter. Babyface was a pretty boy by nature. He didn't try to look like this; he came out of the womb like this.

"Come on," Babyface said as he went to get them a fifty-dollar-a-night hotel room at the P.G. Motel located across the street from the Iverson Mall.

---

The next morning, Babyface left Victoria sleeping in the bed, while he went out to get them breakfast. First, though, he stopped at the mall across the street to purchase her a few pieces of clothes with the little money he had left.

While out, he bumped into an old friend who he met while in Lorton, Young Tom. Now, Young Tom was a smooth nigga, who mostly hung out with the old heads, sucking up all the game he could. Tom had connects with everybody; he was a true hustler. If it was something you wanted, he either had it or could easily get it for you. As Tom pulled up in his brand-new grey Mercedes and got out, he couldn't believe his eyes as he walked up behind Babyface.

"Nigga, you slippin'," he whispered in Babyface's ear. "In jail, you couldn't pay a nigga to walk up on you like this."

Babyface knew whoever this person was standing behind him was right, but fortunately, he knew it wasn't an enemy, 'cause if it was, his brains would have been on the sidewalk thirty seconds ago. As he turned around, he was face to face with an old friend whom he often thought about.

"TOM! My muthafuckin' nigga, what's up?" As he and Tom embraced, Babyface could feel the bulge of Young Tom's .45 Desert Eagle.

"What's up, nigga? I see they finally let your ass out," said Tom as he looked him up and down. "When did you get out?"

"Ah, man, I just got out yesterday."

"Yesterday, huh? So where you staying?"

"I'm across the street at the motel," Babyface replied.

Tom laughed. "What, nigga? You over there buying pussy?"

"Nah, slim, I ain't gotta buy no pussy. Me and my girl got a room." As the words left his mouth, Babyface couldn't believe he had referred to Victoria as his girl.

"Damn, it's good to see you, Babyface. Hey, has anybody hit you off yet?" Tom asked.

"Nah, you know I don't fuck wit a lot of niggas. I grew up in the system. The only niggas I know is either dead or in jail."

"Well, nigga, that's an understatement, 'cause I'm alive and outta jail," Tom replied. "Matter of fact, take this. It ain't much, but it will hold you for a while till you can get your own." Tom peeled off a thousand dollars and gave it to Babyface, who needed it after having spent close to four hundred dollars on a few things for Victoria and himself.

"Thanks, Tom."

"Yeah, slim, you alright. If I can help a good nigga out, I will. But look here, write my cell and pager numbers down. You already know my profession, so whenever you're ready to get your grind on, give me a call."

As Babyface walked away, Tom's words repeated in his head as he wondered how he would take care of Victoria with only thirteen hundred dollars to his name. He knew it would only stretch but so far. Therefore, he had to find a hustle, and he had to find one fast.

---

As the weeks passed, Babyface and Victoria did everything together. They talked and got to know each other without detailing their childhood. Most evenings, they stood on the balcony of the motel and watched the pimps roll up in their flashy cars to pick up their hoes and take them down to the track on 14th Street. Babyface admired the cars, loved the hoes, but looked at the pimps as though they were some straight up bamas from outta town, with their loud-colored, tailor-made suits, pink gators, walking canes, and Jeri curls.

One night as they stood on the balcony, a pimp from Chicago, by the name of Royal, pulled up in his Benz. He was smoother than the rest of the pimps they saw. Yes, he wore suits, but only Armani and Hugo Boss, and although he wore too much jewelry, he still was a smooth nigga.

"Babyface, that nigga tried to holla at me yesterday when I was out here by myself," Victoria said, while pointing down at Royal.

"Oh yeah? What'd he say?"

"I don't even remember. I just walked back in the room," she replied.

Babyface's expression became serious. "Hey, Victoria, would you ever do that?"

"Do what?" she asked.

"You know...sell pussy?"

"Nah, I couldn't see myself out there like that."

"What if your life depended on it?" he pressed.

"Only if my life was worth something to depend on," she said. "Now my turn to ask, would you do that?"

"Fuck no! Fuck I look like selling my dick?"

Victoria laughed. "No, silly, I mean pimp hoes."

"Oh, hell yeah, but for real, it would have to be a last resort. Besides, I don't think I can get a broad to do that, and another thing, I ain't feeling the shiny suits and shit."

Victoria laughed at Babyface's answer.

"Come on, you wanna go see a movie?" he asked.

"Yeah, but let me get dressed first," Victoria replied.

When Victoria emerged from the bathroom dressed in her Calvin Klein outfit, Babyface's mouth damn near hit the floor. Her jeans fit perfect, as if made just for her, defining her wide hips and plump ass. Her nipples protruded from underneath the wife beater Babyface let her borrow, and the matching jacket, with only the last three buttons snapped, revealed just the right amount of cleavage. Victoria was fine, and on a scale from 1 to 10, no doubt she'd be a 10 1/2. Victoria had a body like Lisa Raye and a face like Beyonce.

Babyface couldn't help but to express himself to her. "Damn, you look good as shit. You's a bad muthafucka."

"Come on, Babyface, you're making me blush, and besides, look at you."

Babyface was dressed fresh in a brand-new blue and white Iceberg sweat suit, with a fresh pair of blue and white Air Force Ones Nikes on his feet.

"Yeah, I'm alright, but, Victoria, you're a dime piece for real. Whoever gets you will be one lucky muthafucka. I'd tilt my hat to 'em."

"Well then, why don't you tilt your hat to yourself," Victoria said shyly as she walked up to Babyface and pressed her chest up against his, then looked him directly in the eyes.

She took a deep breath, scared of being rejected by him. Victoria was already in love with Babyface without him having even touched her. Today, though, she knew she had to make the first move. He was too much of a gentleman to try his hand first after witnessing what she'd been through.

Victoria closed her eyes and gently placed her lips on his, slipping her tongue inside his mouth and kissing him with built-up passion. As they passionately kissed in an ecstasy neither ever knew, they embraced each other so hard that both of them could feel the other's heartbeat.

As they continued kissing, Babyface unbuttoned her jacked and gently took it off, caressing her perfect breasts through the wife beater. She then pulled off his sweatshirt and discovered he wasn't wearing a t-shirt. As she kissed on his chest, she ran her fingers up and down his chiseled six-pack, touching him as if she was exploring a fine art sculpture. After pulling off her wife beater, he caressed her round, firm breast as he began to gently nibble on her nipples.

As she rubbed on his swollen dick through his sweatpants, she wondered if she would be able to take all 9 1/2 inches. It didn't matter to her, though. She wanted him, regardless of what pain she may have to endure. She took out his dick and began to caress it, slowly running her soft palms over the head of his dick as she kissed on his neck.

Babyface, I want you inside me," she whispered in his ear. "I've wanted you inside me ever since I met you."

The sound of her soft, erotic voice sent chills straight to his dick, causing it to stand at supreme attention. He unbuttoned her pants, pulling them off only to witness that she was wearing no panties at all. After he laid her on the bed, he gently played with her clit, rubbing his fingers in a circular motion and causing her to reach a climax while still kissing her soft nipples.

"Oh, Babyface, please...I want it inside. Come on, please," Victoria moaned.

He continued to tease her by getting on top of her and rubbing his dick on her clit, causing her pussy juices to soak the sheets. Victoria couldn't believe what she was feeling. No one ever made her feel this way. He took her on a high unknown to her, and she loved it.

"Put it in me...I can't take it no more...stop teasing me."

Babyface ignored her begging and continued to make her want it more by running his tongue down to her navel and ultimately to her thighs. As he continued, the curiosity of what he was about to do made her more heated. Finally, he began kissing on her clitoris, licking it up and down slowly while feeling the wetness of her walls.

"Oh god, Babyface! Damn that feels so good. Why you make me wait so long? Come on, put it in me, please."

After licking her pussy with perfection, Victoria was on the brink of another climax. She couldn't take it anymore. She had enough of his teasing. He teased so much that she began to cry real tears. Victoria wanted him inside her so bad that she grabbed his dick, pulling him on top of her and guiding it straight to her pussy.

As he penetrated her walls, loud moans of ecstasy escaped from her mouth. From the sound of it, Babyface couldn't figure out if he was hurting her or pleasing her. He began digging deeper, ignoring the cries but obeying the passion. Her pussy gripped his dick so tight, it felt like he was pulling her body with his dick every time he motioned in and out. As his dick pounded her pussy, he could feel the juices dripping off his balls. This was the best pussy he'd ever had.

"Damn, Victoria, this pussy is good," he panted, while reaching his climax. Moments later, Victoria reached an orgasm, as well.

As Babyface laid back on the bed in a daze, Victoria sunk her head in his chest, wiping her tears with his body. "Babyface, I love you. I now have something worth living for."

"Me, too, Victoria. I have a genuine tuff love for you. No matter what, I'ma always be there for you and do whatever it takes to protect you."

After planting a kiss upon her lips, Babyface laid there in silence while contemplating their next move. With only three hundred dollars left, they needed money and fast. The room was paid a week in advance; therefore, he could save as much as he could without worrying about where they were gonna sleep. Still, they were broke, and he had to do something fast.

As he rose from out of the bed, he felt the wetness on the sheets and figured he would get a towel to soak it up. As he pulled the comforter back, he was shocked at the puddle of blood that had soaked the motel's clean white sheets. He looked at Victoria in disbelief.

"Damn, Victoria, why you ain't tell me you was on your period?"

Victoria put her head down in shame. "Babyface, I ain't on my period. You're the first nigga I gave it to."

"You can't be a virgin," Babyface argued. "What about the situation wit Wayne?"

"I guess he ain't get it in all the way. You must have saved me in time. Either that or his dick was just too small to bust my cherry."

"Damn, so I'm your first, huh?" Babyface boasted.

"Yeah, nigga. Like I said earlier, go 'head and tilt your hat to yourself. You are now the proud owner of this pussy. Babyface, I'm your bitch fo' life.

━━━━━━━━━━━━

As he laid down the diary, Babyface sat back and reminisced about the first time he made love to Victoria. He remembered her declaration to her...*bitch fo' life*...and she sure did live up to it.

# CHAPTER 7

## THE COME UP

Knowing they needed to hustle up some cash fast, Babyface came up with the idea of him and Victoria boosting designer clothing and unloading them at the pool hall and on the streets.

As they entered the pool hall, it seemed like everything stopped and everyone's attention was drawn to Victoria. The old heads tapped one another and pointed in their direction, nodding at Babyface as if to say, "You a smooth ass young'n to be pullin' a broad that fine." Even the pimps sat back admiring her beauty and Babyface's class.

As Babyface looked around, he spotted Tom coming out of the back room called the Casino, where the big gamblers hung out.

"Hey, Tom!" Babyface yelled.

"Ah, my muthafuckin man Babyface! Wazzup, nigga?"

"Look, slim, I got some Coogi sweaters I'm tryna sell."

"Where they at?" Tom asked.

Babyface nodded at Victoria, who held the bag of sweaters. Without saying a word, she walked over, planted a kiss on his cheek, and handed him the bags. Then she walked back to the spot where she was patiently waiting and took her position.

Tom looked in the bag, and then asked, "So what you want for these sweaters?"

"I'm tryna get at least $250 for each one," Babyface replied.

"Look, I'll go ahead and give you two G's for the eight sweaters, but for real, slim, I hate to see you out here boostin'? Why don't you wanna hustle and get you some real bank?"

Babyface thought for a minute. Even though he never really

sold drugs before, he always thought about getting into the game.

"Slim, I never really hustled before. Shit, I grew up in the system and never had time enough in the streets to hustle."

"Well, look here, since you ain't tryna hustle, why don't you do something else that'll get you a nice bankroll?"

"Like what?" Babyface asked.

"Look here, if you can get me a presidential Rolex, I'll pay ten G's for it. Shit, that's a nice start-up bank for you."

Babyface contemplated on Tom's offer. He was right. There was no way he could take care of him and Victoria by only stealing clothes. Eventually, that shit would play out. Also, with ten G's, he figured they could get an apartment somewhere and a reliable car to get around in until they could decide what they were going to do next.

"Okay, Tom, you got that. I'ma work on that A.S.A.P. I'll holla at you later." Babyface then turned and guided Victoria out of the pool hall, as all eyes followed them as they left.

---

"Wake up, Victoria," Babyface said, while gently shaking her from out of her sleep.

"What, boo?" she said groggily.

"Baby girl, I got a plan. We're gonna go over to the mall and buy some business clothes, then head down to Georgetown to the Rolex dealer. But first, I'ma buy one of the fake Rolex replicas they be selling on the corner by Roy Rogers. After that, I'ma go in the dealer first and act like I wanna purchase a watch. Then you come in like your looking for something nice for your fiancé's birthday."

"Uh huh, go head, boo," Victoria said, now propped up on her elbows and paying full attention.

"Okay, when I ask to try on the watch, pay attention to my every move. As soon as you see the salesperson hand me the watch, get their attention fast, and that's when I'ma make the switch. If we do this right, we got 10 G's, baby."

"Damn, Babyface, I ain't never seen 10 G's in my life."

"Well, if you get your ass up and get ready you'll be seeing it today," Babyface said.

"Okay, boo, give me five minutes."

---

After exiting the taxi, Victoria and Babyface instantly went separate ways. Victoria walked on the opposite side of the street, keeping Babyface in sight as he walked to the vending stand and purchased a platinum replica Rolex. Afterwards, he shoved the watch in his jacket pocket, and then scanned the area to make sure no one had seen him. Before entering the Rolex dealership, he looked across the street to make sure Victoria was in place. So far so good.

As he entered the store, with briefcase in hand, he smiled at the woman behind the counter and proceeded to look around.

"Hello and welcome to our store. Is there anything in particular you are looking for," asked the woman in spectacles.

"Ah, yeah and no. Let me just browse for a moment before I'm in need of your time." Babyface looked and talked like a young black stock broker.

As he studied the watch selections, Babyface fixed his eyes on his mark. When he saw the platinum presidential with diamond bezel, he almost chocked. He wanted to bust the glass, snatch it and run, but he knew Georgetown was one of the busiest districts in Washington D.C., so it would be impossible to pull it off. Instead, he stuck with the plan.

"Excuse me, ma'am, can you tell me a little about this watch here?"

The woman walked over to the glass with her key, unlocked the case, and had him point out which watch he was referring to.

"Well, sir, this is the new Rolex Presidential. There were only two hundred made this year. It's a platinum watch with a Swiss-made platinum rotator. Basically, it is totally made of platinum, except for the diamond bezel, which is a total of five carats of VVS quality cut Rolex diamond."

"Well, what is the price?" Babyface asked.

Just as the woman was about to answer, Victoria entered the store, as if in a rush. "Ma'am, where's your ring selections?"

The woman pointed to the ring selection, then turned her attention back to Babyface. "As I was saying, there were only two hundred of these made, so if you purchase one, it would be making an investment. The price for this particular watch is fifty thousand."

"I once owned a 18k gold Rolex, but recently had it auctioned off at the Jewelry Exchange Convention," Babyface lied.

The woman's eyes lit up at the thought of the commission she would make from the sale. "Well, in that case, would you like to try it on?"

"Sure," Babyface coolly replied as the woman proceeded to remove the watch from the case.

As soon as Babyface placed the watch on his wrist, Victoria came out of nowhere and distracted the woman.

"Oh, oh, Miss, come here. How much is this? I want it. I want it," Victoria exclaimed in a loud, whiney voice. And within a tenth of a second, Babyface made the switch that would earn him the most cash he'd ever had in his life.

After calming Victoria down, and assuring her she would attend to her once she finished with the customer she was currently assisting, the woman turned her attention back to Babyface, who removed the fake Rolex from off his wrist and handed it to her.

"Thanks, ma'am, but I think I'll pass on that. It's a nice watch, but a little too rich for my blood."

Disappointed that the sale fell through, the woman placed the watch back in the case without even looking at it. Eager to make a sell to him, she quickly tried to offer other watches, but Babyface declined.

The whole time, Victoria continued to call out for the sales lady to help her. "Miss, can you please come over here and tell me how much this ring cost? I'm in a rush and I want it."

By now, the woman had become irritated with Victoria. "I said I'll be there in a minute."

Babyface felt that now was as good a time as any to make his getaway. "Ma'am, I think I'll come back some other time. Do you have a card?"

Sadly, the woman handed him her card and then shuffled over to attend to Victoria, who placed her hands on her hips and instantly went into ghetto mode.

"I asked you to help me, not him," Victoria griped.

"Well, miss, couldn't you see that I was in the middle of a deal? Your irrational behavior cost me a sell. Now what would you like to see?" the sales lady shot back.

"How about I don't like your attitude. Since you already lost one sale, why don't you make it two? I'm outta here. I'll buy my jewelry at Tiffany's."

Needless to say, the woman was so angry she almost cursed Victoria out as she left the store. However, she wasn't as angry as she would be once she realized she now had a faux Rolex on her hands.

---

The next morning, Babyface woke up early, showered, dressed, and left to go meet Tom. As Babyface entered the Feed Bag, he looked around, taking in his surrounding. At a nearby table, Tom motioned for Babyface to join him and another gentleman. When he got to the table, Tom immediately got up to embrace Babyface, and not because he was happy to see him, but to check to make sure Babyface was not strapped.

Babyface looked over at Tom's company once he was cleared.

"Oh, Face, this is my man, Petey. Petey, this is Babyface, the one I was telling you about."

Petey got up and extended his hand. "What's up, Face? Glad to meet you. Have a seat."

Babyface sat down opposite of the two, facing towards the door entrance so he could see everyone who entered the establishment.

"Look, Face, I wanna get right down to business. I brought Petey here because he is interested in what you got," Tom informed him.

"But I thought I was just dealing with you," Babyface said, feeling a little uncomfortable about the situation.

"You are dealing wit me, but unfortunately, I lost a lot of money gamblin' last night and I know you tryna get that thing off so you can get yourself together. So, I called my man here."

"It's cool. So what's up? You tryna cop this piece or what?" Babyface asked, looking at Petey.

Petey admired his approach, seeing that Babyface was straight about business. "Yes, I'm interested in what you got."

"Well, let me set my price. This joint is a collector's item straight from the dealer," Babyface said, pulling up the sleeve of his Coogi sweater to expose the finest jewel they had ever seen. "The whole watch is platinum, inside and out. The tag on it says fifty thousand, but I'll give it to you for twenty g's."

"Look, Face, I want that watch, but I can't give you twenty thou' for it. That's a little steep for a watch stolen from the official dealer. After all, I wouldn't be able to sell it to nobody after I'm done flossing it. You know them joints are traceable, especially if it's really a collector's item. But what I can do is make you a nice offer, though," Petey said.

As bad as Babyface wanted to get up and leave, he couldn't. He needed the money. Tom looked at Babyface with an expression as if to say, "At least hear the man's offer."

"Look, Face, right now my bank is tight, but I do have some work. Let's say I give you a half a brick and 5 g's for it," Petey offered.

"Half a brick? Man, I don't hustle. How I'ma move that shit?"

Tom interrupted. "Face, you could push that shit up here in the pool hall wit me. The spot stay jumping 24/7. You could get it off in like two days, maybe one if you really 'bout your money. And besides, nigga, I need the company. Ain't nuthin' like hustlin' the same spot with an old friend."

Babyface contemplated Tom's suggestion. He knew Tom had his best interest at heart, 'cause if he didn't, he would have never suggested he hustle in the same spot with him. Also, a half brick "wholesale" was going for 10 g's alone. If he broke it down to all ounces and sold them for a thousand a piece, he'd come out with eighteen, plus the five thousand. That would total twenty- three altogether. Either way, Babyface would come out on top.

"Okay, Petey, I'ma take you up on the offer."

"Thank you, Face, and in the future, I hope we can continue to do business. One thing, though. I can't get to my shit right now 'cause I got a flight that is leaving shortly. So, in the meantime, hold on to the watch and take this five thousand as a down payment."

*Damn, the nigga don't even know me and he's giving me five g's as a down payment,* Babyface thought. "When will you be back in town?"

In about a week, and when I get back, I'll have a half brick of some of the best coke in D.C. waiting for you."

"Cool. Well, I must be going, fellas. It was a pleasure doing business with you," Babyface said as he rose from the table and made his way to the exit. "This shit turned out better than I thought," he mumbled under his breath as he walked out the door.

---

Once Babyface got back to the motel, Victoria ran to the door to greet him. She had been impatient and nervous the whole time Babyface was gone, but knew she had to follow his instructions of staying put in the room until he returned. As soon as he walked in the door, he grabbed Victoria up and gave her a deep kiss. Out of curiosity, and as validation that everything went well with the transaction, she looked down at his wrist, and to her surprise the watch was still there.

Victoria bombarded him with questions. "Daddy, why do you still got on that watch? What happened? He didn't want it or something? What went wrong?"

"What makes you think something went wrong?"

"'Cause you still got on that watch," she replied.

"Vic, Vic, Vic…never doubt my work. Ain't nothing in this world I can't do." He pulled out the 5 g's and slammed it on the nightstand. "Now pack our bags. We're going looking for an apartment today."

Victoria jumped up at the sight of seeing the money, and she held Babyface so tight that he had to tell her to let go. To her, Babyface was beyond a hero; he was invincible.

# CHAPTER 8

## MOVING ON

Victoria and Babyface moved into the Marlboro Plaza High-rise on Good Hope Road in southeast D.C., which was the best place they could find for the money. The seven-hundred-dollar a month, one-bedroom apartment located on the 8th floor had wall- to-wall carpet and a modern kitchen. Victoria was so excited to have a place to call home. In fact, she hadn't had a place to call home since she was nine years old.

After scantily furnishing the apartment with a king-size bed and a cream-colored living room set, Babyface visited Wild Bill's Auto and purchased his first car with the fifteen hundred dollars left. Although he hated the battered 1978 Ford Granada with the busted taillight, he needed it so he could get his grind on, especially since he was near broke and would need to hustle hard.

Nine o'clock the next morning, as Victoria lay wide awake on Babyface's chest watching him as he slept, the telephone rang. She quickly picked up the receiver, wondering who it could be since they just got the phone turned on the day before.

"Hello," she answered in a sleepy voice.

"Excuse me for calling so early. I didn't mean to wake you, but is Babyface in?"

For a moment, she was gonna tell whoever was calling to call back later, but she decided to find out who was on the other end first.

"Who's calling?" Victoria asked.

"Tell him Petey."

Victoria knew this was the person Babyface was waiting to

hear from.

"If he's sleep, I can call back," said Petey.

"Oh no, hold on," Victoria quickly replied, while shaking Babyface so hard that he jumped out of his sleep startled. "Daddy, it's Petey on the phone."

Babyface took the phone. "Hello," he said, while wiping the sleep from his eyes.

"Ah, Face, I'm sorry for calling so early, but I thought we could meet up so you can pick up this package now since I'm going to be busy later on."

At the sound of picking up the package, Babyface instantly became fully awake. "Where you at, Petey?"

"I'm down at the 51 Liquor Store off of Southern Ave," he replied.

"Oh shit, you ain't but down the street and around the corner. Give me ten minutes. Matter of fact, I'll be there in seven."

Petey laughed. "Yeah, okay. I'll be in the parking lot, sitting in a burgundy Cadillac DTS."

"Okay, Petey, and I'll be pullin' up in the worse bucket you ever seen in your life."

They both laughed before ending the call.

As Victoria watched Babyface get dressed she wanted badly to ask could she go with him, but she knew her position. If he wanted her to come, he would have told her to get ready. She was happy for him, and she saw it in his eyes that he was happy, also. Finally, he would start seeing some real money. Even though she didn't like the fact of him dealing in drugs, she kept it to herself. She figured after he had made enough money to quit, then she would voice her opinion.

═══════════════

After Babyface left to go meet up with Petey, Victoria busied herself with cooking cheese omelets and turkey bacon, while waiting on him to return. Her anticipation on seeing her man come up kept a smile on her face ever since he left. She fantasized of them having nice things, traveling, and shopping at Prada, Chanel, Gucci, and Versace. She even thought about getting pregnant, birthing a few babies, and having a loving family she always longed for. She knew she had a real man, and she knew nothing in life could keep them from being together. Babyface was hers for life, and she was his.

---

Once the transaction had been completed, the Rolex in exchange for the half brick that Babyface planned on turning into a million dollar enterprise, he couldn't get back home fast enough. The old hooptie constantly backfired while going down Alabama Avenue. Babyface was so hungry that he could almost smell the delicious breakfast he knew Victoria had cooked for him. Also, the thought of having a side order of pussy crossed his mind, as well, giving him more than enough reason to press harder on the gas pedal as the traffic light turned yellow, warning him to slow down.

Babyface figured the old hooptie that he called Silver Bullet could make it through the light. He smiled, figuring he had made it; however, he was soon distracted by the loud sound of sirens and the bright flashing red lights of the D.C. police, who were pulling him over for a traffic violation. For a second, he thought about trying to outrun the police, but he knew it was impossible since the engine would cut off if Silver Bullet went over forty-five miles per hour.

Babyface had to do something, and it had to be done fast. Here he was driving with no license, violating a traffic signal with a half a kilo of pure Columbian cocaine sitting in the console of his car. He wanted so badly to kick himself in the ass for this major fuck up.

"Shit! Damn! Fuck!" he said.

While pulling over, Babyface quickly retrieved the coke out of the glove compartment. He had made his decision; he couldn't go back to jail. Besides, Victoria wouldn't know what to do without him. Therefore, there was only one option. Babyface had to get out and make a run for it.

As soon as he swung open the car door, he leaped out and was set to do a Carl Lewis sprint through the ghettos of southeast, only to be hit and bumped to the ground by an unmarked police car. Babyface still didn't give up, though. He was determined to get away. As he struggled to pull himself up off the ground, he got to his feet and took one step before collapsing. That's when he realized his leg was broke. When he looked up, he found himself staring into the barrels of two police issued Glock 9mm handguns.

━━━━━━━━━

Victoria's father, Toney, pointed the .38 revolver in her mother's face and was about to pull the trigger, when the ringing of the phone saved her from remembering the nightmare. Instantly, she jumped out of her sleep, sweating and breathing heavily. The phone rang once again, and as she was picking it up, she looked around for Babyface, who wasn't there. She then looked at the time and realized she had slept all the way till seven-thirty the next morning after having waited for him to return from his meeting with Petey.

"Hello," she answered in a low, sleepy voice, wondering who could be calling so early. As soon as she heard the recording, her heart instantly fell into her stomach.

"This is a collect call from...*me, baby girl*. If you wish to accept this call, dial one now."

Immediately, Victoria pressed one.

"Hello baby girl."

"Face, where are you? Please don't tell me you're where I think you're at?" she asked in a fearful tone.

"I'm in jail, Vic. These muthafuckas got me in a jam."

"NOOO! NOOO! Please tell me I'm dreaming. Why you do this shit to me, Face? Why? You said you wasn't ever gonna leave me. NOOO!" she cried out loud. Nothing could describe the pain she felt; she was literally broken down.

"HEY, VIC!" Babyface screamed in his most aggressive voice. "Look, what the fuck I tell you about that muthafuckin' crying. I don't need no crybaby in my corner. I need a trooper. Now suck that shit up."

"Okay, Face," Victoria replied as she continued to weep; only this time she did it silently.

Her whole world was falling apart faster than it was put back together. Victoria saw herself starting over from where she just came from...nothing. No matter what Babyface said the tears still poured from her eyes like waterfalls.

"Vic, you there?"

"Yeah, I'm here," she said, while trying to mask the fact that she was crying.

"Look they got me for possession with intent to distribute. I'm down here under the fake name Gary Jones, and my bond is five thousand dollars."

"Five thousand! Face, where am I gonna get that type of money? All we got is five hundred to our name."

"Look, just come down here tomorrow, and we'll talk about it then," he told her.

Why can't I come now?" Victoria asked.

"'Cause visits don't start till tomorrow. Don't worry, baby girl, everything is gonna be alright. Okay?" he assured her.

"Okay. I'll be there first thing in the morning, Daddy. I love you."

"I love you, too," Babyface replied before the phone line went dead.

*Damn, I hope Face got a way outta this shit. How the fuck we gonna get up five g's? Well, whatever he wants me to do it's done. I vowed to Face that I'ma be his bitch fo' life...down till the end. I owe Face everything. I owe him my life.*

The next morning, Victoria was up and ready to catch the first bus down to the D.C. jail. In fact, she'd been up all night crying. No matter how hard she tried not to, she just couldn't stop. Victoria felt the same way she did when she was nine years old; she felt the same way when Sheila came and took her away from her friends; and she felt the same way when Rico and Wayne Wayne violated her.

As she entered the visiting room, all heads turned in her direction. She was dressed to kill in her brand new Prada outfit with matching Prada shoes that Babyface bought for her. She wanted to truly represent, and the outfit did the job. The tight- fitting beige skirt with matching top, along with her laced up Prada boots, made her look like she was a model for a Prada magazine ad photo shoot.

As she sat behind the glass waiting for Babyface, she began to get impatient. "Excuse me, C.O. I'm here to see Gary Jones. I've been here for twenty minutes, and they've brought out everyone but him. What's the hold up?"

"He'll be up in a few, miss. We had to send somebody down to medical to get him."

"Thank you," Victoria said, and then thought, *Medical? What the hell is he doing down in medical?*

Minutes later, she noticed somebody pushing a wheelchair towards the end of the booth where she sat. As they got closer, she almost fain'ted when she realized the wheelchair's occupant was Babyface. There he sat on the other side of the partition, with a cast that went from his foot clear up to his thigh. Victoria stared at him for a few moments, trying her hardest to hold back the tears, before picking up the receiver which they would use to communicate through the thick glass.

"Vic, you better not cry," were the first words out his mouth.

"Boo, what did they do to you?" she said in her lowest voice.

Babyface proceeded to explain every detail of his misfortune, the charges he was facing, and the need to get the bond money so he could be released before his true identity was revealed.

"Face, how we gonna get that type of money?" Victoria asked.

"Look, baby girl, I want you to go up to the pool hall and find

Tom. Tell him everything about what happened, and tell him that if he loans me the money, I'll pay him back double."

"But what if I don't find Tom?" Victoria asked with concern. "What if he says he ain't got it?"

Victoria's eyes began to well up, and Babyface could see she was about to start crying. He hated to see her cry. Victoria was his life, his heart, and deep down inside he knew he had failed her.

"Vic, I'm telling you…you better not cry."

Victoria couldn't help it, though. She hated seeing him in this predicament. "Babyface, you are my life. You're all I got. What am I supposed to do? And how am I gonna get that type of money? Babyface, I can't do nothing without you. What am I gonna do?" With that, the tears gushed from her eyes.

Unable to take seeing her in so much pain, Babyface lashed out at her. "You figure it out!" he yelled out in a harsh tone, then hung up the receiver and wheeled his chair out of the visiting hall.

Victoria couldn't believe he left like that. However, she knew he was right. This was a cold world and only the strong survived. The world was now on her back, not her shoulders. She knew she had to be strong, not just for her but for him also. Therefore, from that day on, Victoria made it her business to prove to him that she was the strongest bitch ever. She vowed she would do whatever it took to get him out. She just didn't know how.

Victoria went home to wait for his call, which never came. As bad as Babyface wanted to call home, he couldn't; he had to teach Victoria a lesson. He had to make her realize that nobody in this world is going to do anything for you, unless you do it yourself. He had to teach her how to survive on her own, how to be strong. It was her turn now to return the favor since he was in no position to take care of things himself. His fate lay in her hands. He left her with enough game. Now, it was up to her to figure out how she would play it.

# VICTORIA'S SECRET

After reading a few more pages of Victoria's diary, Babyface couldn't help but to wipe his own tears. He felt bad he'd left her with that much burden, but he also felt good because Victoria proved to him that she was strong. She let it be known as a proven fact that everything he taught her she had lived up to it to the fullest.

═══════════════

The next day, Victoria ventured out on her first mission of finding Tom. As she walked in the pool hall, all eyes were on her, as she franticly scanned the room in search of Tom. The only people she saw were a few pimps, who managed to wink at her in the half second of eye contact she gave them, and some old timers in the back shooting pool. Over to her right were a couple of hoes who looked Victoria up and down while frowning. They didn't like the fact she was stealing their shine without saying a word. As she studied everyone in the room, she decided to ask the old timers had they seen Tom.

"Excuse me. I don't mean to interrupt y'alls game, but I'm lookin' for Tom. Have you seen him?"

The two older men stopped shooting pool to officially check Victoria out. The younger of the two was Jeff, a regular at the pool hall. Jeff was kinda short but real smooth. He never wore a pair of tennis shoes, nor did he own a pair of blue jeans. He only dressed casual, and he kept his hair cut perfectly blended into his full beard with a precise shape-up. Everybody who frequented the pool hall knew him. In fact, he stayed up in there so much that people use to think he was part owner of the spot, but what they didn't know was if it wasn't for Jeff loaning the owner some money the Pool Hall wouldn't have even been open. So, in all actuality, he was part-owner; it just was not legally documented.

"What's your name, sweetheart? I've never seen you up here before. And why you looking for Young Tom?" Jeff asked.

"My name is Victoria, and my reason for finding Tom is personal."

Both men looked at each other.

"Ay, Petey, you hear that? She said it's personal," Jeff said.

"Yeah, I heard her," Petey replied.

At the sound of hearing Petey's name, Victoria instantly knew he had been the one who called that morning.

"Well, sweetheart, we kinda got some bad news for you," said Petey as he lustfully looked Victoria up and down while licking his lips. "Unless you're one hell of a lawyer, your personal days with Tom are over. Now, if you happen to be in need of a replacement, then I'm sure I can accommodate you."

"Nah, it ain't even like that with me and Tom. In fact, I was doing a good friend a favor by coming to holla at him," Victoria informed him.

"Well, sweetheart, Tom's just been indicted in Federal Court," said Jeff as he clinched tight to his pool stick while eyeing Victoria's titties.

Victoria didn't know what to do. She was disturbed. Tom was their only hope, and now she learned he was locked up, too. Petey could tell something was wrong by Victoria's flushed face, so he took advantage by playing the nice guy role.

"What's up, sweetheart? You okay? You look like you just lost your best friend."

*This nigga must think I'm dumb. I know he's tryna fuck me,* Victoria thought as she contemplated whether or not she should let him know she was Babyface's girl. "Nah, I'm okay. I'm just a little tired."

"How about I take you to get something to eat?" Jeff offered.

"Nah, that' cool," she replied as she turned and headed for the door. She wanted to cry, but she knew she couldn't. In fact, she was tired of crying. She had to do something.

At the sight of Victoria's fat, round ass, Petey's dick began to swell. He had never seen a bitch this bad come in the pool hall, and he wanted her for whatever price he had to pay.

"Hey, shorty, hold up for a second," he called after her as he followed her out front.

Victoria turned around to face him. "What's up?"

"What's up with you is the question," Petey replied.

"What you mean by that?" she asked, being clueless.

"Look, shorty, I ain't gonna beat around the bush. I'ma get straight to the point, and it's up to you if you take my offer. How much would it cost me to play?"

Victoria knew what he was getting at, but still she played dumb. "What you mean how much would it cost you?"

"Look, shorty, I'm tryna hit that, and I ain't got no problem giving you what you want. Matter fact, I'll even tip you good if it's as good as you look."

"I'm sorry, but I think you need to go talk to them bitches in the Pool Hall. You got me confused. I ain't no ho," she shot back at him.

"Everything got a price on it, shorty. What if I make you an offer you can't refuse?" asked Petey.

"Yeah right," said Victoria. "I tell you what, nigga. Give me five thousand."

Victoria couldn't believe the words that came out of her mouth. She was actually willing to sell her pussy to get Babyface out. She then thought back to the time when she and Babyface were standing on the motel's balcony having the discussion of whether or not she would consider prostituting and him pimping. Then, she wondered what Babyface would think or say if he found out. Hell, he couldn't be mad at her since he told her to "figure it out", or would he be? She didn't know any other way to come up quick. Sure, he taught her how to be a master thief, but she needed a partner for that. She didn't know the first thing about selling drugs, or who to even sell to. And if she got a job at some fast food joint, it would take her years to save up the money needed to bail Babyface, while still paying bills and feeding herself. Victoria had no other choice. She was about to free her man by any means necessary.

"Five thousand!" Petey shouted. "Bitch, you done lost your mind. Yeah, you a bad muthafucka. I give you that, but five thousand is a down payment on a house. Ain't no pussy in the world worth that unless your shit come with a lifetime guarantee. Now, I tell you what, since I'm horny as a muthafucka and you're the baddest bitch I've seen in a while, I'll give you a thousand. But for that you gotta do whatever."

Victoria evaluated his offer, while looking him up and down. Right before she was about to deny him, she thought of Babyface sitting in that jail, waiting for her to come through for him.

"A'ight, nigga, where we going?"

---

Once inside the motel room, Petey started grabbing all over Victoria.

"Hold up, nigga. Slow down. You gonna get it."

"What the fuck you mean slow down? I'm paying for this shit. Now take off your clothes," Petey ordered her.

Victoria started getting nervous. Petey would be only the second man to ever put his dick in her pussy. She began to hesitate, but within an instant, a rush came over her. This was it; this was how it was gonna be done. She wasn't going to be into it, just let him do his thing and get it over with. To her, it would be business and nothing more.

As Victoria removed her clothes, Petey slid a condom on his erect dick. She then laid on her back and spread her legs open wide. She allowed her mind to drift off, not thinking about how it felt as Petey pounded away with his little dick. All she thought about was getting Babyface home soon.

"Damn, this pussy feels good," Petey commented as he pulled his dick out of her sweet, wet pussy. "Damn, shorty, I had to take it out 'cause I ain't tryna cum yet. This pussy's good as a muthafucka."

Victoria could see that this nigga was a true trick, so she used game and played with his ego. Grabbing his dick, she started jerking it and making him hornier with dirty talk.

"Damn, baby, this big dick is good. Come on and fuck me some more. I wanna feel this big dick in my pussy."

"A'ight then, bitch. Turn around. I want it from the back."

As Petey pounded her pussy from behind, Victoria held her ass cheeks open, giving him a clear view of her clean shaved pussy. She continued talking dirty in hopes of making him cum faster.

"Yeah, baby, that's it. Fuck me! Fuck this pussy…oh, fuck this pussy good! Your big dick feels so good in this pussy. That's right…fuck me harder!

When he started pounding her harder and faster, she knew he was at the peak of busting a nut. So, to speed up the process, she began to fake an orgasm.

"OHHHH…YES, baby, you fuckin' the shit outta me. Oh, baby, I'm 'bout to cum. This pussy's 'bout to cum all over that dick. Oh, yes, baby, fuck me harder. Fuck me…yes…I'm 'bout to come, baby."

As Petey pounded away, he was sucked in by her dirty talk. You like this dick, don't you, bitch?"

"Yes…yes, I love this dick!"

"That's right, bitch! I'm punishing this pussy, ain't I?"

"Yes…you're fucking me good!"

Within seconds of Victoria speaking those words, Petey exploded, and before his dick had a chance to stop pulsating, she immediately got up and held out her hand.

"Okay, where's my money?" she said, looking Petey directly in the eye.

"Damn, bitch, let me catch my breath first."

"Nigga, I gave you what you want. Now own up to your end," Victoria replied.

"You a feisty lil' bitch, ain't you?" said Petey, as he reached into his pocket and peeled off ten Benjamins. "Here you go, and I'ma give it to you, shorty, that pussy is worth way more than 5 g's."

"Yeah, well, why you only give me one?" she asked, hoping he would reconsider and throw her off another four thousand.

"'Cause that's what we agreed on, and anyway, you'll never get another nigga to pay that much for pussy. Matter of fact, I'm probably the only nigga that'll give you a thousand. You lucky you caught me at a horny time. By the way, you can keep the room for the night, if you want. I won't be needing it."

After Petey left, Victoria ran herself a hot bubble bath to wash away the filth of Petey's sweat. While soaking in the tub, Victoria began to analyze what she'd just done, and to her surprise, she didn't feel bad. She felt her actions were justified.

Back at the D.C. jail, Babyface was playing dominoes with Bones, a fellow convict, who was a tall, light-skinned dude with wavy hair, and the first pimp from D.C. that Babyface ever met personally.

"Ay, Bone, let me ask you a question," Babyface said, curious to know how he got in the game.

"As long as it's not incriminating go 'head," Bone replied.

"There you go with your slick ass tongue." Babyface laughed.

"Nah, go 'head, Face. Ask your question."

Face looked Bone straight in the eyes. "How in the fuck did you become a pimp? Ain't no pimps come outta the southeast where you're from. Only killers is raised on the Southside."

Bone laughed. "Face, pimps don't have no region where they come from. It's just in a nigga's blood. It's the hoe that brings the pimp out of a nigga. If you can talk to a bitch and spit realness, and she bites the bait and start breaking you off that bank, then you's a pimp, nigga. It's just up to you to take it to another level."

"Yeah, I feel you," Babyface agreed.

"Face, you mean to tell me you ain't never pimped before?"

"Nah, Bone," Babyface replied.

"Yes, you have; you just didn't know it. I see the way you got that C.O. bitch, Ms. West, running around here bringing you street food and shit. Hell, I know where you be getting that weed from. I bet you ain't even fuck the bitch yet, let alone give her a kiss, and she up here breaking the law for your ass. Nigga, if that ain't pimpin', then I'm in the wrong profession."

Babyface laughed. As he sat in a light daze baffled by Bone's sharpness, he was interrupted by a loud slam on the table.

"By the way, Face, DOMINO, nigga! Give me my cigarettes!"

Babyface just laughed, and then made a mental note to talk to him more about the business of pimping later.

———

As Victoria was coming out of the motel, Royal pulled into the parking lot in his burgundy 600 Benz, dropping two of his hoes off so they could get ready to go trick down on 14$^{th}$ Street. Victoria shook her head at the thought of fucking and sucking all night, then handing over her money to a clown-ass pimp.

*Dumb ass bitches,* she said to herself as the two girls got out of the car.

Victoria could tell by the way they dressed and the shopping bags they carried from the designer shops that they were well-kept and had plenty money. One carried a Versace shopping bag that looked so heavy she could imagine that the clothes were worth more than Babyface's bond. The other had a Gucci bag. The more she studied the girls, the more familiar they looked. The tall one was light brown-skinned with long pretty hair, and looked a lot like Vivica Fox in her glory days. The other wasn't all that pretty, but had a body out of this world. She had ass like the rapper Trina and titties rounder than Janet Jackson's. However, the long scar running down her right cheek, which looked like a burn from a curling iron, distracted Victoria. Instantly, Victoria started thinking about Penny.

*Nah, that can't be Penny. Penny would never be a ho. Besides, she hated pimps,* Victoria thought.

As the tall girl headed to the room, she turned around to call her friend, who was lagging behind with her bags. In a familiar, husky voice, the girl yelled out, "Goddamn, Penny, hurry your slow ass up! You know we ain't got that much time to get ready. Royal will be back in about an hour."

Victoria couldn't believe what she just heard.

"Dang, Liddy, why you gotta be rushing me? You see I got all these bags."

Victoria almost lost her mind. The only two people she loved other than Babyface, and who she hadn't seen in over five years, were standing right in her presence and she hadn't even recognized them.

"Penny!" Victoria yelled while running towards her.

As she got closer, Penny's eyes started to water. "Victoria! Is that you?"

"Yeah, girl!"

"Oh my God...oh my God! Hey, Liddy, come out here!"

Penny and Victoria embraced so hard that the tension only reminded them of the day they parted.

"Girl, what the fuck you call me out here for?" Liddia asked, unaware of the shock she was about to receive. Upon seeing her friend whom she thought she'd never see again in life, she instantly froze where she stood. Liddia pinched herself to make sure she wasn't dreaming. "Victoria! That can't be you."

"Liddia, you look so good," Victoria commented as they embraced.

That day, Victoria swore the three of them would never part again.

---

As the three sat in the room talking, Victoria revealed the truth covering the whole five years of her absence all the way up to the present, including how Babyface saved her from Wayne Wayne. Although she knew he'd be mad if he found out she'd told them he killed Wayne, she felt she had to. She couldn't hold anything back. These were her sisters.

Liddia and Penny were shocked at Victoria's stories. Although their trials couldn't compare to Victoria's, Liddia and Penny had also gone through their share of shit. They told her how Liddia ran away after Sheila took Victoria, and how Liddia returned for Penny after having met Royal. Liddia was the one who turned Penny onto hoeing. Even though Penny didn't like the fact of giving him her money, she did it for Liddia.

Although she wasn't necessarily proud of her actions, Victoria told her story of how she had just turned a trick. Once again, the three women had something in common.

"Bitch, what you charging for that pussy?" asked Liddia.

"I only did it once; I got a thousand for it," Victoria replied.

"Bitch, you is lying," said Liddia. "You can't be serious. A nigga really gave you thousand dollars? Damn, bitch, what you do…lick his ass, let him cum in your mouth, let him fuck you in the ass, or better yet do the R-Kelly?"

"No, Liddia. You're stupid," Victoria said, laughing. Then in a sincere tone, she said, "I had to do it y'all. I gotta get my man outta jail."

"Damn, Vic, you must really love that nigga."

"I do, Penny. I swear I do. I owe him not only my life, but two lives, and I only got one."

"So what you gonna do, Vic? You coming down the track wit us tonight?" asked Penny happily.

"Shut up, Penny. You know damn well she can't come down the track without any pimp."

"Oh well, I guess I won't be going then, 'cause I ain't giving my hard earned money to no pimp. FUCK THAT!" said Victoria with conviction.

"I see you still the same old feisty Victoria," said Liddia. "Well, how you gonna get the money to get him out?"

Victoria looked both her friends in the eye with built-up tears that she fought back. "Can y'all PLEASE help me? I swear to God on everything I love, me and Babyface will both pay you back double."

"I don't know about that, Victoria," Liddia said with hesitation. "Royal don't be playing about his money. Plus, he just took us shopping. He wants a bitch out there working to get all that back plus more."

"He ain't pay for them clothes. You did. You don't owe him nuthin'," Victoria argued.

"Royal takes care of us," Liddia retorted, defending him.

"Oh yeah? Well, tell me where's your Benz? Where's your house? I bet you don't even know his real name."

"I might not know his name, but I know one thing…he ain't in jail," Liddia shot back.

Penny interceded. "Oh, Liddia, now that was a low blow. You don't even know Victoria's man."

"And she doesn't know Royal, either."

"It ain't like she wasn't telling the truth," Penny said.

As the girls were talking, Royal's horn beeped out front.

"Well, Victoria, that's our ride. I'm sorry we can't help you, but if you tryna survive, come out here with us so you can meet Royal."

"Nah, I don't need no pimp, Liddia. Babyface is all I got, and besides, ain't no nigga gonna be shaking me all out in public," Victoria replied.

"Yeah, well, you stupid then. Come on, Penny, let's go."

As Liddia walked toward the door, Penny sat on the bed with tears in her eyes.

"Come on, Penny, before Royal gets mad."

Penny looked Victoria in the eye and said, "Promise me you won't ever leave me again."

"I promise, Penny. I swear to God I won't leave you."

"Bring your stupid ass on," Liddia said from the doorway.

Penny looked at Liddia. "Tell Royal I'm not coming. I choose Victoria. There can never be a greater love than her." Penny then turned to face Victoria again. "I hope I'm doing the right thing, and Babyface better be a cool ass nigga," said Penny as she smiled with tears in her eyes.

As Victoria and Penny embraced, Liddia expressed her anger. "Y'all some stupid-ass bitches! Look at the two of you broke-ass bitches with a broke-ass pimp in jail who don't even know he's a pimp yet. Y'all got to be the dumbest bitches on the face of the earth."

*Beep...beep...beep!*

Bitches, y'all better hurry y'all asses up out here. It's money to made," Royal yelled from his car.

Before Liddia slammed the door, she looked at both her friends one last time.

"Liddia, you don't have to go out there if you don't want to. Come with us. Y'all can come live with me," Victoria pleaded.

"Bitch, please! You think you can just pop up in a muthafucka's life after five years and run shit. Victoria you got me all fucked up, and Penny you's a dumb bitch. She ain't gonna do nothing but leave you again after she get that nigga out. Fuck both you dizzy ass bitches."

With that, Liddia slammed the door in their faces, crushing both their hearts. They loved her more than she could have ever known.

═══════════

After reading a little more of Victoria's diary, Babyface smiled from ear to ear. "Damn, baby girl, you worked your shit, huh? Turned a nigga into a pimp overnight, and got bitches choosing me that didn't even know me. You's a bad muthafucka. Your loyalty is what got us this far. If it wasn't for that, I wouldn't be here. I'd be somewhere stuck for twenty years. Can't a pimp in the game fuck wit my pimpin', and ain't a ho out there that can fuck wit you.

═══════════

After Liddia left, Victoria and Penny spent hours talking, with Penny running down the ho rules for 14th Street.

"Never look a pimp in the eyes?"

"Why, Penny?"

"'Cause once he gets your attention, he'll think you're disloyal to your pimp, and then he'll be tryna cop you all night long."

"Well, we don't have a pimp, Penny," Victoria reminded her.

"Oh, yes, we do. They just haven't seen him yet. Another thing, don't let these hoes know how much you got from a trick."

"Why?" Victoria asked.

"'Cause if it's a lot, then the next time that trick rolls up, she'll be taking your clientele. Also, and most importantly, never suck a dick without a condom on it."

"You ain't gotta worry 'bout that one. I'm strapping up twice on every trick."

Both girls laughed.

After a few hours, Penny had schooled Victoria on most of what she needed to know when it came to the art of hoeing. Now, it was time to put everything she had learned to a test.

# CHAPTER 9

## GET MONEY

That night, Victoria and Penny caught a cab down to New York Avenue and checked into a room at the Downtown Motel, where all the hoes on 14th Street took their customers to turn a trick. They would get a room for thirty dollars, and turn so many tricks that the thirty would multiply by twenty by the end of the night.

"Most tricks would rather feel comfortable in a room than pulling down their pants in an alley and risk getting arrested or robbed," explained Penny.

"Ay, Penny, how much money we gonna be making out here?" Victoria asked, wanting to know how long it would take for her to be on the stroll before being able to bail Babyface out.

"Well, Vic, on a good night you might end up with anywhere between six hundred to a thousand dollars. I, on the other hand, will not do as well. Most tricks bypass me when they see pretty hoes like you and Liddia. I'm not pretty, so I might end up with three or four hundred."

"Penny, don't say you ain't pretty."

"Come on, Vic. We ain't lil' girls no more. Face reality. My face is tore up, simple as that. But you know what? I got a body like a stallion, I give the best head, my pussy stay wet, and I got a fetish for taking it in the ass. If a trick can get pass this ugly ass scar on my face, guarantee I can make him cum in less than five minutes."

"Damn, bitch, who you…Wonder Ho?" Victoria said, laughing.

"Nah, Vic, I leave that up to Liddia and Precious," Penny

replied.

"What! Precious still a ho?"

"Vic, once a ho always a ho. Right now, Precious is still the reigning queen. She got the stroll on lock. Bitches envy her, especially Liddia. But you ain't gotta worry 'bout that, though, Vic. You gonna get a lot of money. You're the prettiest ho I ever seen. I know for a fact you gonna take Precious' place. You just gotta get familiar wit the game. Now, let's stop talking and go out here and do the damn thing."

By the time Victoria and Penny hit the ho stroll on 14$^{th}$ Street, the whole strip was packed with pimps pulling up in all kinds of whips: Benz's, Jags, Caddy's, and Range Rovers. They mostly stood on the corners, watching their hoes jump in and out of cars and bragging to each other about who got the best hoe on the block or the most hoes in their stable. Often times, they betted on which pimp would knock the next pimp's bitch. Further down the street, in front of one of the many alleys in which hoes turned tricks, was where most of the hoes gathered every night to gossip about everything from what pimp got what, who's pimping who, what pimp got locked up, what ho got whipped, what ho got money, etc., etc. The pimps nicknamed this alley Ho Valley. If they looked out on the stroll for one of their hoes and she wasn't out there, he'd figure his bitch got lazy and went down to Ho Valley to catch a rest. Most of the time when a pimp pulled up on Ho Valley, it meant bad news. Somebody was either gonna get smacked or pushed back out there on the stroll.

"Come on, Vic. I'ma take you down to Ho Valley so you can meet your new family."

"What new family, Penny?"

"Vic, even though most hoes don't like each other, we still gotta stick together and watch each other's backs out here. We call each other Ho Sistahs."

After Penny grabbed Victoria's hand, she walked them into the crowded alley of gossiping women and interrupted whatever they were doing to introduce them to the baddest ho 14th Street ever seen.

"Hey, y'all, listen up," Penny said as the women began to gather around. "This here is Victoria, and we go way, way back. Tonight is her first night on the stroll, so be easy on her, alright?"

All the girls introduced themselves, except Precious. Victoria wondered why. All the other hoes were polite, so why wasn't she? Didn't she know that Victoria looked up to her ever since she was a little girl?

Just then, another "working girl" joined them. She came over and gave Penny a hug. "Damn, girl, where you been for the last two days?"

"I've been bonding with my long lost sistah. Candy, this is Vic. Vic, this is Candy."

"Hey, Vic, nice to finally meet you, girl. Penny talks about you so much I feel like I know you."

Candy and Penny were close ho sistahs. In fact, Candy showed Penny the game, and mostly because Liddia was constantly getting tricks. Since Candy and Penny were out-shinned by most of the pretty hoes, it left them enough time on the stroll to bond. Candy was an old-timer. She had been in the game ever since back in the day and only had one pimp the whole time, and that was Bone. Although she gained weight with her age, she still looked good enough to make at least four hundred a night.

"Candy, this is her first night and we really need the money to help get her man out of jail. So, if you can help us get some tricks, we'll gladly return the favor."

Candy looked at Victoria from head to toe. "Shit, Penny, it don't look like she'll have any problems getting no tricks. Hell, we should be asking her to get us some. Besides, where's Liddia?"

Penny told Candy about what happened back at the motel.

"Liddia is stupid. Well, anyway, what the hell we in this damn alley lollygagging for? Let's get this money so she can get her man out, and before these lame ass pimps try to put y'all under pimp arrest for being out here without a pimp. Penny, you know you breaking the rules to the game wit this shit."

Penny shrugged her shoulders. "Rules are made to be broken, Candy."

"Yeah, whatever. Come on."

While Victoria was down on 14th Street turning tricks, Babyface was in jail inquiring about the pimp game.

"Hey, Bone."

"Yeah, whazzup, Face?"

"You really think I can do it?" he asked.

"Do what, Face?" Bone was clueless as to what Babyface was referring to.

"You know…pimp."

"Pimpin' ain't something you do, Face," Bone replied. "It's something that's already done. It comes with the territory of what type of nigga you already are. Ain't no instructions on how to pimp. Pimpin' is power, and do you know what power is? Power is the ability to influence others. Most pimps don't even know they're pimps until a ho turns her first trick and brings him back that money. Do you got a girl who loves you, Face?"

"Yeah, I do," Babyface replied with certainty.

"Well, I bet you a hundred your girl would do anything to get you out right now, even if she gotta sell her pussy."

"Nah, Bone, I love my girl. I couldn't pimp her."

"Nigga, a pimp's girl is his first hoe." Bone laughed at Babyface's naivety. "I love my bitch, too, but I know she out on that hoe stroll as we speak tryna get this bond money together, and you know what? I'd be a fool to stop her. So what she turning tricks. That's life, baby; that's all I know. Shit, Face, a bitch ain't got but one hustle. It's sad but true, and it's right between her legs, and whoever is the nigga who got control of that pussy, he got the keys to Fort Knox."

"Bone, you a wild nigga." Babyface laughed.

"Nah, Face, I just know what I know. I'm a pimp, and I pimps hard. Think about it, Face. It's a lot of money to be made."

"Yeah, I hear you."

———

After only one week of hoeing, Victoria had made a name for herself, and all the other pimps out there were trying to get at her. They even had their other hoes trying to convince her to join the team. Penny even got better, but only after Victoria upgraded her with some cosmetic surgery, covering up the burn mark with a dark brown blush. Penny was so pleased with the results that she could hardly stay out of the mirror. All the other hoes became jealous of the two, except for Candy, and they mostly hated Victoria for giving Penny so much confidence. Penny started working the stroll as if she was the baddest bitch out there. Still, regardless of how many tricks she turned, nobody turned more than Victoria, not even Precious.

Tonight would be their last night working the stroll before bailing Babyface out the next morning. Then, their pimp would be "official." Although they had reached their goal of five thousand dollars, Victoria insisted on making more so she'd be able to buy Babyface some nice outfits upon his release and have a nice start-up bank for them.

After Victoria turned her twentieth trick for the night, she caught up to Penny and Candy who were walking up and down the stroll. "Well, tomorrow's the big day, and I'm so excited," Victoria voiced with enthusiasm.

"Speaking of tomorrow…here, Vic, take this girl. Tonight was my best night ever," said Penny. "I pulled in eight hundred."

"Damn, girl, you're on a roll," Victoria commented while taking the wad of money.

"So, Vic, do you think Babyface is gonna like me?" Penny asked. "Better yet, do you think he'll be accepting of what we did to get him out?"

"Girl, I know Babyface will love you, and I also know he'll be grateful."

Penny tried to find comfort in Victoria's words, but she was still a little uneasy. "Hey, Vic, you still gonna do this when he get out?"

"I'm pretty sure I will. Me and him talked about this before. I asked him would he ever be a pimp, and he said, 'Hell yeah'. And, Penny, Babyface don't go back on his word for nobody. He feels that's all he's got other than me."

"Well, in that case, we done just birthed a pimp," said Penny, laughing.

"And you know that's right. But, Penny, he's gonna be the best pimp ever. He'll love us, protect us, and most of all, he'll be loyal to us. Babyface gonna change the game in pimpin'. He gonna be the smoothest pimp out here and the most paid. You know why?"

"Why?" Penny asked.

"'Cause he got two of the best hoes in the game at the top of their peak."

"Hell, I'll be glad when he comes home because y'all bitches talk too much," Candy said. "Speaking of pimps, here comes that nigga King."

King was the most paid pimp on 14th Street, and Precious was his bottom ho, meaning his best and most loyal ho. A bottom ho is the highest title a ho can get.

"What the fuck does he want," said Victoria. She was getting tired of almost every pimp trying to get at her. She was tired of ignoring them. To her, these niggas were bammas who wore loud suits, too much jewelry, and tried to rhyme every sentence that came out their mouths. It was as if these niggas were stuck in the 70's.

They jumped out of the street and onto the sidewalk as King damn near ran them down while pulling up in his pearl white Jaguar XJS. Instantly, he started spitting game at the hoes.

"You hoes is in violation. Now get your asses off the sidewalk before I place you hoes on probation. Ho, don't snooze. Y'all breaking the rules. Now get back in the street and walk the beat."

They knew they were breaking the rules to the game since a ho's position is in the street. It was disrespect to a pimp if he caught her on the sidewalk, but in this case, he would have ran them over if they hadn't jumped onto the sidewalk.

"Matter of fact, I been peeping you hoes for about a week," King continued. "Who's your pimp? Hurry up and speak."

Penny, Victoria, and Candy all looked at each other. *This nigga is trippin'. Who the fuck he think he is,* Victoria thought to herself.

"Now, if you hoes ain't got a pimp and you in need of the best, then I suggest you hop in this ride before I place you under arrest."

At that, Victoria had enough. "Nigga, please roll out. We ain't stuntin' that shit."

Penny and Candy looked at Victoria in amazement. They couldn't believe she was talking to the biggest pimp on 14<sup>th</sup> Street like that. Everybody respected King, and plus, hoes don't talk to other pimps in public.

"Bitch, where your ho manners at? Don't make me call one of my bitches over here to teach you some."

"Nigga, you can call any bitch you want, and the first one to jump out here is getting fucked up. That'll be one less bitch you gotta worry about," Victoria spat back.

"Look here, ho, I'm not gonna argue wit you. Now you breaking the rules. If you ain't got no pimp, then get the fuck off the stroll. If not, I can make it real possible that you don't turn another trick," King threatened.

Penny and Candy knew he spoke the truth. If a ho didn't have a pimp, she was out of bounds, and if she didn't want to leave or choose a pimp, then the pimps would follow her and every time a trick would pull up, they'd blackball her.

Penny spoke up. "We got a pimp."

"Well, ho, don't blemish his game. State his name."

This time, Victoria spoke up, playing along with his pimpin'. "Our pimp's name is Babyface, and ain't a nigga out here can take his place. So, you better speed on before you get peed on."

Penny and Candy laughed hard at Victoria's attempt at rhyming.

"Fuck you, bitch," King said as he pulled off.

"You gotta pay me first, nigga!" Victoria yelled at the speeding car.

# CHAPTER 10

## P.I.M.P

"**J**ones! Hey, Jones! Jones, you hear me talking to you?" Not used to his fake name, Babyface kept playing dominoes with Bone, not realizing that the C.O. was calling him.

Bones looked up as the C.O. started toward their table. "What the fuck he coming over here for?" Bone said, looking at Babyface.

As soon as Babyface turned around, the C.O. looked at him. "What's wrong, you deaf or something?"

"Who you talking to?" said Babyface.

"I'm talking to you. Ain't your name Jones?"

Babyface had been caught off guard. "Oh yeah, I'm Jones. Sorry, C.O., I was all into this game. What's up?"

"Pack your shit. You made bond," the C.O. informed him.

"What?!" Babyface looked at Bone.

Bone smiled and shrugged his shoulders. "Nigga, you better get your ass outta here."

"Yeah, you made bond. Someone posted it about an hour ago. What's wrong, you wanna stay?" the C.O. asked in a smart tone.

"Hell no! Let's go. I ain't got no shit to pack."

Babyface stood to embrace Bone. He felt kind of fucked up with having to leave his newfound comrade behind, but there was no way he could help him. Bone had been indicted on another charge right before Candy came to pay his bond. Now he had no bond because he had to use the money for a good lawyer.

Bone broke the embrace and took a step back. "Take care of yourself, Babyface, and remember, nigga, you's a pimp. You just don't know it yet. But when you do realize it, PIMP and PIMP HARD."

"A'ight, Bone. Look, if you need anything, just call me."

"Face, I'm alright; you know that. Just get yourself straight. That'll make me happy."

They embraced one final time before Babyface took his first step to freedom. When he got downstairs to where inmates were taken so they could change back into street clothes, the C.O. handed him a bag.

"Here, your people brought you this to wear out. You're lucky I can't fit it, 'cause I was 'bout to keep the shit for myself."

Babyface reached in and pulled out a black and grey Prada sweat suit, then opened the shoe box which contained some matching black and grey Prada tennis shoe boots. As he put on his new outfit, a smile swept across his face. His baby girl did it. She stayed loyal, and on top of that, she made sure her man stepped out in style. The only thing puzzling him was how she did it.

As he walked out the front door of the jail, Victoria noticed he had a slight limp, which actually enhanced his walk, making him look smoother than he already was before his injury. Thanks to the jail's poor medical staff, they took his cast off too early, causing his leg to heal on its own, which left him with a permanent limp.

"Damn, Vic, he's cute," said Penny. "And he got a cool ass walk. Ohh, look at his curly hair. Damn, Vic, I'm jealous already."

"Shut up, Penny. You's crazy."

As Babyface approached the two, he wondered who the girl was standing next to Victoria. *Damn, this bitch is phat as hell,* he said to himself.

Victoria jumped up and wrapped her arms around Babyface's neck so tight that he couldn't help but to think about their past and all they went through. This was his love, his bitch for life, and she proved it to him when she paid his bond. The kiss that followed was so long and passionate they both almost forgot Penny was standing there watching them. After embracing Victoria, Babyface looked over at Penny, who smiled as if she was just as happy to see him out as Victoria was. Oh face come here I have somebody I want you to meet. As Victoria held both of their hands, she introduced them.

"Babyface, this is my best friend, Penny. She is responsible for helping me get you out. Penny, this is Babyface, the love of my life."

Babyface looked at Penny, and then looked at Victoria. "Is this the Penny you cried for, the Penny you longed for, the Penny who meant everything to you, Vic?"

"Yes, Face, this is her in the flesh," Victoria replied.

Babyface then grabbed Penny and embraced her with his strong arms. "Thanks, Penny. I owe you, and whatever you two did to get me out I'm grateful. Thanks. I'm just curious as to how you two found each other after all these years."

Penny looked at Victoria to answer her man.

"Well, Daddy, that's a long story. After we celebrate your first day home, I'll sit down…I mean, *we'll* sit down and explain every detail. I just pray you don't misjudge us."

"How the fuck can I do that? There's nuthin' in this world that can make me pre-judge your loyalty. I love you, Vic, and, Penny, since you part of the family now, I love you, too."

Victoria looked at Penny and smiled. "See, I told you."

"Shut up, Vic. You make me sick," Penny replied while blushing.

---

Babyface put down the diary as Ms. Winters came in the room to check on Victoria. "How's she doing?"

"Well, it seems like she's getting her vitals back up. Hopefully, she'll start breathing on her own soon," Ms. Winters replied, then left.

Babyface smiled at the fact that Victoria was doing a little better. He couldn't wait for the moment when she finally came out of her coma.

"Damn, baby girl, I remember the first time I met Penny. She was so damn shy and sweet. I'm sure glad y'all found each other, 'cause if you didn't, I'd probably still be in jail facing a rack of time." He then leaned over to kiss Victoria on her bandaged head. "I love you, Vic."

After sitting down, he buried his face back in her diary. He wondered if the events that were about to come up would be accurate. So far, Victoria's diary was all truth, but he couldn't understand how someone with a history as wicked as hers had enough guts to write about it.

---

After taking Babyface shopping on Wisconsin Avenue to boutiques like Hugo Boss, Armani, Versace, Everett Hall, and Neiman Marcus, they went down to Georgetown and ate at Toney & Joe's Restaurant, which sat on the waterfront overlooking the Potomac River. They watched as wealthy customers pulled their yachts up to the dock, while the restaurant waiters served them their dinners on the boats.

"Now that's some fly ass shit," said Babyface. "Look, this nigga got bitches catering his food to him while he's laid back on the deck of his boat chillin'."

"That could be you, too, Face," Penny told him.

"Yeah, Penny, I wish."

"Well, your wish just came true, Daddy," said Victoria.

"Oh, so now you gonna buy me a yacht? What y'all do, rob an armored truck?" Babyface laughed.

"No, but I tell you what, if you want a boat, then we gonna do whatever we gotta do to get it for you," Vic replied, trying to prepare Babyface for what he was about to soon hear later.

After a long evening of shopping and eating, the three went to their apartment. The whole time while driving in Victoria and Penny's new ride, which was an old 1985 Honda Accord, Babyface wondered where these bitches got all this money from.

So many questions were running through his head, and he was anxious to get home so he could get some answers.

Once inside the apartment, Babyface couldn't believe his eyes. The cheap pleather sofa they once had was replaced with a genuine leather sofa. Where the small television set once sat was now a miniature movie screen, and when he went into the bedroom, he found a king-size bed taking up most of the room. As he looked around, he spotted a bottle of Hennessey XO and three glasses sitting on the nightstand. He wondered if Victoria was fucking somebody on the side, and once she got what she wanted, decided to dump him. Babyface wanted to know how she got all these things. He was tired of playing the waiting game, and his patience ran out.

"Alright, Vic, you gonna tell me how you got all this shit or what?"

"Are you ready to hear it, Face?" Victoria asked hesitantly, unsure of how he would respond to her revelation.

"Baby girl, I wish you would just go 'head and tell me."

"Okay…well, you might wanna sit down on the bed first," Victoria suggested.

As Babyface prepared to hear what was soon to be revealed, Penny went over to the nightstand and poured three glasses of Hennessey XO. "Here, I think you might need this."

With a confused look on his face, Babyface took the drink. He then started to wonder if they were gonna tell him they'd been fucking each other. If so, he wouldn't need a drink, 'cause he was down with that. Hell, one of his fantasies was to have two bitches at the same time. So, they certainly wouldn't hear any objections from him.

"Now that I'm sitting down with my drink, I think I'm settled enough to hear what the hell is going on."

"Okay, Face, here it goes." Before Victoria began, she motioned for Penny to take hold of Babyface's one hand as she held the other. "Face, before we tell you this, promise me that you'll never hold it against us."

"Vic, just stop bullshitting and spit it out!"

"Okay then...Face, for the last month Penny and I have been selling our pussy on 14th Street. That's how we bailed you out and got all this shit."

Her words stunned Babyface, and all he could think about was what Bone had told him. *Bone was right,* he said to himself. Babyface looked Victoria deep in eyes, then looked at Penny. He knew he couldn't go back to hustling; it was too risky. Besides, these bitches made more money in thirty days than he did in his whole life.

"Vic, you know I don't go back on my word," Babyface stated.

Immediately, Victoria knew what that meant. "So you're saying you're down with it?"

"You muthafuckin' right I am. I'd be a fool not to be."

"Well, in that case, since we down on our knees, we gonna do this the right way," Victoria said.

Once again, Babyface was confused, but not for long. As Victoria and Penny looked up at him with the most sincerity in their eyes, they began proposing to their new up and coming pimp.

"Babyface, do you take Penny and me as your loyal hoes for life and promise to protect us and love us forever?"

Babyface couldn't believe this shit. These bitches were real serious, on their knees pledging their loyalty and life to him. For sure, he obliged.

"You muthafuckin' right I do."

"I now pronounce us pimp and hoes for life," said Penny.

After Babyface guzzled Hennessey, he looked at his two hoes, still in shock. These bitches just made him a pimp, and he vowed to himself that he was going to be the best pimp in the game. Things were about to change.

"Well, since the ceremony is over now, it's time to celebrate," said Victoria, as she and Penny began removing their clothes.

Babyface sat there, stuck on stupid. Here it is he gets the best news of his life and a fantasy come true...he was about to fuck both these bitches together.

# VICTORIA'S SECRET

Babyface's first night on 14th Street was a memorable one. He instantly picked up on the game. As he walked up and down the sidewalk watching every alley that Victoria and Penny took their tricks into, he carefully timed them no longer than ten to fifteen minutes. As the other hoes passed by, they never gave him any contact, but still stole glances at his handsome features. The older hoes didn't like his style of dress, while the younger hoes dug his style. He had on his Prada sweat suit and tennis shoe boots. He was cute with a smooth ruggedness. They all knew who he was, and he could hear them talking about him as they walked past.

As Babyface walked down the block where the other pimps were hanging out, he could feel the cold stares from the pimps with the funny-looking hats and loud-colored suits and Gators.

"Hey, young blood, what's up?" said one pimp.

"Ain't nothing," replied Babyface.

"Dig, playboy, you pimpin'?"

"Most definitely," Babyface answered in a secure manner.

"What's your name?"

"They call me Babyface."

"Oh shit, so you the pimp that got that bitch Victoria, huh?" the pimp asked.

"Yeah, that's me," Babyface replied proudly.

"Say, young blood, from the way you look, it don't look like you'll have that ho long."

"Well, looks are deceiving," Babyface responded.

"Nah, what I'm saying is that you look like you just came from a rap concert by the way your dressed."

With that, all the other pimps laughed.

Royal knew who Babyface was because Liddia had told him how Penny chose him while he was still in jail. This made Royal look bad to the other pimps since he had lost his ho to a young nigga in a sweat suit and with no car.

"Oh yeah? Well, you dressed like you just came from the circus," Babyface said, looking Royal up and down.

"Nah, baby, you got it twisted. I'm Royal, the flyest pimp you'll ever see. It ain't a pimp in the game that can fuck wit me. Don't get mad 'cause you can't afford no Gators; tell them hoes you got to stop holdin' back and pay a playa."

"Slim, whoever the fuck you are, I advise you don't get in the rap game, 'cause that shit you saying out your mouth is weak. You've watched the movie The Mack one too many times. I advise you to get out of the 70's and jump into the new millennium. It's a new era of time now."

"Yeah, young blood, I hear you," Royal said. "But look at yourself. You out here tennis shoe pimpin'."

Again, all the other pimps burst into laughter.

"Yeah, I may be tennis shoe pimpin', but I can bet you that *one* of my hoes bring me more bank than all of yours put together."

"Young blood, I think you better reconsider that, 'cause I've got ten bitches in my stable…"

Babyface interrupted. "Make that nine bitches, 'cause after tonight, I'm knocking one of your hoes."

Finished with their tricks, Victoria and Penny stood at a distance looking at Babyface with the crowd of pimps. They could tell from the commotion that the other pimps were trying to make fun of Babyface. After all, he didn't have a car, jewelry, or any other flashy stuff. To them, he was just a pup in the game.

"Hey, Penny, I got an idea that'll make all them pimps mad right now," Victoria said.

"What's that, Vic?" asked Penny.

"How much money you got?"

"Shit, Vic," Penny said, while pulling out her money, "I only turned a few. I got like two hundred."

"Okay, give it to me. I got like seven."

"What you gonna do, Vic?"

"Just come with me."

Victoria and Penny entered the Rite Aid drug store and

exchanged all the money into one-dollar bills, except for two twenties. They then purchased some rubber bands and split the money up into two fat-ass stacks bound with the rubber bands, making sure the twenties were on the outside and visible. The stacks were so fat it made the rubber bands look like they would pop. One would think each stack held about three thousand a piece.

Victoria then handed Penny one stack. "Take this and watch what I do. After you see me do it, you come right behind me and do the same thing."

"Whatever you say," Penny replied.

As Babyface stood there getting ridiculed by Royal and the other pimps, Victoria and Penny walked up to him, making sure none of the pimps caught their eye. The pimps grew silent.

Victoria approached Babyface first, with her sexiest walk and sweetest tone of voice. After kissing him on the cheek, she whispered, "Here you go, Daddy. There'll be even more after tonight." She then pulled out the fattest stack a pimp ever seen a ho give her man on 14th Street.

"Okay, baby girl. Now get out there and get the rest of my money," Babyface said, patting her on the ass. He knew her game and played along.

Penny then walked up, switching her ass from side to side, and making sure Royal could see her every move, she knew what she was about to do would be his biggest embarrassment...to see one of his former hoes give another pimp a bankroll way bigger than she ever gave him. Penny was more than happy to pull this stunt. She was killing two birds with one stone: humiliating Royal and making her new pimp shine.

"Here you go, Daddy. I know this is a little less than usual, but I promise I'll triple that after tonight."

She then kissed Babyface and handed him over the fat-ass bankroll. The rubber band was so strained that it popped during the exchange. She then walked away swiftly, while every pimp on the corner stood in awe at how this young nigga received more bank in one night than all their hoes do in one week.

Instantly, the respect came raining down on Babyface. One pimp, named King, liked what he just saw, mainly because he and Royal didn't get along ever since Royal knocked one of his hoes.

Royal had a vicious hate for Babyface, yet kept it real in the pimp game and gave him his props. "I see you, young blood. Even though you got on tennis shoes, you pimpin', baby. Pimp on nigga. Pimp on."

As Babyface was about to leave, he turned around to face all the pimps, and in the smoothest, casual way, he said, "Oh, and by the way, my name ain't 'young blood'; it's Babyface and don't ever forget it."

# CHAPTER 11

## HO KNOCKIN'

E ight weeks later, Babyface had enough money to purchase his first car. Babyface and his girls went out to Arlington, Virginia to Eastern Motors, right across the D.C./VA borderline. Arlington, which was only ten minutes from the city, is where most hustlers and pimps came to purchase a car, mostly because of its wide selection of cars and dealerships. But they really purchased from there because one could drop as much money as they wanted and them muthafuckas wouldn't report shit to the I.R.S. They were greedy foreigners who loved to see a young nigga pull up with illegal money.

The first car Babyface looked at was a silver AMG S500 four-door Benz. The sight of this car made his dick hard.

"Damn, boo, this is a serious whip," said Victoria.

"Daddy, if you get this, muthafuckas is gonna hate. You think they hatin' now, but if you get this, they really gonna hate," said Penny.

"Yeah, baby girl, that's what we want 'em to do."

"Hey, Face, I know this is your dream car, but look at the sticker price. I think we need to go back down the stroll and put in some more work," Victoria said.

As Babyface looked at the price, he couldn't believe his eyes. True, the car was really nice, but he just didn't have the bank right now. They wanted seventy-five thousand for it, which in reality wasn't bad for a car that just came out that year. Anyway, the color is not what Babyface wanted. He always said that when he got his Benz, it would be a pearl white 600 AMG.

As they continued looking around, a short, light-skinned saleswoman, who appeared to be in her thirties, came over to help. "Hi, I'm Alice. Are you looking for something in particular?"

Babyface could see that this woman was digging him. Out of all the customers at the dealership, she chose to come help him. He made eye contact with her, and then made her eyes follow his as he slowly looked down at her cleavage, then down to her pussy, and back up to her face.

"As a matter of fact, Alice, I'm looking for something in particular. Something short but sleek, with a lot of curves and light-colored with a sense of style."

Alice blushed at the handsome man as he indirectly complimented her. Victoria and Penny could see that Babyface was about to work his charm, so they stepped back as if they weren't with him.

"Well, are you looking for something rough or something with a smoother ride," asked Alice, as she glanced at the bulge in his pants.

"Depends on the mood I'm in," he replied, smiling at her.

Again, she blushed, but this time it was obvious she was stuck. Babyface went in for the kill. "Look here, Alice, let's cut to the chase. What about we exchange numbers and talk about this over a candlelight dinner, and maybe, depending on the mood, breakfast in Cancun?" Babyface looked her directly in the eyes, showing her that this just wasn't an attempt to improve his game, but this was serious.

Never had she met a man so aggressive and smooth at the same time. As Alice wrote down her digits, she looked up at Babyface once again to study his body language. She wasn't totally sure that he wasn't trying to run game like most of the young hustlers did when they came to purchase cars. However, Babyface had class and didn't bend corners. He was straight to the point, and to add, he was too damn sexy.

"What's your name?" she asked, looking him in the eyes.

"Babyface, sweetheart. So now that we've gotten past all the formalities, are you gonna sell me a car?" He flashed a warm smile.

"I tell you what. Since we're going to Cancun, I might as well save you as much money as I can. Whatever car you want I'll get it down as much as I can, plus you can keep my commission. So, Babyface, how much are you planning to spend?"

"I've got forty-five thousand, but I want something that'll make my money stand out."

"You know what? I got something for you. I think you'll like it; it'll fit your style."

Alice then took Babyface around back where they kept their most exotic cars for personal customers. The first car that caught his eye was a brand new 600 CL Benz. However, he knew it was out of his budget.

"I'll be right back," Alice told him, leaving him to gawk at the Benz.

Alice returned, driving an emerald green, four-dour Lexus LS 430 with cream leather and wood grain interior. This top of the line Lexus just came out four months prior. Babyface's eyes lit up.

"This joint cost sixty thousand brand new, Alice. I know it ain't dropping that much."

"Yeah, you're right, Babyface. We were planning on selling it for fifty-six thousand, but like I said, I'ma get you the lowest price I can, plus take off my commission."

"Okay, boo, work your shit."

Alice went inside to talk to Ahmed, the owner. She told him that Babyface was her brother who'd just come home from overseas on some basketball shit. She then promised him she'd stay at work late to repay him for his favor. At the idea of Alice sucking his dick again, Ahmed told her to give him the car for the same price the dealership paid for it at the auction and to keep fifteen hundred for commission.

═══════════

While Babyface was in the car dealership working his pimp

game, Victoria and Penny got in their car and stepped off. They figured he'd be better off working his charm on Alice if she didn't know they were with him, and plus, Victoria had an idea that would make tonight even better.

"Where we going, Vic?" asked Penny.

"We're gonna make Babyface happy today. We gonna get something he always wanted. Just come on and play along."

As they pulled into the parking lot of the pool hall, Petey was out front leaning on his Caddy and talking on his cell phone.

"Yeah, he got it on," said Victoria.

"Got what on, Vic? And who is that?"

"The watch, Penny. That's the nigga Petey."

"You talking 'bout the trick that paid you a thousand dollars?"

"Yeah, that's him," Victoria replied.

"So what we come up here for?" Penny asked; she was confused as to why they were there.

"We came to get Babyface's watch back. He's gonna be so happy."

"How we gonna do that? That nigga ain't much of a trick to give his watch up for some pussy, is he?"

"No, stupid, we gonna steal it from him."

"Oh, I see. You wanna give him a ménage a trios and fuck his brains out till he falls asleep."

"Yeah, Penny, we gonna suck the skin off this nigga's dick. He's a straight trick."

"And what if he doesn't go to sleep, Vic?"

"Then we take matters into our own hands. We on a mission, Penny. We gotta get Daddy that watch."

As Victoria and Penny exited the car, Petey couldn't resist remembering the last time he saw Victoria. He used to kick himself in the ass for not giving her his number back then. Ever since that day he always thought about fucking her again. He even jerked off thinking about her. As they walked past, they faked like they didn't see him, giving him the chance to look at their ass cheeks bursting from their daisy duke shorts.

"Goddamn," Petey said, and instantly told the person he was talking to on the phone that he would call them back. "Hey, shorty, come here!" he called out, walking up behind them.

Victoria and Penny turned around as if to find out who was calling them.

"Oh, hi. I forgot your name. I was just looking for you," Victoria said.

"Oh yeah? Well, I've been looking for you ever since that day. So what's up, and who's your friend?"

"This is my girl. We were just riding past and I thought about you, so I pulled over to see if you was here."

Petey looked at Penny. Although she wasn't as pretty as Victoria, she was still fat to death. Her body made his dick hard, and Victoria's beauty almost made him cum on himself.

"Yeah? So what's up with you two?"

"It depends on what you saying, shorty. Can you handle both of us?"

When Petey heard that, all types of freak shit entered his mind. "What's it gonna cost?" he asked.

"Since you was so good the last time, I'ma give you a discount, and my girl here is willing to join in for free after I told her how good you are in the sack."

Petey's dick almost erupted right there on the spot. "Come across the street. Let's get a room."

———————————————

While Penny sucked his dick, Victoria sat on his face, making him eat her pussy. They did everything to him, any position, and any kind of way he wanted it. They even put on a girl-on-girl show for him while he jerked off. After about a half-hour of doing almost everything, Petey still wasn't tired. With the way things were looking, they figured Plan A would fail, so they contemplated on pulling out the box cutters. However, right before they come to that conclusion, Penny had one more trick up her sleeve: she would let Petey fuck her in the ass. Petey's eyes got so big that Victoria knew the excitement would drain him. Penny talked so dirty to him while he fucked her asshole that Petey soon found himself on the brink of exploding. After he came, he laid back and smoked a blunt. Victoria could see that he was tired, but it was taking him too long to fall asleep. She wanted Babyface to have the watch, and therefore knew she would have to pull out all stops. She never did it before, not even with Babyface, but she reached in her purse for the Vaseline and invited Petey to fuck her in the ass, as well.

"Come on, baby, you fucked her in the ass so good I got jealous. I'm a virgin in the ass, and I want you to be the first. Come on, fuck my ass."

Petey immediately jumped up at the fact that he would be her first ass-fuck. Victoria packed much Vaseline in her ass, and looked at Penny as prepared for the worst. She couldn't believe Penny had a fetish for this excruciating pain she now felt. Victoria didn't like it, but she just hollered and took the pain in hopes of satisfying Babyface. After hearing her cries, Petey couldn't take it no more. As soon as he came, he plopped down on the bed.

While Penny caressed his nuts, his eyelids grew heavy. Victoria dressed first, and then switched with Penny while she put hers on. Penny wanted to do the honors of clipping his watch, so Victoria continued playing with his nuts until his eyes finally closed. As soon as the caressing stopped, though, Petey's eyes opened. When he saw Penny pulling his watch, he tried to snatch his arm back, but it was too late. They got up and ran out the room as Petey tried to put his clothes on to chase after them. By the time he came running out of the room, they were pulling out of the parking lot. They both laughed as they looked at him out of the rearview mirror, standing in the motel's parking lot with no shirt on and barefoot. They knew there wouldn't be any retaliation. Petey was a major hustler, and he'd lose all respect if somebody found out two hoes tricked him out of his watch all because he was a freak nigga. This was a loss…a major loss that had to be chalked up.

---

As they pulled into the driveway, Babyface pulled in right behind them. When Victoria and Penny got out the car, they became excited with seeing him pushing a Lexus.

"That bitch, Precious, is gonna be fucked up when we jump out of this," Penny said.

"Oh yeah, and them pimps gonna be fucked up at you, especially Royal." Victoria added. "Candy already told us how them bitches be asking 'bout you. You 'bout to run 14th Street. By the way, Daddy, we got a surprise for you."

"What's that, Vic?"

She pulled the Rolex out of her purse and placed it on his wrist. Babyface was ecstatic at the watch that looked so similar to the one he and Victoria stole.

"Daddy we went through some serious shit to get that 'cause we wanna see you happy," said Penny. "Whatever you do, keep it on. It's a signature of our love."

At that moment, Babyface wanted to get sentimental, but he refused to shed a tear and show his soft side that he kept well hidden. After hearing the detailed story, except for Victoria taking it in the ass, Babyface was amused at how much of a trick Petey turned out to be. Before the incident, he had a little respect for the guy, but after hearing how stupid Petey was, he felt no sympathy for him.

"Damn, y'all some wicked bitches. You ain't gotta worry 'bout him, though. That nigga is so embarrassed he won't tell a soul."

---

Tonight was the perfect night. There was a light breeze, and for some reason it seemed a special night for every pimp and ho in the city. Niggas from all over the globe were on 14th Street. As

Babyface pulled up on the scene, he could hear their admiration and curiosity to know who sat behind the wheel. With the pimps feeling threatened, they immediately instructed their hoes to go down the street. Indirectly, these niggas were insecure with their pimping.

Penny, who was seated in the back, was the first to get out. Her dark silky skin complemented her sky blue and cream outfit. The Coogi skirt sat so high off her ass that you could see her bottom ass cheeks jiggle with every step she took. The whole strip stood in shock; never had they seen Penny look this good.

After Penny got out and walked to the driver's side, Victoria stepped out of the front passenger's side with freshly pedicured toes set in her gator sandals. Muthafuckas couldn't believe that she had on a Coogi skirt the same color as the exterior and interior of the car. That shit set the whole strip off. Victoria looked like a star strutting down the red carpet with her long golden hair. As Victoria walked over to the driver's side and stood next to Penny, she, too, struck a seductive pose. After both of them made their grand appearance, it was Babyface's turn.

He popped in his CD, "P.I.M.P." by 50 Cent, and nodded for Victoria to open his door. Victoria held the door open, as Penny extended her hand to escort him out of the car. As Babyface stood upright, everybody check him out from head to toe. He was dressed to impress in his perfectly tailored cream Versace slacks that laid over top his cream Versace slip-ons. To complete the look, he wore a cream and beige sweater, and accessorized with his fifty thousand dollar Rolex and three karat diamond in the left ear.

Babyface smiled while looking Royal directly in the eye. Royal grinned at the young pimp. Even though he hated Babyface he still had to give him his props. Yet, he still was sarcastic when doing so.

"I see you, young blood. You pimpin', baby."

Babyface knew Royal called him young blood as a sign of disrespect, but the others didn't. He made a mental note to get Royal by himself and check his ass one last time. King couldn't resist the young nigga's class; he had to give him his props, too.

"Hey, Babyface, that's a tight ass whip. I recognize a pimp when I see one, and, young nigga, you pimpin' hard," said King.

After King broke the silence, other pimps came over to shake Babyface's hand, offer advice, and even invite him over to their parties. Babyface thanked them for their advice, but despised them for their fakeness. These were the same muthafuckas that wouldn't even talk to him when he first came out of jail.

On the other side of the street, Victoria and Penny stepped in Ho Valley liked they owned the place. As all the other hoes where complimenting them, Precious walked passed the alley and rolled her eyes at Victoria, while Liddia lagged behind her, rolling her eyes at Penny.

"Look at them bitches, Liddia. Out here stylin' and profilin' when all the time they need to be turning as many tricks as they can to help that nigga pay his high ass car note," said Precious.

"I know that bitch ain't just say that. Our man paid cash for his shit. What the fuck he look like wit a car note?" Victoria retorted.

"Fuck that bitch, Vic. She just jealous 'cause King's been pushing the same ol' Jag for three years now. You know how Precious is," Candy said.

"What the fuck is Liddia doing wit her?" asked Penny.

"Oh, y'all ain't heard? Liddia chose King last night," Candy informed them.

"What!" shouted Victoria and Penny in unison.

"Yeah, Royal been whippin' her ass since Penny left."

Just then, Penny felt bad; she had a good feeling that Royal was going to take it out on Liddia when she left him.

"Y'all need to get your girl back. Y'all come too far to let this shit go down like this, and I know y'all are not just gonna sit around and watch her get used and abused," Candy said.

"Hey, Vic, we gotta get her back," said Penny.

"I was just thinking the same thing," Victoria replied.

As Victoria and Penny tried to catch up with Liddia, Babyface sat in his car watching them, wondering why they were walking at such a fast pace. Sensing that something was wrong, Babyface continued to watch from a distance.

Right before they reached her, Liddia jumped into a trick's car, which pulled into the next alley. They waited nearby, knowing she would be finished within the next ten minutes. When she came out, their plan was to convince her to leave King and come with them.

As they predicted, the trick's car pulled out of the alley ten minutes later. After five minutes passed and Liddia still had not emerged, they became worried.

"What the fuck is she doin', Vic?"

"I dunno, Penny. She should've been come out by now."

"Maybe she caught another trick on her way," said Penny.

"I dunno, but she needs to hurry her ass up."

After a few more minutes passed, they heard a loud scream, which had almost been muffled by the sound of the passing cars.

"Did you hear that, Vic?"

"Yeah, Penny. It sounded like a scream."

Just then, they heard it again. Victoria and Penny looked at each other, and then at the same time, they hollered, "Liddia," before running towards the alleyway. When they reached the alley, they could see Royal standing overtop Liddia and stomping her brains out.

"Bitch, I'm Royal! I'll kill you! Never leave a nigga like me," he said as his pointy toe gators crushed her skull. Liddia was bleeding badly, and every time she tried to get up, he'd stomp her even harder.

"Muthafucka, what the fuck you think you doing? Get the fuck off her!" shouted Penny.

"Bitch, mind your business!"

"She is our business, nigga! Now, get the fuck off her," said Victoria, as she pulled out her box cutter.

"Bitch, I'll kill all three of y'all back here."

"Well, that's what you gonna have to do then," Penny said as she swung at Royal. Royal ducked her punch and came up with a right hook to her chin, instantly knocking Penny unconscious.

"Nigga, you crazy, bitch!" Victoria shouted, as she lunged at him with the box cutter.

Royal grabbed her wrist in mid air, kneed her in the stomach, and twisted the box cutter out of her hand. As Victoria fell to the ground, he grabbed her by the hair and held the box cutter to her throat.

Just then, Babyface appeared.

═══════════════════

Babyface put down the diary, sat back, and looked at Victoria still in her coma. "Damn, baby, it seems like I always pop up to save you at the right time. I'm sorry, Vic. I swear I'm sorry. Just pull through, and I swear I'll make it up to you, baby girl.

# CHAPTER 12

## BIG PIMPIN'

fter killing Royal, the word spread around 14th Street that Babyface broke the rules to the game. He killed a pimp over a ho. While the pimps hated him for such an act, the hoes secretly admired him. To them, he was a savior. Bitches were waiting for Babyface to come down to the track so they could choose him, but he couldn't. He had just killed a pimp and broke the rules, and also he heard from Candy that homicide was down there asking questions. They even knew his name. Babyface wondered which pimp or ho gave his name up. So many haters ran through his mind, and he vowed if he ever found out who dropped the dime on him, they, too, would get the same thing Royal got.

"Hey, Daddy, we gotta do something. Candy just called and said the detectives were all over the stroll last night asking for you. They got the spot so dry hoes can't even pull a trick."

"Damn!" Face said as he looked at Liddia. It was all her fault. *If this bitch would've listened to her friends from the beginning, none of this shit would be happening,* he thought.

"What we gonna do, Face," asked Penny.

"Ain't too much we can do but go on the run," he replied.

"Yeah, but where to?"

"We can go to Atlanta," Liddia said.

"What you know about ATL," Victoria asked.

"Well, Precious used to talk about it all the time. It's where King's from. She said they made so much money there, but had to leave 'cause the F.B.I. was looking for King on some other shit. Plus, they got all them strip clubs and be having so many events.

I'm telling you, Face, we could get some real money in Atlanta," said Liddia.

Babyface looked at Liddia and thought, *This bitch better get her ass out there from sunup to sundown, 'cause she's the cause of me losing money.*

For some reason, Victoria felt responsible for this crisis in Babyface's life. She thought about how Face's life would have turned out if he never walked up and found her in Wayne Wayne's car. She thought about what he would be doing if she didn't turn him into a pimp. In a way, she was responsible, yet she also realized this life was desired for him. He was a pimp by blood. It was in him; he just didn't know it.

"What we gonna do, Daddy?" Victoria asked, while looking him in the eyes. "And whatever decision you make, you already know we down till the end. Make no mistake about it."

"Vic, I knew that the day I met you."

"Well, Face, whatever we're gonna do, we gotta do it fast," Penny voiced, stating the obvious.

"Yeah, Penny, I know. I'm contemplating on this ATL thing. Liddia, your ass better be right," said Babyface.

"I am, Daddy. I know we gonna get paid, and I wanna thank you for what you did. I'm sorry for not choosing you in the first place, but I promise to make it up to you."

"Bitch, you better," Victoria said with attitude.

"Don't tell me what to do," Liddia retorted.

Babyface could sense the tension between the two of them and quickly intervened. "Y'all better cut that shit out. We ain't got time for no bullshit."

Victoria and Liddia looked at each other and smiled.

"Bitch, I love you," said Liddia.

"I love you, too," Victoria replied, and for the first time since they last saw each other, they embraced.

"Now, since you two made up, you wanna give me a hand packing this shit?" Babyface said.

"So where we going, Face?" Victoria asked.

"ATL, baby girl, and Atlanta better watch out because here we come. The realest nigga in the pimp game is 'bout to turn that town upside down."

***

After the eight hour drive to Atlanta, Babyface was tired and needed to rest. They checked into the Marriot Hotel on Peachtree Street in downtown Atlanta, where all the happenings were at: strip clubs, bars, night clubs, etc. Downtown was like the Las Vegas of Atlanta. Every pimp, ho, player, hustler, thug, and whatever night crawler Atlanta had was downtown on Peachtree Street.

"Oh, Daddy, let's go to Club 112; the one they be talking about," said Penny.

"No, let's go downtown to Club Cheetah. They say that's where the pimps and hoes hangout," Liddia said.

"I heard the Gentleman's Club is where all the ballers and rappers be hanging at," said Victoria.

Babyface had no energy left in him to hit any of the spots they were naming. "Whatever you bitches do y'all better bring some money back. I don't care where y'all go; just be careful."

"You're not coming, Daddy?" said Penny.

"Baby girl, I just drove eight straight hours, and I'm tired as a muthafucka. Matter of fact, take the keys to the Lexus, but there better not be a scratch on my shit when you bring it back. Here, Vic," Babyface said and handed her the keys.

Penny walked over to him, kissed him on the lips, and whispered in his ear, "You sure you don't want me to stay here with you tonight and make you feel comfortable."

"Not now, Penny. I'm tired. But I'd love to wake up in the morning with my dick in somebody's mouth." He smiled and patted her ass.

The next morning when Babyface woke up, Penny was sucking his dick so viciously that he had to literally pry her head away so he could get up to go wash his face. Next, Victoria came in, sat on the toilet, and began performing fellatio. She sucked and licked his dick like it would be her last time doing it. Babyface gently pushed her head off his dick and went into the small kitchen of their penthouse suite. As he was looking in the fridge for some juice, Liddia, who was a pro at deep-throating, came over and began sucking his dick, damn near swallowing the whole 9½ inches. While in the process of sucking his dick, she pointed her finger in the direction of the nightstand. Looking toward where she had pointed, Babyface's eyes fell upon the biggest bankroll they had ever made overnight. At the sight of the money, he instantly came in Liddia's mouth.

*Damn, what the fuck? Is my dick a breakfast bar or something? Every morning these bitches take turns sucking my dick,* he said to himself.

═══════════

For the next three weeks, Victoria, Penny, and Liddia worked Atlanta so hard that Babyface was holding close to having thirty thousand stashed. He enjoyed Atlanta so much that he even considering staying. Houses in ATL were cheap and the atmosphere was all love. Babyface liked going to all the clubs, especially the Gentleman's Club, which was a favorite spot for him and his hoes. This is where they made most of his money. They no longer had to jump into tricks' cars. Their whole style of clientele changed. They mostly turned tricks with the ballers. Whoever was getting money in that town knew who Victoria, Penny, and Liddia was. They were considered fresh pussy on the scene.

While most of the biggest ballers paid thousands to fuck Victoria, Liddia and Penny would only be getting paid hundreds to fuck their workers. Penny was satisfied getting five and six hundred from one trick. Hell, at home she'd have to turn at least twenty tricks to get that type of money.

On the other hand, Liddia wasn't satisfied. She felt Victoria always tried her hardest to outshine them by bringing Babyface the most bank, and in return, this is why he neglected her and showed Victoria the most attention. Out of the whole time they were down in Atlanta, Babyface fucked Liddia only once; he never cuddled and watched T.V. with her like he did for Victoria and Penny; and he never massaged her feet like he did them. Liddia didn't like being the third ho; she was use to being in charge. All their life Liddia was the one who called the shots, and with the tables now turned, she couldn't take it that Victoria was now in her position.

Babyface never took time to understand Liddia, especially since he was bitter towards her for her mistakes. Also, he didn't care for the way she treated Penny, always taking advantage of her. Another thing he picked up on was Liddia's attempt to start something with Victoria by picking on Penny. She knew Victoria was overprotective of Penny, and always stood up for her when she wouldn't stand up for herself. Even though he didn't like Liddia's character, he still kept her in his stable. He needed her. Liddia was a pro and didn't take any shit from nobody. Not to mention, the money she brought in was good. Babyface knew he had to start showing her some affection; he just had to do it in a pimp's way.

*Pimpin' ain't easy, but somebody gotta do it. And when you do, you gotta pimp hard,* Babyface said to himself while thinking about his friend Bone.

He wondered about his old comrade, the one who taught him the game and damn near prophesized all this shit. *Damn, I gotta go visit my nigga. I hear he's now in Atlanta federal penitentiary. I know this nigga gonna be happy to see me. In fact, I'ma pay my man a visit tomorrow since the penitentiary is only ten minutes away.*

=========

One night, Babyface wanted to go down to the Gentleman's Club, where he had been working his charm on the pretty bartender for the last week. At first, she was reluctant to talk to him, but after three minutes into their first conversation, she couldn't resist Babyface. Every time he came to the club, she would leave a customer she was tending to go talk to him. Her boss knew what Babyface was up to, so every time he'd see them talking, he'd come over and give her more work to do. Tonight, though, Babyface was sure to bring her to his stable. He would put it down like a true pimp.

"You bitches better hurry up and get ready. I gotta get down there and work this ho before her boss comes in," said Babyface.

"Okay, Daddy, give us one minute!" Liddia yelled in response.

"Hurry up, Liddy," said Victoria, as she and Penny was already dressed to go.

"Damn, bitch, can't y'all wait? Anyway, I don't feel too good. Can I stay here, Face?" Liddia asked.

"No," Babyface replied. "Now hurry your ass up and come on. It's money out there to be made." He wasn't being hard on Liddia because she was arrogant; he was being hard because Liddia was the one responsible for them being there in the first place. He felt she had to make up for the loss back in D.C., so he couldn't give her a rest. She owed him.

After only thirty minutes in the Gentleman's Club, Victoria and Penny ran into Fat Rick and his worker, Lil' Tank. Rick and Tank were one of the biggest hustlers in Atlanta. They moved ten bricks a day wholesale. Rick loved being with Victoria. Ever since they came down there, Victoria and Penny became their regular pussy on almost a daily basis. They got so comfortable with them that on some occasions they'd even take them to their stash houses to fuck. Victoria liked Rick. He was cool and didn't have a problem breaking off at least a thousand for that pussy. As for Tank, Penny had that nigga wide open. So open that he'd pick her up just to give him some head while he made runs for Rick. He even opened his stash spot in his Cadillac Escalade right in front of Penny. She observed Tank's every move, but from all the buttons he pushed, she was confused at how his dashboard would pop up exposing all the bricks. She made a mental note to keep watching, though.

While Victoria and Penny left with Rick and Tank, Babyface

sat at the bar working the young bartender. You could tell from the smile on her face that Babyface had her in a trance. He figured he wouldn't let up. He wanted this fine young stallion. He pictured her making just as much as the rest of the girls.

As he was talking, Liddia came over and interrupted them. For a second, Babyface was a little angry, but from the way she looked, he could tell something was wrong. "Damn, girl, you alright? What's wrong?"

"I'm telling you, Daddy, I'm sick. I can't work tonight. I don't know what's wrong, but I've been throwing up ever since we got here. Daddy, can I please go back to the room and get some rest?" she asked.

Babyface knew he was wrong for bringing Liddia out after she had expressed not feeling well earlier. He was supposed to take care of his hoes, not work them to death. He felt a little sympathy for Liddia, and plus, she was fucking up his pimping as he was try-ing to bring in a new ho.

"Here," he said, handing her the keys, "take the Lexus, but come back and pick us up in a few hours. Take some aspirin, and when we get back, I'll run you a nice hot bubble bath. If you ain't feeling better by the morning, I'ma take you to a doctor. Okay, baby girl? Now go 'head and get you some rest."

"Thanks, Daddy," Liddia said as she planted a kiss on his cheek.

After a few hours of working his charm, the young bartender still had not given in, but Babyface wasn't giving up. He got her to agree to let him come pick her up from work the next day. That's all he needed. He figured after one night of lovemaking, the next morning she'd want to do any and everything to make him happy.

Victoria and Penny returned to the club after they finished with Rick and Tank. Rick gave Victoria more than the regular amount, tipping her an extra five hundred since she let him do anal penetra-tion. Penny, however, ended up with her usual six hundred. Since Victoria had a total of fifteen hundred dollars, way more than the amount Penny pulled in, she decided to give Penny five hundred more so she, too, could make Babyface happy.

"Daddy, where is Liddia?" Penny asked.

"Oh, she wasn't feeling too good, so I let her go back to the room to get some rest."

"Well, the club is about to shut down. How are we gonna get back to the room?" said Victoria.

"She should be out front right now waiting on us. I told her to come pick us up in a few hours. Penny, go out front and see if you see her."

While Victoria and Babyface talked about the possibility of bringing another ho in his stable, Penny returned with a confused look on her face.

"Daddy, she ain't out there."

"Damn, this bitch don't follow no instructions! Call the hotel, Penny, and tell her to get her ass down here now!"

"Calm down, Face. She probably fell asleep. You did tell her to take some aspirin, didn't you?" Victoria said.

"Yeah, she was looking kinda fucked up. I hope this bitch ain't pregnant or got some fucking disease."

"Nah, I doubt that, Daddy. Liddy's a pro. She ain't fucking without no protection. She's probably just tired."

Penny came back again with the same look. "She ain't answering the phone. I hope she's alright."

"Penny, call a cab. This bitch probably in there knocked out."

As the cab pulled up in front of the hotel, they spotted the Lexus parked in its usual spot. When they got off the elevator, though, Babyface could see the door was halfway open.

"Damn, what the fuck is wrong with this bitch? She ain't even close the door."

After going inside, they all stood with a shocked expression.

"I know this bitch didn't," Victoria said as they looked around at the ransacked room.

Babyface immediately ran to where he kept his money stashed. As he pulled out the boxes from the closet, instantly his heart fell to his feet. Everything was gone, even his clothes.

"I'ma kill that bitch!" he yelled as they searched the room looking for any valuables they had left.

"Oh, Liddia, why?" Penny cried out. "Why would she do this to us? Why?"

Babyface knew why. He just couldn't admit it. "Vic, call down to the receptionist to see if this bitch caught a cab to the airport. Maybe we can catch her before she gets on her flight."

Even though he'd just taken a thirty thousand dollar loss, he still held his composure. He couldn't let Victoria and Penny see him in a rage. So, instead, he held his pain inside. Although they knew he was hurt, they admired his calmness.

"This bitch done lost her mind," said Babyface. "Damn, she even took our clothes. I swear I'ma kill this bitch. Vic, why the fuck you ain't call down to the lobby yet?"

Victoria turned around to Babyface with tears in her eyes and a piece of paper in her hand. "I don't have to call down to the lobby, 'cause she left us a note."

*Dear Face, Vic, and Penny,*

*I'm a ho, a true ho. I do what I gotta do for my pimp. Please understand you fucked up when you let the wrong ho in your stable. There's no sense in tryna find me. I'm now back with my true family. So fuck all y'all, and do remember this...never trust a ho.*

*Sincerely,*
*"Liddy & Precious"*

After crumbling the note, Babyface balled his hand into a fist. Liddia played her friends, and King played him. All those props King was giving him were bogus. The whole time he had a hidden agenda, and Liddy was under Precious' spell and not his. So, in turn, Precious worked Liddy to turn on her friends. That way, King's name wouldn't be tarnished for violating the rules of the game. Pimps were not supposed to rob other pimps. Therefore, if it was ever brought to his attention, he could always blame it on a no-good ho.

# CHAPTER 13

## PIMPIN' AIN'T EASY

The next morning, Babyface woke up and took a deep breath before reminiscing about what happened the night before. "Damn, this bitch done fucked my game up," he said to himself.

He noticed that Victoria and Penny were still fucked up at what happened, but to him, it wasn't that big of a deal. In actuality, he didn't lose that much. It only cost him thirty-thousand to get rid of a ho he never wanted, but for Victoria and Penny they lost a lifetime friend who they loved since childhood. For some reason they felt responsible for bringing Liddia in the stable, and Babyface saw it.

"Why the fuck y'all looking so down? I know she was y'all friend, but she threw your friendship away a long time ago. You just didn't see it."

"I know, Face. I'm sorry."

"What you sorry for, Vic. Never could I hold you two responsible for her actions. She was the one disloyal."

"What we gonna do now, Daddy?" Penny asked. "We don't have enough money to pay for the room for the week."

"Look, baby girl, suck it up. It ain't that bad. We come too far to get discouraged now. This ain't nuthin' but a minor setback. We gonna do what you been doing, and the same thing that got me outta jail, got my Lexus, and got this Rolex. You're gonna use what's sitting right between your legs to get what we need, baby girl."

"Face, we gonna get all that back and more," Victoria voiced, regaining her confidence. "The bitch mighta stole our money, but she could never steal our hustle. That bitch got the game fucked up. That shit ain't do nuthin' but make us wanna get more money."

"That's right, Vic. That's what I wanna hear." Babyface knew he had a winner in Victoria, who was strong in any situation. That's why she got the bottom ho title, because she knew her position. "Now, Penny, I want you to promise me you'll put all this shit behind you," he said as he held her chin in the palm of his hand and looked into her eyes.

"I promise, Daddy, I'ma do whatever I gotta do to get you back that money and more."

"Now that's the Penny I know," he said as he kissed her lips. "Look, I want y'all to go down to the video shoot they are doing for Lil' Jon and the Eastside Boys that I heard they are filming today, and get them bamma's bank. If you can get in the video go right ahead, but your main mission is to get that money. While you're doing that, I'ma head up to the prison to go visit my man Bone."

"Okay, Daddy, but hold on a sec. I still ain't had my breakfast yet," Victoria said as she dropped to her knees to give Babyface some head.

"Me, either," said Penny as she joined in.

═══════════

After putting his charm on the fat, unattractive C.O. and offering to take her out to dinner at the end of her shift, Babyface had no problem getting into the prison without being on Bone's list. She let him straight through.

When Bone came out in the visiting room, he had no idea who was coming to see him, especially since he had told Candy not to come down any more because it cost too much money for her to travel back and forth. He would rather see the money in his account then spend a few hours talking about the same thing they could talk about over the phone.

As Babyface stood, Bone couldn't believe his eyes. Happy to

see Babyface, he embraced his friend tightly, and then held him by both of his arms, stepped back, and looked at the young pimp dressed in his Gucci sweat suit and tennis shoes. His eyes couldn't help but to also notice the platinum Rolex shining on his wrist.

"Damn, boy, you look good. What the fuck brings you all the way out Atlanta? I know your ass ain't come all the way from D.C. just to visit me. And how the fuck you get in here? You ain't even on my list."

Babyface smiled at his friend. "Bone, I got some shit to tell you, man. A nigga's been through some rough shit, but it ain't all rough. A nigga had some good times, too."

After Babyface and Bone sat down, Babyface filled him in on everything that had happened since he left him back at D.C. jail. He didn't have to tell him about Royal, though; Bone already knew from the last time Candy came to visit him.

A few hours later, visiting hours were over. It was hard for Bone to see Babyface leave. He was more than happy to see his young protégé come up in the game, and Babyface had stayed loyal to their friendship, as well, Babyface would give Candy a steady bank once a month to send to Bone. That in itself was enough to prove his loyalty, but the fact he came to visit was a true honor.

"Face, this visit is almost over, but before you leave, I gotta tell you something."

"What's that, Bone?"

"For one, your biggest mistake was not going back to knock that ho at the dealership. Never leave a potential ho behind. Two, you neglected Liddia by showing Vic and Penny more attention than her. Try not to show a ho that you love another more than the other. Keep it all the same and show the same love. And three, never let a ho know where your stash is at. You shoulda known that one, Face. You can't trust a ho."

"Yeah, you're right," Babyface agreed after having learned his lesson the hard way.

"Hey, look, Face, I'm bout to give you something I've had

since I was sixteen years old. I ask that you treat it with respect. I got twenty years, so ain't no sense in me holding onto it. Plus, from everything you just told me, you gonna need it.

"Thanks, Bone, but I don't need no gun. That bitch can have that money," Babyface said, assuming he knew what Bone wanted to pass onto him.

"Nigga, I ain't talking bout no gun."

Babyface looked at him with a puzzled expression. "What you talking 'bout then?"

"Nigga, I'ma give you Candy. Take this number. She'll be on the first flight out of D.C. to Atlanta."

Babyface stood for a moment looking at him in shock, unable to digest his words at first. "Bone, I can't take your ho."

"Look, Face, you ain't hearing me. Nigga, I got twenty years…not months, but years. By the time I get out, that pussy be done turned to dust. Now Candy may be a little up there in age, but she still look good and plus she's a vet. She knows how to ho, and better still, she's already friends with Vic and Penny. Nigga, they ho sistahs, so they'll be happy to have her on the team."

Face thought about it. He could use Candy. He'd just lost one ho, but he'd be gaining another. Plus, Candy was loyal; she'd do anything for Bone.

"Now, Face, if I happen to win my appeal, you gotta give me my ho back. Deal?"

Face looked at his friend. Bone was a real nigga. Pimps don't give up there hoes, but in this case, he just wasn't giving up a ho. He was giving Babyface a part of him.

"You got a deal, Bone." He then embraced his friend.

"Ay, Face, learn from your mistakes and make sure it don't happen again. Nigga, you a true pimp. Pimp hard, young nigga."

═══════════════

While Babyface went to see Bone, Victoria and Penny were down at the video shoot at Magic City.

"Hey, Vic, we gotta get Face that money back. Did you see how he was looking? He was hurt, just couldn't tell us."

"Yeah, I know, Penny. I hate to see him like that. We gotta get this money and make our boo happy."

"Come on, ho, let's go in here and catch these tricks," said Penny as they walked in Magic City switching and bouncing their asses.

Once inside, every nigga in the club was following behind Victoria and trying to spit game. She had so many niggas trying to get at her she didn't know which one to choose first.

"Damn, Penny, these niggas are tryna fuck, ain't they?"

"Yeah, Vic, they are. This one nigga over there is talking 'bout he'll take me to Cancun. I told that nigga he can take me to the nearest hotel and give me the money."

Both girls laughed.

While she and Penny were talking, Victoria spotted Rick and Tank standing over by the wall checking out some other girls. She knew they probably wanted to fuck, yet wasn't willing to waste the time of trying to get the pussy.

"Hey, Penny, look over there by the wall."

"Oh, Vic, that's Rick and Tank. Sure nuff bank. I bet them niggas' dicks are hard as a rock thinking 'bout fucking them bitches."

"Yeah, Penny, I know, but they ain't got the time to be here all day tryna get them bitches. These bitches wanna be in that video and ain't leaving till the producer says 'Cut'."

"Come on then," Penny said. "We can get this money and then come back to get the rest of these lames."

As Victoria and Penny walked over to the crowd of horny niggas where Rick and Tank stood, other niggas couldn't believe a bitch this bad was coming up to Tank's ass. Tank was more than pleased to see Penny, and he wanted every nigga in the spot to know he was fucking a bitch this phat.

"Whazzup? I know you two ain't tryna stay here and watch these bitches when you could fuck us?" Penny said.

"You got that right," replied Rick, as he pulled Victoria by her hand to take her to an inn not too far from Magic City.

After working Rick damn near to death, Victoria quickly got up and put her clothes on. "Hey, Rick, I know we usually spend more time together than this, but I gotta hurry up and go back down to the video shoot."

"Why, you got some nigga you wanna get?" he asked, sounding a bit jealous at the thought of her getting with some other nigga.

"Nah, Rick, I'm just tryna get in the video."

"Yeah, right. You probably got a nigga waiting on your ass."

"Okay then, Rick, whatever you say," Victoria replied, not wanting to waste time by going back and forth with him. "Can you just hurry up and take us back."

Rick lay on the bed sprawled out, tired. Even though he could have gotten up to drop them off, he wouldn't. He didn't want the rest of the ballers to see him drop her back off at the club after leaving with him. Ultimately, they'd put two and two together, and figure out that he was Victoria's trick.

"Look, Vic, I'm tired. Here's a thousand. Go tell Tank I said to drop y'all off."

Okay, Rick. You the realest," she said, kissing his cheek.

"Yeah, I bet I am."

Knock...Knock

"Who is it?" Tank called out.

"It's Vic. Open the door!" she answered from the other side.

Tank swung open the door. "What, girl? We ain't finished yet."

"Damn, Tank, we got somewhere to be. Can she come back?"

"No," Tank replied flat out.

"Come on, Tank. Don't be mean," Victoria pleaded.

"I tell you what, Tank. We can drop Vic off and then come back, 'cause I ain't finished with your ass yet either," Penny suggested while licking her lips.

At the thought of Penny sucking his dick again, Tank quickly agreed.

"Well, what the fuck you still standing there for? Let's go," Tank said.

While on their way to Magic City, they passed a Church's Chicken.

"Oh, Tank, can you stop at Church's? I'm hungry as hell," Victoria said from the back seat.

"No," answered Tank, "I'm taking your ass straight to Magic City, and then me and Penny going back to the room."

"I'ma tell Rick how you treatin' me. You won't even let me get something to eat. That's fucked up, Tank," Victoria whined. "I thought we was cool."

"We are cool, Vic, but telling Rick ain't gonna make me turn around."

"Come on, Tank. Let the girl eat. She ain't had nuthin' all day, and I'm hungry, too. Besides, I know you gonna want something to eat after you hit this ass," said Penny as she rubbed his dick through his pants.

Tank looked over at Penny and instantly made a U-turn.

"Thanks, baby, and when we get back, I'ma let you fuck me in my ass," Penny whispered in his ear while caressing his dick.

Tank pulled up in the parking lot. "Go 'head, Vic, and hurry up."

"Tank, my feet hurt from being in these heels all day. Can you get it for me?"

"Damn, Vic!" Tank shouted, becoming impatient with her.

"Go head, baby. Listen, I'ma do something extra for going through all this trouble," Penny said while leaning over. "I got this lil' trick I'ma show you with my tongue."

Upon hearing that, Tank's dick grew larger and harder. "What your ass want, girl? And I ain't making no more stops for your ass either."

"Thanks, Tank. You know you my man," Victoria said.

After getting their orders, Tank jumped out of the truck, leaving the keys in the ignition so they could listen to the radio.

"Alright, Penny do you remember how to pop the stash?" Victoria asked, while looking around to make sure Tank went into the restaurant.

"I dunno, Vic. He be pushing so many buttons."

"Well, try it, bitch. We ain't got all day."

Penny pushed damn near every button, but the spot still didn't open. "Damn, Vic, I can't get it to open."

"Try again, Penny."

Penny tried again.

"Hurry up, Penny. He's at the counter now."

"I am, Vic. This shit ain't working."

"Shit! Watch out," Victoria said as she climbed into the driver's seat.

Penny looked at Victoria nervously. "I know we ain't 'bout to steal his truck."

"Shit, Penny, there's money in this muthafucka. Fuck Tank. Our main concern is Face."

As Victoria reminded Penny of their purpose for being there, Penny fumbled with the buttons even more. All she wanted to do was make Babyface happy. "Come on, muthafucka! Open up, bitch!" said Penny, growing impatient.

While Victoria pulled off, Tank came running out the store, food dropping out of his hands. "I'ma kill you bitches! Come back here!"

---

When they pulled into the back of the hotel, Penny was still fumbling with the spot. By this time, Penny was near tears from not having gotten the spot open yet. She felt she had failed Babyface.

"Vic, I gotta open it for, Daddy!"

"Okay, Penny, calm down. I know you're upset. We're gonna open it, boo. Just slow down and think, Penny…think."

Suddenly, something popped into her mind. "I got it, Vic! I got it! Watch this."

After Penny reclined her passenger seat all the way back, she hit every button she remembered, and just like magic the whole front dashboard opened up to expose the most money they had ever seen at one time, along with two bricks and a 9mm Taurus.

"Shit, Vic, how we gonna carry all this?" Penny asked.

"Look in the back for sumthin'."

Penny came back up front with a big gym bag. She emptied the contents and they started placing the money inside, stacking it on top each other like cinder blocks. As Penny reached for the gun and bricks, Victoria stopped her.

"No, Penny, leave the coke and gun."

"Why, Vic?"

"'Cause, Penny, Face don't need that shit. Coke is what got Face locked up. He don't need to hustle; he got us. So what he need that shit for?"

"Yeah, you're right."

Penny left the bricks, but as Victoria was getting out the truck, she stashed the gun on her, thinking Babyface may need it.

*Boom...Boom...Boom*

The banging on the door alarmed Babyface. For a moment he thought it was the police, until he heard them yelling, "Face, open the door! Hurry up!" As he opened the door, they rushed in.

"Damn, where's your key at? And what the fuck you outta breath for?"

"Come on, Daddy, hurry up and pack. We gotta go," Victoria said.

"Go for what?"

"You gonna be happy," Penny said with excitement, "but we ain't got time to explain. We'll tell you once we get on the road."

"Explain what?" Babyface asked.

"This, Daddy!"

When Victoria pulled open the gym bag, Babyface couldn't believe his eyes. He didn't bother to ask any more questions; he just hurried and packed his things.

As they were leaving, he looked at the two people who meant the most to him in this world, and he vowed never to fail them. "I swear to God I love you bitches to death."

"We love you, too, Daddy. Now, let's go," Victoria said, rushing him out the door.

After they were on the road, Babyface drove straight to the airport. Once they pulled up to where passengers of arriving flights would exit, he announced he had a surprise for them, as well.

"What surprise you got for us?" Victoria asked.

"That surprise," Babyface replied as Candy emerged from the sliding doors of the airport.

"Oh my God! No you didn't!" Victoria shouted.

They both hugged Babyface and kissed him before jumping out to greet Candy.

"CANDY!" they yelled as they ran to her, almost knocking her down.

"Damn, y'all bitches sure know how to greet a ho," Candy said as they hugged and kissed her. "I missed y'all."

"We missed you, too," Penny replied.

As Babyface grabbed her bags and placed them in the trunk, he looked at Candy. "Thanks, Candy. Glad to have you on the team."

"No, thank you, Face. You saved me. From this point on, I'm considered your ho, and whatever position you put me in, I'll work it to the best of my ability. From now on, unless Bone happens to get out, you're Daddy to me."

"Well, in that case, hop your ass in the car, ho."

They all laughed as they drove off.

After driving for about an hour, Babyface pulled into the Motel 6 right off the highway. Once inside, he started counting the money.

"Damn, Vic, there's a hundred thousand dollars here! My bitches hit the jackpot!" He then went to the other room to put the money up and came back.

"Daddy, where we going to?" asked Candy.

"I don't know yet. I ain't made up my mind."

"Well, Daddy, it says here that the three biggest cities for pimpin' are Chicago, Memphis, and Milwaukee," Penny said, with her face glued to the magazine.

"What the fuck you over there readin', baby girl?"

"Oh, I picked up this F.E.D.S. magazine outta Tank's truck while we was ripping him off."

"F.E.D.S. magazine?"

"Yeah, Daddy, this is that new magazine. It's way better than that other shit. It's straight street. I'm reading this article on some guy name Pimpin' Ken. He's in here puttin' it down for real," she told him.

"Pimpin' Ken...I heard of him before. Niggas on 14th Street used to talk about that dude. Ain't that the dude that be hanging with Too Short and Snoop Dogg?" said Babyface.

"Yeah, Daddy, that's him. There's a picture of him in here wit Snoop, Bishop Don Won, and a few other pimps."

"Let me see that magazine." As Babyface read, he was amused by the article. He couldn't hate; he had to give the nigga his props. "Damn, this nigga done made movies and all, huh?"

"Yeah, Daddy, but we can't do no movies."

"I know, Penny, 'cause my ass will be indicted on everything. But what we can do is go to them cities and get that money. Damn, this nigga got legit bankroll," Babyface said as he continued reading. "That's what I need. If my bank was legit, I'd get a strip club. It's money in that shit."

"Well, Daddy, if you want a strip club, then we gonna get one," Victoria said as she danced in front of him.

"Babyface, you can get all that shit, and you better believe us bitches gonna ho it up and get all that shit. We gonna get it done like it's supposed to be done," Candy added.

"Well, that's good to hear, 'cause tomorrow we're on our way to the windy city. Chicago, here we come. There's a new pimp in town and his name is Babyface, and can't a pimp in the game take his place."

They all laughed when Babyface recited his motto.

Victoria and Penny were happy to see him smile again. They knew he was proud of them for what they had done, but they vowed to make him prouder by getting that strip club, which was their next mission.

# CHAPTER 14

## PIMP JUICE

As Babyface's Lexus slowly eased up on Chicago's Westside on Roosevelt and Cicero Streets, it seemed as though all eyes were on the green machine. So many hoes and pimps walked up and down the street of old factories and buildings that have been up since the days of Al Capone. These streets were a ho's heaven. Most hoes in Chi-town knew the game before they could grow tits. Chicago was one of the biggest cities for pimping, and the city was known for breeding pimps and hoes. Every family on the Westside of Chi-town had at least one member of their family in the game.

As hoes damn near broke their necks to see the passengers in the emerald green Lexus 430, the pimps welcomed Babyface by tipping their hats. Babyface nodded back while opening his sunroof, giving the pimps a fair warning to lock their hoes behind closed doors. Only if one would understand crisp music that now blasted from his speakers, one would know that this young nigga came to PIMP. As Babyface coasted down the strip at two miles per hour, those looking on could hear the rapper Nelly screaming, "Pimp Juice...I think I'm 'bout to let it loose."

"Ohh, Daddy, we 'bout to turn this muthafucka out," said Penny.

"Yep, this ain't nothing but a big-ass lollipop waiting to get sucked. We gonna drain this town," Victoria added.

Since Candy was up on the game, she felt the need to warn her fellow hoes before they got in over their heads. "Now, look here. These ain't no lames out here. We ain't in no playground, although it may look like one. These muthafuckas is slick and they got game, so, bitches, be careful and play by ho rules."

Having been to Chicago before with Bone, Candy knew they couldn't sleep on this town. Even though it looked like a hoe's heaven from all the steady business rolling through, it still was a pimp's hell, where other pimps shook hands with each other, bought each other drinks, and then stole each other's hoes.

"Candy, since you've been here before, tell me where's the best place to eat, somewhere all the playas and hoes go."

"Oh, Daddy, keep straight on down Roosevelt. There is this spot called Hoaday's, and they got some good ass food," said Candy.

"I hope so, 'cause I'm hungry as shit," Victoria replied.

"Me, too," Penny said.

After Babyface pulled up in front of Hoaday's breakfast spot, Victoria and Penny got out and did their signature routine while Candy held the restaurant's door open for Babyface as if he were a king approaching his thrown. Every playa in the spot turned their heads, some checking out Babyface and others checking out his hoes. Yeah, Chi-town had some bad-ass hoes, but so far, none could fuck with Victoria. Babyface still had the baddest bitch in the game.

"What's up, young playa?" a short pimp said, while nodding in Babyface's direction.

"Ain't nothing, old playa," Babyface replied, looking him in the eyes.

"First time in Chi?" asked another pimp dressed in all red.

"You can say that, but it won't be the last," said Babyface as he looked the man up and down.

"Well, in that case, welcome to playa paradise. I'm Tookie, and I got hoes all over the muthafuckin' Westside and Southside. You can find me at the Rose Lounge down on Madison and Central. Come on down, playa, and I'll buy you a drink."

Tookie held his hand out to shake Babyface's. As Babyface shook his hand, he could see that the hoes with him were stealing looks at the new pimp on the scene, and Babyface felt pretty sure that he'd be able to knock one. Shit, they were in Chi-town where all the rules were damn near handed down from birth, and still, these bitches were breaking them.

"Yeah, Tookie, I just might do that," Babyface replied.

"By the way, playa, what's your name and where you from?"

"Babyface, and I'm from the Nation's Capitol, drama city."

"You from D.C., eh? I know a few players who been down your way. Come by the lounge, Babyface. We'll talk," Tookie said before getting up to leave, with his ho entourage following close behind.

Babyface liked the other pimps' style in Chi-town. They knew how to greet another player. It wasn't no instant hate like what happened back at home. *I guess 'cause it's so much money to be made by all out this muthafucka,* Babyface thought.

"Where's the nearest motel, Candy?" Victoria asked while eating her breakfast of steak and eggs.

"The best spot for us is at the Shamrock Motel. We passed it on our way here."

"You talking 'bout that rundown looking joint with all that traffic? I saw a lot of truck cabs parked there," said Penny.

"Yeah, Penny, it may be rundown, but that's where all the money's at. Tricks come thru 24/7, especially them truck drivers. They be up at four o'clock in the morning looking for some pussy," Candy informed them.

Victoria's eyes got big at the thought of all the money they could make. "Well, that sounds like the place we wanna be, huh, Daddy?"

"I guess so, Vic, but I know there're more spots around here than that one. Right, Candy?"

"Oh yeah, Daddy, there're a few hooker joints we can go to. There's a spot down on Madison Street called The Grand Motel. It ain't a coincidence they named it that, 'cause a bitch can make a grand in a couple hours if her ho game is right."

"Well, in that case, I know I'ma be seeing a lot of money from The Grand Motel 'cause all my bitches' ho game is tight," said

Babyface.

"There is this other hooker spot, too, Daddy, on Lake Street and Cicero. That's where all the pimps gather to watch their hoes work, and down the street from there is the 7-up Strip. That joint be pumpin', too," said Candy.

"We'll plan to visit all these spots in the next couple of hours," Babyface said as he patted Candy's ass.

"Hey, Face, you never gave me my initiation on the team yet," Candy reminded him, while rubbing his dick.

"Soon, Candy, soon, but first I gotta see what type of money that product brings in."

"Oh, Daddy, you'll see. I'ma vet. I'll break my ankles to get your bank."

Babyface knew he couldn't fuck Candy on the first day. He had to make her wait, make her want it more, and from the stories Victoria and Penny shared with her, Candy really wanted it bad, which would make her ho even harder. She was a vet, so he had to treat her like one. The things Victoria and Penny did candy had already done for Bone, so it was nothing for her to get the money. She just needed something to make her wanna get out there and get it, and Babyface held out on her for that purpose alone, just so she could show her work and prove herself.

═══════════════

After checking the girls in at the Shamrock Motel, Babyface went downtown to check into the biggest Holiday Inn he'd ever seen. He got a penthouse suite away from where the girls hoed at. That way, after they finished the night's work, they would have a nice place to lay back and rest. Besides that, Babyface didn't want to lay his head nowhere close to the strip for various reasons.

Once he unpacked, he went down to Polaski Street to the nearest post office, but first, he went across the street to Track Auto and purchased a front and back end bumper to a Lexus the same model as his. He took the bumpers out of the boxes, then placed fifty

**123**

thousand dollars in one and forty-five thousand in the other. He kept five thousand for himself. After going into the post office, he mailed the packages to his own P.O. Box address back in D.C. Babyface planned things ahead of time. Before they left D.C., he purchased a P.O. Box plus extra storage. He never knew what may happen while out of town, so he got the P.O. Box for security reasons, and now it was paying off. Babyface was sending home his biggest stash ever…ninety-five thousand dollars. After knowing that his stash was safe, Babyface then set out on one of the coolest, meanest pimp towns in the world, and started laying down his pimp game all over the Westside of Chicago.

On his way back to the Shamrock Motel, Babyface stopped at Bob's boutique on California and Harrison Streets. He figured since he was in a town with classy pimps, he had to be classier. He was gonna show this town how Babyface, The Pimp, put it down.

Once inside, he peeped the tall pimp he saw earlier at Hoaday's, getting his black and gold Versace suit tailored. This time he wasn't with his hoes; he was talking to two guys dressed in urban street gear, who looked more like drug dealers than pimps. While Babyface checked out some outfits, he couldn't help but notice Tookie hand the two guys a large sum of money.

At first, he thought maybe they were conducting some type of drug transaction, but as the two young guys were leaving, Tookie yelled out to them, "Okay, young lords. Let Lord know I'll get back at him next week."

Babyface instantly knew what that meant. He then started putting two and two together. For one, Tookie and the two young fellows were wearing black and gold, the colors that represented the biggest gang on the Westside of Chicago, the Mighty Vice Lords. Also, Tookie walked with a cane, which represented the staff of justice, another Vice Lord sign. On top of that, he wore a brim hat that represented shelter, which is another Vice Lord sign. Then there was the funny-looking, signature handshake Tookie gave them. From that, Babyface knew Tookie was a member of this organization and that these guys came to collect his dues.

It was rumored that Vice Lords were trying to get away from gang bangin' and venture into politics, and for all those who still dealt in any criminal activity, they had to pay extra dues. The fact that the leader of the organization didn't accept pimps hoeing a black woman, their dues would be taxed higher than others. If a pimp was a part of this organization and didn't want to abide by those rules, then he'd either have to stop pimping or leave town. And in Royal's case, this is what led him to Washington D.C.

"Hey, Babyface, whazzup, young playa? I see you ain't have no trouble finding somewhere to get fly" Tookie said as his tailor measured his suit.

"Yeah, one of my hoes put me down wit this spot. You know a pimp gots to stay fly," Babyface replied.

"Look here. Why don't you come on down to the House of Blues tonight? Be my guest. We got a fine up and coming new R&B singer putting on a show tonight."

"Oh yeah? What's her name?"

"Saleena. There girl's a stallion, and plus, she can blow."

"Yeah, maybe I'll come down and check her out."

"That's good, Babyface. A playa would love to show you some hospitality in his town, and when you come down, just ask for me and they'll escort you to the VIP section."

"Yeah, okay, Tookie, I'll be there."

Babyface accepted Tookie's invitation. This in itself would give Babyface a chance to show his recognition and let everybody know there's a new pimp in town. Soon after his grand appearance, every ho in Chicago would want to choose the young, handsome pimp.

As the Lexus pulled up at the Shamrock Motel, Babyface could see Candy and Penny out front talking to another ho. *Damn, these bitches ain't been here twenty-four hours and they tryna cop me a ho already.*

# VICTORIA'S SECRET

The moment Victoria, Penny, and Candy checked in at the motel, Meeko instantly introduced herself, and within a hour, she had told them everything and anything about putting down their ho game in Chicago. To Victoria, Meeko was too friendly, but to Penny and Candy, she was just a ho sistah trying get to know them.

"Come on, Meeko, you wanna meet our Daddy?"

"Nah, Candy, I'm already breaking the rules by looking at him. If Mousey found out I was looking at a nigga that fine, he'd kill my black ass and put me out on the street."

"Damn, if he's that evil, then you really need to come meet Face," Penny said as Babyface was getting out of his car.

Meeko stood in a trance. She adored his coffee complexion, dark curly hair, thick eyebrows, and his sense of style. Babyface looked her directly in the eyes, and when he spoke, his words came at her in slow motion.

"How you doing, sweetheart?" Babyface asked in his most soft, but aggressive tone.

Meeko blushed. "Fine. How are you?"

Just as Babyface was about to answer, a red Cadillac Fleetwood pulled up and the windows rolled down. Instantly, Penny and Candy knew it was another pimp, and being the true hoes they were, they turned their backs to the car, only exposing their fat, round asses.

"Ay, Meeko, get your ass over here now!" the pimp yelled.

"Okay, Mousey," Meeko said as she hurried over and got in the car.

"Y'all can turn around now," Babyface said to Penny and Candy, who were still playing their position.

"Damn, Face, that nigga interrupted you pimpin'," said Penny.

Candy looked at him with a look of certainty. "I guarantee, Face, within the next seventy-two hours that bitch'll be tryna to break her heels to get you that money."

"Yeah, I sure could use a stallion like that. Speaking of stallions, where the fuck is Victoria?"

At that moment, Victoria emerged from the room with Rick

and they said their goodbyes. She then turned to Babyface and said, "Here you go, Daddy," as she handed him six hundred dollars.

Penny and Candy followed suit by handing him over a total of eight hundred.

"Damn, you bitches only been out here a few hours, and y'all got fourteen hundred dollars already. Look, since it's our first day here, and since y'all pulled in so much already, we're gonna go out tonight and celebrate bringing Candy on the team. Plus, I wanna show these niggas the type of nigga they got pimpin' in their town.

═══════════

As the street lights reflected off of Babyface's chrome rims, one couldn't help but stare as the emerald green Lexus made its way down Wells Street. Babyface pulled up in front of the House of Blues, and as soon as Victoria opened his door, the soothing sounds of Ronald Isley filled the air. Everybody standing in line instantly turned around, all eyes were on Babyface and the three baddest hoes Chi-town ever seen. As they walked by the crowd of people waiting in line, the bouncer took one look at Babyface and opened the velvet rope to let them in.

"Whazzup, my man? I'm Babyface. Tookie…"

Before Babyface could finish, the bouncer cut him off. "I know who you are. You're Tookie's guest. Come on. I'll take you to your seats."

Victoria, Penny, and Candy all looked at each other. Damn, Babyface had made a name for himself there already.

As the bouncer led them over to Tookie's table, Tookie smiled as they made room for the young, smooth nigga who just stole his shine. For a minute, he thought to himself he shouldn't have invited Babyface, but he had to show his hospitality like a real pimp is supposed to.

Tookie got up to greet Babyface and extended his hand for a shake. "Babyface, I'm glad you could make it."

"Glad to be here," Face replied.

"Have a seat," Tookie said as he motioned for them to sit down.

Victoria sat on Babyface's right and Candy sat on his left, while Penny stood behind him with her hand on his shoulder.

From the various Cristal bottles on the table, Babyface could see he was about to enjoy his night. He nodded to all the players who came past their table and introduced themselves. All introduced themselves except for the short pimp he saw with Tookie at Hoaday's Restaurant. He just looked at Babyface, nodded his head, and touched his hat, which is a sign letting one know that he digs his style. The pimp then whispered something in Tookie's ear and left.

"Okay, Mickey, I'll catch you later," Tookie said.

As the pimp departed, Babyface knew he had seen Mickey somewhere before besides earlier that day, but he couldn't put his finger on it.

After conversing with Tookie for a while and watching the soulful singer, Saleena perform, Babyface got up to leave. "Well, Tookie, I had a nice time and you really showed a pimp true hospitality. One day, if you ever drop through D.C., it's only right that I return the favor."

Tookie got up and pulled Babyface to the side. "Look here, playa, I know you're a pimp, but I can tell by the way you carry yourself that pimpin' ain't your only hustle."

"What you tryna say, Tookie?"

"Look, Face, I'm looking for a connection. I need some blow, and I know they got that shit for cheap where you from."

For a second, Babyface wanted to scold Victoria for not getting those two bricks back in Atlanta. He just missed a come up that could have been helpful to his bankroll. "Damn, Tookie, I ain't got no coke."

"Nah, Face, I'm talking about heroine. That shit moves like hotcakes out here. I got all the major spots and a loyal team, but the shit we getting' up here is some garbage. I need a new supply, and, Face, don't tell me all you do is pimp, 'cause every pimp got a side hustle."

Babyface wanted so bad to tell him, "Yeah," but he couldn't. Instead of saying no, though, he asked to see what he was trying to purchase.

"How much you talking, Tookie?"

"I'm tryna get two kilos."

"Well, I ain't gonna make you no promises," Babyface replied. "But I'll keep you in mind."

"Okay, Face, that's a blessing in itself. Thanks, playa. Here's my cell and pager number."

Babyface couldn't believe what he just did, but at the thought of making at least two hundred thousand, he couldn't flatly turn him down.

---

For the next three weeks, the girls worked every ho spot on the Westside of Chicago. After about a week, every pimp and ho in Chi-town had heard of Babyface and his three hoes. Candy's name came up the most since she was a vet. All the young hoes at the Shamrock Motel looked up to her, especially Meeko. Candy and Penny liked Meeko, but Victoria didn't. She got a bad feeling from her. Also, she could sense that Meeko was jealous of her bottom ho position. Meeko wanted to choose Babyface so bad, but it seemed that every time Babyface was about to put down his game, Mousey would pop up out of nowhere. Still, tonight was supposed to be the night.

While Babyface was enjoying his talk with his hoes, his cell phone rang. "Who's this?"

"This Tookie. I was calling about some business."

"Oh, whazzup, Tookie?" Babyface asked.

"I'm calling 'bout that talk we had at the House of Blues about a month ago. Have you heard anything yet?"

*Damn,* Babyface said to himself. He wanted so bad to tell him yeah, but he couldn't. The thought of robbing Tookie had also crossed his mind. Shit, according to what he did to Royal, he'd already broken the pimp rules in the eyes of another pimp. Besides, Babyface always said if he ever became a pimp, he'd change the game a bit, and that extra two hundred thousand sure would come in handy. All he needed to get out the game and get his strip club up and running was half a million.

"Hey, Tookie, I got something nice about to fall through. I'ma call you within the next couple days. Just be ready."

"Okay, Face. I knew you'd pull through for an old playa."

As soon as Babyface hung up his cell phone, it immediately started ringing again. "Hello?"

"You have a collect call from Candy. Will you accept the charges?" asked the operator.

*Damn, I hope ain't nothing happen to this bitch.* Babyface replied, "Yes, I'll accept."

"Hello, Face…"

Before she could say another word, he cut her off. "Bitch, where the hell you at?"

"I'm down at the Cook County Jail."

"For what?!" Babyface shouted.

"Face, I had a trick that was undercover. They played me real good. He even touched me, and he ain't supposed to do that. Not only that, but before the negotiation, I asked him if he was a cop and he said no."

"Then why the fuck are you in jail?"

"Face, you know how these people play. They're some dirty muthafuckas."

"Yeah, alright…look, how much is your bond?" Babyface asked.

"I ain't got no bond, Daddy. I got a one-hundred-dollar citation."

"You ain't got one hundred dollars on you?"

"No, Daddy," Candy replied. "They confiscated a thousand dollars from me."

"Aight, I'm on my way, baby girl. Just sit tight."

After he finished the call, Penny looked at him and asked, "What's up, Daddy?"

"Candy done got her ass locked up for solicitation. Look, I'ma go on down there to pick her up, then I'ma head on downtown to my room. I'll be back in a few hours."

"I wanna go," Victoria said.

"Sure, baby girl, let's go."

As Victoria and Babyface got into the Lexus, a young-looking white ho walked up to Penny and started talking. Babyface never saw her at the Shamrock before and didn't remember her from Hoaday's Restaurant.

"Whazzup with that white girl, Vic?"

"Oh, that's Shelly, Mousey's bottom ho. She's kinda nosey. I don't talk to her too much, but her and Penny are kinda cool. You know how Penny is, always tryna cop you a new ho."

"Yeah, well, she ain't doing nuthin' wrong, and your ass needs to stop being so naive all the time and start talking back to them bitches."

"Oh, that's our roll, Daddy. That's how we bait 'em. I always act nonchalant, makin' 'em wonder how I am. Then, Penny comes in on the friendly tip, and next thing you know they end up telling all their business."

Babyface smiled at Victoria's cleverness. "Your lil' pretty ass swears you smooth, huh?"

"Yeah, Daddy, look who I got it from, the smoothest nigga on the planet, Babyface, and can't a pimp in the game take his place."

"You better say it," Babyface said as they both laughed.

---

While Babyface and Victoria were on their way to pick up Candy, Penny was being questioned to death by Shelly.

"Hey, Penny, how long you been hoeing in D.C.?" Shelly asked her.

"Shit, ever since I had titties," said Penny, laughing.

"So, where's the strip at in D.C.?"

"Oh, that's downtown on 14th Street."

"I heard it was across the street from the White House. Is that true?" Shelly asked. "'Cause if it is, y'all some crazy ass hoes in D.C."

Penny laughed at Shelly's curiosity. "No, Shelly, it ain't across the street from no damn White House, but it's a few blocks away."

"Well, I heard they go to this lil' hangout on the stroll called Ho Valley. Is that true?"

"Yeah, Shelly, Ho Valley's the shit. That's where all the hoes hangout at."

"Damn, I bet y'all was down there doing your thang, puttin' it down."

Shelly was digging too deep, so Penny tried to throw her off. "It's money everywhere, Shelly. You'd have to ask my pimp that question."

"Oh no, Penny, you know I'ma bottom ho. You'll never catch me talking to a pimp other than Mousey. I'm loyal to my man till death. Ya heard? So tell me, what made you leave D.C.?"

"Girl, stop asking me so many questions," Penny said, becoming uncomfortable with Shelly's interrogation.

"Okay, but I got one more question?"

"And what's that, Shelly?"

"While you were in D.C., did you ever run into a pimp named Royal?"

Instantly, Penny's heart started racing. "No! There are so many pimps in D.C., and the only one I've ever been with is the one I'm with now."

"I never asked you had you been with him. I asked did you know him." Shelly was relentless.

"Well, to answer your question, Shelly, no, I don't know him."

# JASON POOLE

While Penny was at the Shamrock getting the third degree from Shelly, Babyface was at the front desk of the Cook County precinct trying to get Candy out.

"Excuse me, officer, but I'm here to pay my sister's citation. Her name is Candice Paine."

The fat baldheaded desk sergeant looked Babyface up and down from head to toe. Instantly he knew the flashy, well-dressed young man standing in front of him was a pimp coming to bail his ho out.

"Well, she's got a one-hundred-dollar citation and a ten-dollar fingerprint fee. You know she wasn't carrying any I.D.," the sergeant informed him.

"Nah, I ain't know that, and since when do you pay for fingerprints?"

"Since the department told us to," the sergeant replied with an attitude. "Now are you gonna pay or what?"

Babyface quickly gave the officer the money.

"Well, that's good that you paid the citation and all, but I have bad news for ya. It seems like she won't be getting out any time soon."

Babyface looked at him with a puzzled look, waiting for an explanation.

"Her fingerprints just came back," the officer continued, "and she's wanted in Washington D.C. on credit card fraud and grand larceny. So the authorities are going to come pick her up and transfer her back to D.C."

Babyface couldn't believe what he just heard. *This shit can't be happening,* he thought. *Why the fuck Candy ain't tell me that she had warrants? Damn, just when I think I'm getting ahead, something else happens to throw a monkey wrench in my game.*

Babyface hurried out of the precinct and jumped into his Lexus, slamming the door.

While Babyface and Victoria were on their way back to get Penny, Shelly was still playing prosecutor.

"Hey, Penny, you sure you don't know Royal?"

"I said no. Why you keep asking me that?" Penny was becoming nervous.

"'Cause Royal is Mousey's brother and he was killed in D.C. over some ho. When Mousey called down there, some pimp named King said Royal had a ho named Penny."

At that, Penny's heart raced so fast she wanted to run, but she couldn't. She had to play it off until she got somewhere safe to call Babyface. "Shelly, there're three hoes on 14th Street named Penny, and like I said, I don't know Royal. I'm sorry if something happened to him, but hey, that's D.C., the murder capital of the world. Niggas get killed all day everyday. Hold on a sec, that's my trick right there. I'ma get back wit you, Shelly. Don't go nowhere."

"Oh, I ain't goin' nowhere," said Shelly, with her arms folded as she watched Penny enter her room with the trick.

As soon as Penny got in her room, she grabbed the phone and went into the bathroom. "Excuse me for one minute, Greg. I got an important phone call to make. This is only gonna take one minute, so do me a favor and go 'head and get that big dick hard and ready for me."

"Don't be too long. You know I gotta be back on the road soon," Greg called out to her.

---

"SHIT!" Babyface shouted as he hung up the phone.

"What's wrong, Face? Is Penny alright?"

"We gotta go get her. She just found out that this Mousey nigga is Royal's brother."

"WHAT!" Victoria said.

"Yeah, plus King told 'em that Royal got killed over a ho named Penny," he added.

"Face, we gotta hurry up and get her." Victoria was close to being hysterical.

"I know, Vic. I told her to lock her room door and sit tight till we get there. She'll be safe in her room." As they were talking, his phone ran again. "Hold on. This might be Penny. Hello."

"Hey, Face, whazzup, young playa?"

"Who dis?" Babyface asked.

"This is Tookie, baby. What, you don't know my voice by now?"

"Nah, Tookie, a nigga just movin' kinda fast right now. What's up anyway?"

"Oh, well, I was just calling to tell you my bankroll's ready when you are. What you throwing them at me for?"

Babyface thought for a second. *Maybe I could go 'head and pull a move on Tookie, get the two hundred thousand, pick Penny up, and head on to Memphis since I already told Tookie I was headed to Milwaukee next. Shit, a nigga needs that money, especially since Candy got caught up in this jam. That's an easy, free two hundred thousand.*

"Tell you what, Tookie. You ready now?"

"Hell yeah, Face. I'm tryna get down. It's almost the first of the month."

"Where you at?" asked Babyface.

"I'm over at the Grand Motel, Room 312."

"Okay...I'm charging a hundred for each one."

"Cool, nigga, you just did me a favor. How long you gonna be?" Tookie asked.

"Give me a few minutes."

Babyface turned his car around and headed to the Cabrini Green projects on the north Westside of Chicago.

"Face, what you doin'? We gotta go get Penny."

"Just sit back, baby girl. I'm 'bout to make a move that's gonna put us on the map for good.

"What about Penny?"

"As long as Penny stays in that room, she'll be safe. It won't be long before we get her. Just sit tight, baby girl. I know what I'm doing."

Babyface pulled up at Cabrini Green projects, which was G.D. territory, the Gangster Disciples. They were one of the biggest gangs in the whole nation, and became nationally known because of their strict rules and discipline. Also, the leader of the organization ran this gang from inside the penitentiary walls. They were heavy into politics, mainly trying to get black people to vote for other blacks to get into office. The gang's structure went from negative to positive, and after seeing such an influence, they even renamed the organization Growth and Development. After hearing the organization's leader in a telephone conversation from prison on one of the Geto Boyz CD's, *The Resurrection*, you could tell by the sincerity in his voice that he was conscientious man, yet still kept it gangsta by letting the world know that a real gangsta would get his ass off the block to go to the voting polls and make a difference in the community. Unfortunately, some of the G.D.'s still remained in the game. Some had no other way to feed their family and others just did it because it was the only life they knew.

Babyface got out his car and called a guy named Future over, who he met about two weeks ago at the club called the 50-Yard Line.

"Whazzup, Face? Damn, you smokin' that hard. You just got two ounces off me yesterday," Future said.

"I'm looking for something else. You think you can help me?"

"What you need?"

"About a quarter ounce of H."

"Damn, Face, I ain't got no weight. All I got is 25's. You'll have to wait till tomorrow," he told him.

"Well how many you got?" asked Babyface.

At that, Future's eyes got big at the excitement of selling out to one customer. "I got like twenty bags left."

"Give 'em to me."

"Damn, Face, I ain't know you fuck around, baby."

"Nah, Future, I got a little party going on with these white hoes, and they on this shit hard," he lied.

"Well, in that case, just give me four hundred, okay?"

———————————

Babyface headed to the Grand Motel, speeding as if he'd been living in Chicago all his life. First, he stopped at the Moo & Oink Grocer on Madison Street, not far from the motel. Once back inside the car, Babyface pulled two fresh pound cakes out of a bag.

"Face, what you doing wit them cakes?"

"Baby girl, just watch my move. I ain't got time to explain," he said as he opened the cakes.

He took a razor, carved two circles the size of a half dollar coin into each pound cake, and started emptying ten packages of blow into each hole. Then he pulled out some gray duck tape and wrapped each cake so many times that he damn near used all the tape. Next, he took out a magic marker and placed a small dot on the hole he put the blow in. He then held both cakes in each hand and smiled at Victoria.

"Baby girl, what we have here is two bricks of the finest heroin from Washington D.C."

"Face, what the fuck are you about to do?"

"Baby girl, I'm 'bout to get us a easy, free hundred thousand."

"I hope you know what you're doing. What if the nigga you're 'bout to sell to is the police?" Victoria asked with concern.

"Vic, come on now. I ain't no lame. This nigga ain't no FED. This nigga done snorted coke right in my face."

"Face, I think you're making a wrong move. This shit don't look right. Let's just go get Penny and leave. Chi-town is too wicked. These muthafuckas is tricky just like a pretty apple, sweet on the surface but bitter at the core."

Babyface became angry. "Bitch, you outta pocket! I run this shit; I call the shots. I'm the pimp and you're the ho. Now play your muthafuckin' position like a gangsta. I know what the fuck I'm doing."

Once Babyface saw his word were hitting her like a sharp

sword, piercing her heart, he began to use his pimp strategy to build her confidence. "Now, baby girl, have I failed you yet?"

"No, Face."

"Ever since we first met it, was me and you, right?"

"Yes."

"All them capers we did, it was you and me, right?"

"Yeah."

"Can't you see I can't do this shit without you, Vic. You've always been my Bonnie and I'm your Clyde. I'm your strength and you're mine. We partners, remember?"

"Yes, Daddy."

"Well, baby, I need you to play that position. We do this shit together like no other. Now, come on, baby girl."

Victoria looked deeply into his eyes. "Face, I love you and ain't nuthin' I won't do for you. Now, let's go get this sucker's money," she said.

---

As they pulled into the Grand Motel, Babyface could see that Tookie's jet black Cadillac Fleetwood with gold trimming was parked out front. He pulled his Lexus on the side of the motel, but at an angle where Victoria could see the room and side entrance to the stairs.

"Look, baby girl, this is only gonna take a few minutes. If you see anything funny, just drive off and go get Penny. I can handle myself, but make sure you beep the horn twice if you see anything suspicious."

"Okay, Daddy, I love you. Be careful," said Victoria as she kissed his lips.

"I love you too, baby girl. I got this."

Babyface got out and walked around the back way so no one would see him coming from his car. Victoria watched as he walked up the stairs onto the third floor balcony. After two knocks, someone opened the door and Babyface was let in, not knowing his fate.

"Hey, young playa, for a minute I thought you wasn't coming," said Tookie as he tried to embrace Babyface, who knew what time it was. Tookie only wanted to embrace Babyface to see if he was strapped, so instead, Babyface just stuck out his hand and pressed Tookie's with a hard aggressive grip, letting him know that he was strong.

"Nah, Tookie, I just had a hard time talking my man into letting them go for such a low number. He said I must really like you to give 'em to you for that much."

"Well, Face, I imagine he was right, because for sure, young playa, if I was in your position, I'd try to get it to you for as low as I can."

"Yeah, Tookie, but right now, I wanna kill the small talk and get down to business so I can hurry up and get this nigga his money."

"My kind of man, Face. Right down to business. Now, let's check out the product," said Tookie.

"Let's check out the bank first," said Babyface.

"You got that, Face. Here you go; it's all in here. You wanna count it?" Tookie asked as he opened the shopping bag, exposing stacks on top of stacks.

"Nah, I'll count back at the hotel. If it ain't right, I'm coming to see you."

"I understand, but I can guarantee you won't be coming to see me. Now, let's see the blow."

Babyface pulled out both bricks and placed them on the bed. Before Tookie could get a good look, Babyface took out his razor and cut open both bricks on the same spot he marked them with the magic marker. "Be my guest; dig in."

Tookie pulled out his car keys, opened his coke spoon, and dug into both bricks, taking a small hit of heroine. After sniffing, he waited a second. "Yeah, Face, this some good shit. I think we'll be in business for a long time."

"Me, too, Tookie. Well, it was good doing it with you; now let me get my ass outta here."

"Me, too. I gotta drop this shit off."

After Babyface and Tookie exited the room together, they took off in separate directions. Victoria was all smiles. Her man did it again. Face, The Invincible, pulled off his sweetest caper. As he entered the stairwell, she no longer had a view of him, so instead, she watched Tookie pull of in his black Caddy. After a few seconds, Babyface would be coming down the stairs.

*Damn, Face, hurry your ass up,* she said to herself.

As Babyface descended the stairwell, a man dressed in a black and red Sean John sweat suit was coming up. He had his head semi to the ground, but Babyface could still make him out, the pimp from Hoaday's Restaurant and the one who had whispered in Tookie's ear at the House of Blues. Suddenly, Mickey was standing in front of Babyface holding the biggest gun he'd ever seen right between his eyes. The .45 Desert Eagle looked like a cannon ready to explode.

"Look, nigga, you know what time it is. Now drop the bag."

As he looked at Mickey, he started putting it all together. Tookie was setting him up from the first day they met at Hoaday's, and this nigga Mickey was his partner. Tookie felt that since he was a pimp, he'd be saved by pimp rules never to rob another pimp. So, instead, he got the bricks for the young lords, and when Mickey got the money from Babyface, he and Tookie would split it. Then, if it ever came back to him, he could deny it, saying he had no knowledge of it and that he'd never break pimp rules.

"Man, look, slim, you can have the money. Just let me go," said Babyface, not showing any signs of fear, although he was scared as fuck.

After a minute had passed and Babyface had not emerged from the stairwell, Victoria started to worry. After a few more moments, Victoria couldn't take it no more. She felt something was wrong, and even though he told her to leave and go get Penny if this was to happen, she couldn't. This was the one time she'd go against his wishes.

Victoria reached under the driver's seat and pulled back the rug to expose Babyface's chrome 9mm Taurus. With no hesitation, she grabbed the gun and walked around to the stairwell from the back. As she reached the bottom, she could hear somebody talking and it wasn't Babyface's voice, but she still could make out the words as she crept up the stairs holding the gun with both hands.

"Nigga, I just don't want the money. I want your life, too," said Mickey.

"My life? What the fuck I do to you? I don't know you. You got me mixed up, playa," Babyface said, trying to stall the man as he spotted Victoria creeping up from behind.

"Nigga, you took something from me in D.C.," replied Mickey.

"Man, I don't even know you. I've never seen you in D.C. What the fuck you talking 'bout, slim?"

"Explain all that shit to God, nigga."

Just when Mickey was about to pull the trigger, Babyface ducked as Victoria let off two rounds in the back of his skull. Victoria was so close that Mickey's brain matter splattered all over Babyface's brand new Gucci shirt. Victoria became deranged to see her man almost lose his life right before her eyes. She thought back to her father and how she wished she could have saved him. She loved Babyface, and at the fact of knowing Mickey was about to take him away caused her to snap. Victoria stood over top of Mickey and emptied five more rounds into the already dead man's skull. Before she could let off another round, Babyface grabbed her and held her in his arms. At the sound of the gunshots, people started coming out of their rooms.

"Come on, baby girl, we gotta go now. Give me the gun." He had to damn near pry it out of her hand as he pulled her down the stairs.

Once inside the car, Babyface sped off to get Penny. This felt like the same day when he met Victoria, only it was her that saved him, not him saving her. Victoria always said she owed him two lives, and this was payment for one. He couldn't be more proud to have someone love him as she did.

As he pressed hard on the gas pedal, dodging in and out of traffic, he looked over at Victoria. "I love you, Vic, more than you'll ever know."

"I love you, too, Face. But we gotta get Penny and get outta here."

"I know, baby. That's what we doing now."

═══════════════════════

As Babyface and Victoria were pulling into the Shamrock Motel, flashing lights from the ambulances and various police cars made their hearts beat so fast that they could feel it damn near coming out of their chest.

"Oh no, please don't tell me that's Penny," Victoria said, as they carried a body out of Penny's room with a white sheet covering it.

Babyface was speechless; he couldn't say a word. He knew he had failed Penny. His greed for money kept him from saving the only other person in this world he loved besides Victoria. As the police and homicide branch started putting up tape, Victoria became irrational.

"Nooo, not Penny!" cried Victoria, while watching one officer pull back the sheet to take a look at the murdered prostitute. Victoria tried to get out the car, but Babyface held her back. "No, Face, I gotta get my girl. No, Face, let me go. Penny!" she cried out in anger and hurt. Although it was completely obvious Penny was dead, Victoria still tried to get out. "Let me go, Face! Nooo! Penny!"

"Vic! Vic!" Babyface yelled as he grabbed her, pulling her close to him and placing the crying girl's head on his chest. By now, Babyface, too, was shedding tears.

After regaining his composure, Babyface looked up at the crowd of nosy bystanders only to see Meeko looking back at him. He knew she had answers. Her eyes were swollen and red from crying. As she looked at Babyface, she placed a finger to her lips, as if silencing someone, and motioned her head for him to pick her up from around back.

As he drove slowly around the side of the motel, he held Victoria's face up, looked her in the eyes, and said, "Baby girl, this is the time I need you to be strong the most. Hold in your pain, Vic. You know I ain't letting this nigga get away wit this."

As he pulled into the back, Meeko hopped in and he quickly drove away from the Shamrock Motel.

"Look here, bitch, I ain't cuttin' no corners wit you. You better tell me everything you know!" Victoria yelled as she tried to crawl into the backseat to beat Meeko's ass. "I'ma kill you, bitch! You knew what was up!"

"Vic, I swear to God I didn't know. Why would I do something to Penny? She was my friend. Why would I do such a thing when I'm supposed to be choosing Babyface tonight? Why would I get in this car not knowing my fate? Vic, please believe me. I'm just an innocent lost ho. I don't even know what the fuck is going on. All I know is after I finished with my trick, I saw Mousey coming outta Penny's room ripping his clothes off. I hid behind a truck and watched him and Shelly leave. I waited there for a few seconds, and then went to Penny's room. I knocked a few times, but when she didn't answer, I checked to see if her door was locked 'cause Penny never locks her door. When I opened it, I saw her on the floor. Victoria, it was me who called the police. I swear to God that's all I know and to prove to you that I had no knowledge I'll go up to the police station and testify to that. Vic, I wouldn't ever in my life set up a friend."

Her willingness to go to the police convinced Babyface and Victoria that she was innocent. Babyface also recalled that while on the phone with Penny that she never mentioned Meeko, only Shelly as the one asking questions. There was only one flaw in her story, though. She stated that she saw Mousey coming out of Penny's room, but Victoria knew for a fact that she had murdered Mousey herself back at the Grand Motel.

"Okay, Meeko, you said Mousey and Shelly left together."

"Yeah, I swear to God that's what I saw."

# VICTORIA'S SECRET

Victoria turned around and looked Meeko in the face. "Bitch, you lying! We just saw Mousey at the Grand Motel fifteen minutes before we got here, and from what I know, Mousey ain't in no position to be getting here unless he's a ghost."

However, what Victoria didn't realize is that Mickey and Mousey were twin brothers. The man she killed at the Grand Motel was Mousey.

"Vic, I know what I saw. I ain't lying."

Babyface then looked at Victoria, thinking she may have been trippin' so hard that she never really looked at the man she just killed. "Vic, baby, calm down. That wasn't Mousey at the motel; that was a guy named Mickey."

"No, Face, I know what the fuck Mousey looks like. I see that nigga almost everyday, and I know for sure that was him back at the Grand Motel. I swear this bitch is lying, Face."

"Did you say Mickey?" asked Meeko, crying as she looked at him.

"Yeah, Meeko. Do you know him?"

"That's Mousey's twin brother!" Meeko informed them.

"WHAT!" Victoria and Babyface shouted at the same time.

"Yeah, Mickey and Mousey are twins. They had another brother who used to pimp in Chi-town, but the Vice Lords ran him out 'cause he ain't wanna pay his dues."

Babyface and Victoria looked at one another, and then he really started putting shit together. Tookie was doing the twins a favor by setting up Babyface. Also, he was helping himself out by splitting the money. Mickey did say mention about Babyface taking something from him back in D.C., but he never even thought he could be talking about Royal. Even though Babyface knew Royal was from Chi-town, he always thought he was from the Southside because that's what Royal claimed. Babyface figured now that the only reason why Royal told people he was from the Southside was cause he was too embarrassed to tell them he got ran out of his hometown.

"Damn, Vic, this shit is all fucked up," said Babyface. "These

**144**

bitch-ass niggas knew about us the day we stepped foot in town. That's why every time Mousey pulled up he never get out the car and let me see his face, and the nigga Mickey always stepped off when he saw me."

"Will somebody please tell me what the fuck is going on? Why would they want to do something to Penny?" Meeko asked.

"Bitch, you mean to tell me you're Mousey's ho and he ain't tried to put you down to get no info on us?" said Victoria, looking Meeko in the eyes.

"Vic, why are you tryna put me wit this shit?" Meeko cried out. "I don't know nuthin'. Mousey wouldn't trust me to do no bottom ho shit. He saw how I looked at Face; he saw how I was friendly with y'all. Plus, Shelly done already told him I was leavin'. That's the reason I hid behind the truck when I saw him. I know Mousey. I know he wanna kill me, too. So, please, Victoria, stop tryna put me wit this shit."

They both knew she wasn't lying, but it was a hard pill to swallow being though she was Mousey's ho.

---

Babyface placed Victoria's diary on the stand next to her bed. As much as he tried to hold back the tears of pain and anger when it came to thinking about Penny, he couldn't. His tears burst out his eyes like an orgasm. He always felt responsible for Penny's death. If only he would have listened to Victoria and not his greed, Penny would still be here. Babyface gave up Penny's life for a funky-ass two hundred thousand dollars, and ever since that day at the Shamrock Motel, he regretted it.

He leaned over her body, kissed her lips, and whispered in her ear, "Baby girl, I never thanked you for saving my life. I could never find the words to express that much love; I needed to show you. So come on, Vic, wake up and give me the chance to show you. You can't die. We're a part of each other."

He then kissed her once again before picking up the diary to read more.

═══════════════

As Babyface pushed down Madison Street, he pulled over up the street from the soul food spot Edna's.

"Okay, Meeko, get out," said Babyface, not looking back at her.

"What you mean get out? Face, you can't do this to me. Where am I gonna go?"

"That ain't my concern." Babyface's voice was void of any compassion.

"Face, please, please don't leave me here. Please, I'm supposed to choose you. Face, I swear I'll do whatever it takes to make you happy. I need you, Face, please. I can't go back to Mousey; he'll kill me. Plus, I don't want no other pimp," Meeko pleaded.

"Bitch, he said get out," Victoria said.

Babyface looked sharply at Victoria, letting her know she was out of pocket for interrupting his pimpin'. As she took notice, she turned back around in her seat, silently looking at the window.

Babyface knew Meeko was innocent, but he also knew Victoria didn't approve of her. It would be a conflict in his stable. As he sat back and thought about what Bone said the last time they talked, so many things ran through his mind. *Face, never let a potential ho get away.* Bone's advice resounded in Babyface's mind as he looked at Meeko through the rearview mirror. Meeko was a go getter, and the fact that if he took her in he'd be saving her life would make her even more obligated to his pimpin'. *Fuck it. Vic's just gonna have to be mad and deal with it. I'm a pimp. I know how to work around this shit. I can resolve conflict. I need this bitch, and when we get to Memphis, I'ma pimp this ho hard,* he said to himself.

"Now look here, bitch. Personally, I don't think you had nuthin' to do wit it, but on the other hand, you gonna have to do a whole lot more than sell your pussy to convince me that you're worthy to be my ho," Babyface voiced with his most harsh look.

"Face, I'll do whatever, whenever. You're saving my life, and I owe you mines. Please, just make me your ho."

"Aight, Meeko, you're in, but if I have one problem outta your ass, you ain't gotta worry about Mousey 'cause I'ma smoke your ass myself," said Babyface as he looked at Victoria out of the corner of his eye. He knew she was mad, but he was the pimp and he ran the show.

"Thank you, Daddy. I swear you won't regret it. I swear," Meeko said while wiping away her tears.

As Babyface was about to pull off, he couldn't believe his eyes. He had to do a double-take at the red Caddy as it hit the corner of Kedgie and Madison. Mousey was so much in a rush that he didn't even see Babyface's Lexus sitting a few blocks away. Babyface quickly pulled off and turned in an alley. He then grabbed the 9mm and told the girls to stay there.

"Face, where you doing?" asked Victoria. "What you 'bout to do?"

"Sit tight, Vic. It's one more thing I gotta do before we leave Chi-town."

As Babyface swiftly walked up the street, he could see that Mousey was all by himself and in a good mood...so good that when he jumped out of his Caddy to go inside Edna's Soul Food, he didn't bother to lock his doors.

"I can imagine he ain't heard about his twin brother's brains on the steps at the Grand Motel yet," said to himself.

Babyface crept swiftly to the Caddy Fleetwood and jumped in the back seat. He lay down waiting until Mousey came out with his food. Babyface's adrenaline was pumping hard. He knew Mousey wouldn't be able to see him through the dark tinted windows, but if he did, Babyface had his 9mm Taurus cocked and ready to fire.

Mousey got into the driver's seat, and as soon as he closed the door, Babyface popped up, wrapping his left arm around his neck like a chokehold. He pressed his gun into Mousey's right temple.

Mousey was in shock; he couldn't move let alone talk.

"Nigga, if you even flinch, your brains is gonna be stuck on that glass just like that nigga in the movie *Scarface*."

"Who are you?" asked Mousey. "And what you want?"

"Look in your rearview mirror, nigga," said Babyface.

When Mousey saw the image of Babyface, he could have sworn he was looking at a ghost. For all he knew, Babyface was dead and he was on the way to Mickey's house to celebrate the revenge of their older brother, Royal.

"Look at me, nigga," said Babyface as he pressed the gun harder in Mousey's temple. "Yeah, it's me, Babyface the P-I-M-P, and right about now I'ma 'bout to change the game. You wouldn't happen to have any more brothers I need to know about, would you?"

"FUCK YOU!" screamed Mousey, knowing that his life was about to end.

"Nah, nigga, fuck you!" And with that, Babyface pulled the trigger and splattered Mousey's brains all over his dark tinted windows.

# CHAPTER 15

## DOWN SOUTH PIMPIN'

For the whole 6 ½ hour ride to Memphis from Chi-town, nobody spoke a word. They just sat back and let the harsh reality of Scarface's CD, *The Last of the Dyin' Breed*, sink into their thoughts. Everybody had their own personal reason for not talking.

Babyface contemplated his next move, wondering if this pimp life really was for him. He knew life itself had a lot to offer, but he was stuck, addicted to the life of a P.I.M.P.

Victoria's reason for not talking was because she felt Babyface was making the wrong move by letting Meeko into his stable. Meeko could never take the place of Penny, and for all she knew, Meeko could have been in cahoots with Mousey, or at least had knowledge of what would go down. Victoria was seeing Babyface differently. This pimp game was changing him; he was a fiend for money. That's all he thought about…money. It stayed on his mind so much that Babyface started neglecting making love to Victoria. He no longer catered to her needs like he used to. All he worried about was making money.

As Victoria looked over at Babyface, she started thinking to herself, *Look at him. How can he let this game change him like that? What have I done? Damn, Vic, you helped create a monster, but yet and still, you'll always love him no matter what. He's your soul mate, partner, and companion.*

Meeko's silence was for a different reason. She knew not to speak unless spoken to. She also knew Victoria didn't want her with Babyface. Meeko always thought Victoria would feel threatened of her bottom ho position if she and Babyface were to get close. Meeko was pretty, but her body was semi-chubby, much like the build of the actress Kim on the hit TV series "The Parkers". Physically, she couldn't even stand next to Victoria, but mentally, Meeko had some of the same characteristics as Victoria and Penny put together. Meeko knew that in time she'd win Babyface over, but she had to do it in a conflict without words.

As Babyface's Lexus floated down the Memphis highway, he saw an exit sign for lounging and food. Being both hungry and sleepy, he took the Milbranch Street exit. As soon as he pulled off the ramp, he spotted a Hampton Inn sitting right next to a Shoney's Restaurant.

"Y'all hungry?" Babyface asked, breaking the 6 ½ hour silence.

Victoria looked over at him. "Yeah, Daddy, I'm hungry," she replied, while smiling at the man she couldn't stay mad at for at least twenty-four hours.

Babyface added humor when he saw her smile. "Wow, she speaks. For a minute, I thought you went deaf on me," he said as he smiled at the love of his life. He was happy to see her smile. She brought brightness to his day.

"Oh, Daddy, I'm so hungry I can eat a horse," Meeko voiced.

"I bet you can, Meeko, and now that we in Memphis, which is one of the biggest pimp capitols, by tomorrow morning your ass is gonna be eating a whole lotta horse," said Babyface as Victoria burst into laugher.

"I don't know what you're laughing for, Vic. That goes for you, too," Meeko said.

"Bitch, shut the fuck up!" Victoria's mood changed when Meeko opened her mouth, but Babyface intervened quickly.

"Now, Vic, I ain't gonna have this shit. You two bitches gonna have to work your problems out. I can't have two hoes going at it all the time. I need both my hoes to get along. What I look like, a young, smooth pimp coming into a new pimp town with two mad hoes. That shit'll blemish my name."

Victoria looked at him with an expression that showed she was disappointed in herself. "You're right, Daddy. I'm sorry."

"I never had a problem with you, Vic. In fact, I always admired you. I know how close you and Penny were, and I'm sorry for what happened to her. She was my friend, too, and if it wasn't for her telling me how much she loved you and Face, and how much of a family you were, then I wouldn't even be here. I've always wanted to be a part of a family I could love and who would love me in return. Please, Vic, just gimme a chance," Meeko said as her eyes became watery.

Victoria knew her words were sincere, but what really got to her was when she looked into Meeko's eyes and saw Penny, a lost little girl who needed love.

"Come here," Victoria told her as she took Meeko into a tight hug, as if she was hugging Penny. "I'm sorry, girl. You know you my sistah. She then kissed Meeko's tear as it ran down her cheek. "Now stop that crying. You're Babyface's ho, and you know he don't allow that shit," said Victoria as she smiled at Babyface.

"You got that right. Meeko, it's rules in this family and we don't break 'em for nothing," Babyface said, happy that his hoes made up.

"Well, Daddy, I'll be glad when you break *me* in," Meeko replied, while smiling and indirectly begging him to make love to her.

"I'll get around to it, baby girl, but right now, let's go up in Shoney's and eat. A nigga's hungry."

After eating, Babyface checked into the Hampton Inn. Once inside the hotel, they unpacked and settled in. While Meeko took a long shower, Babyface made passionate love to Victoria so good that it felt better than he ever did. This time he took pride in fucking her. He knew he had to make love to Victoria like that. He knew he had been neglecting her. No matter how much Victoria sold her pussy no one ever made her feel like Babyface did. When it came down to sex, he was her first and only love. The sex she had with tricks wasn't sex at all; it was her job and never did she like it. After giving Victoria at least seven straight orgasms, they both became exhausted and fell asleep.

A few hours later, Babyface got up to shower. While standing under the hot water, his thoughts turned to Penny. Even though he didn't permit crying, tears were running down his face as stuck his head under the water to camouflage them. He then thought about Bone, and felt he had failed him to a certain extent. But it wasn't his fault. Candy should have let him know about her warrants before she got with him. Although it may not have made a difference, at least he would have been prepared and took better precautions. Now he had to get as much money as he could in Memphis, and then go back to D.C. to get Candy a lawyer and pay her bond. Next, he thought about his newfound ho. Although she was not as physically attractive like all his other hoes, she still was very pretty. He figured if he placed her on a strict 30-day diet, she'd lose about twenty-five pounds and become one of the baddest bitches he had other than Victoria. Or maybe she'd be running side by side with Victoria depending on her loyalty.

"Damn, I swear this pimpin' shit is gonna be the death of me," said Babyface as he talked to himself in the shower. "Killin' pimps, robbin' pimps, hoes stealing, hoes getting killed, hoes getting locked up…damn!"

As he stepped out the shower, he was startled at the sight of Meeko standing there, towel in hand. "Come on, Daddy. Let me dry you off."

"Go 'head. Be my guest," Babyface replied, accepting the offer.

While drying him off, she paid close attention to his dick, caressing it and getting his dick to full erection. She then dropped to her knees and kissed the head of his dick before placing it inside her warm wet mouth. She bobbed her head up and down as if she was sucking a Popsicle, often times taking it out to jerk it and lick up and down the shaft. As Meeko sucked, licked, and stroked, Babyface almost reached his peak. She performed so well that he figured he'd award her with something she'd been longing for ever since she saw him. Babyface jerked back, taking his dick out of her mouth, and pulled her to a standing position.

"What's wrong, Daddy? You don't like it?" Meeko asked, looking confused.

"Oh, I like it, and I'm 'bout to show you how much. Now turn around and touch your toes."

Meeko loved the aggression; it made her pussy pulsate even more. She damn near had an orgasm just from pulling down her thong and thinking about what was soon to happen. She bent over, spread her legs as wide as she could, and wrapped her hands around her ankles.

As Babyface placed the head of his dick in her pussy, he could feel the wetness as it built up. He slowly drove his dick all the way in her pussy to its maximum length as she moaned in ecstasy. After a few slow strokes, his rhythm increased and her moans became louder. He then held both ass cheeks, spread them apart, and began pounding harder. As Meeko placed her hands on the wall to steady herself, she stuck her ass out to take all of his pleasure. His dick was so good that she fell in love instantly. Meeko came at least three times. Having multiple orgasms was something she had never had, and Babyface was the first man to discover her g-spot.

At the sound of her moans and the wetness of her pussy, Babyface couldn't hold back any longer. He exploded as he held her from behind, fondling her big titties and softly kissing her neck while the tears fell down her face.

"Daddy, please don't ever leave me. I love you and I'll do whatever for you, even if it cost me my life. Just please don't ever leave me. I'm your ho for life and even in my death."

After hearing Meeko's commitment and dedication, Babyface was pleased. He had completed his first mission with Meeko. She was the fourth ho to swear her life to him.

As Victoria lay still sleeping and Meeko got in the shower only to play with her pussy and reminisce about the next time he would make her feel good again, Babyface grabbed the suitcase and started counting the money from Tookie's bitch-ass.

As he counted, Babyface couldn't help but to laugh. "Tookie

put shit in the game all around the board. He was twenty thousand short. Damn, this bitch nigga a cruddy muthafucka. What if those bricks were real? I'd be twenty thousand short. That's a'ight, though, 'cause whoever he give them bricks to, them niggas gonna kill his ass.

He calculated that after mailing this money to add to what he already sent home, he would have $225,000, and only needed another $275,000 to open the strip club, which he would aptly name "Victoria's Cocktail Club".

═══════════

The next day, Babyface took the girls shopping at the Mall of Memphis. After Victoria and Meeko grabbed some things out of Goldsmith's Department Store, it was Babyface's turn to add to his wardrobe so he could be shitty sharp. He chose to patronize Milano's, the most expensive store in the mall where all the ballers and playas came to shop. They had everything from Versace, Gucci, Armani, Caesar Paciotti, Burberry, and more expensive brand names. They also carried colored gators, slip-ons, loafers, etc.

Babyface purchased a grey Versace sweat suit, a pair of black Armani linen pants, and a pair of black slip-ons by Lorenzo Banfi. The most expensive thing he bought was a four thousand dollar Armani dress coat.

As he was paying for his items, a tall, baldheaded pimp stepped up beside him. "Damn, playa, I see you got a helluva taste in clothes. That coat costs a bad muthafucka."

"Yeah, the joint's a'ight. I'm just glad it's the only one they got. I can't stand to see another nigga with the same shit I got on," Babyface said.

"I feel you playa. Me, too. I'm Lonnie B, Memphis' finest," the pimp said as he stuck his hand out, exposing two diamond encrusted rings. He had so many diamonds in his shit you could tell if the metal they were set in was gold or platinum.

"And I'm Babyface, D.C.'s most valuable playa."

"From the way you look and the fact you got them two fine pieces over there with you, I take it you and I are in the same profession. Pimp recognize pimp," said Lonnie B.

"It's only right that we do. Character always reflects lifestyle," Babyface replied.

As he spoke, Lonnie B's eyes almost popped out of their sockets at the sight of Babyface's Rolex that was worth almost his whole stash.

"Damn, playa, that's serious timepiece you got there."

"Yeah, it's just a lil' gift from my girls to show their pimp some appreciation."

"How long you been in town, Babyface?"

"Just got here two days ago."

"Damn, playa, I take it you ain't been down the track yet," said Lonnie B.

"To be honest with you, I don't even know where it's at yet."

"Well, let me be the first to turn an outta town pimp on to some money. The stroll is on Brooks Road. We got a few shake joints down there we work out of. You'll love it. It's a real pimp's atmosphere. You do know this is one of the biggest and best pimp capitols, right?"

"I wouldn't be here if it wasn't, playa," replied Babyface.

Lonnie B grinned. "I like your style, Babyface. Why don't you come on down to the shake joint tonight? I'll show you some southern pimp's hospitality."

"What the fuck is a shake joint?" asked Babyface, looking confused.

Lonnie B laughed. "Oh, that's right. You from outta town so it's gonna take a minute to catch our lingo. The shake joint is where the bitches dance and the playas shoot game."

"Oooh, okay, you mean the strip club. Where's it at?"

"We got a few," Lonnie B replied, "but most of the time the fly playas hang out at Pure Passion. Come on by tonight. I'm sure you'll like it."

"I just might do that," Babyface said as he paid for his things and exited the store, with Victoria and Meeko following closely behind.

═══════════

As Babyface pulled up in front of Pure Passion, he checked out the many luxury cars lined up along the curb. While everybody looked at the Lexus wondering who was inside, Victoria killed all the curiosity by stepping out dressed in her new DKNY outfit. When she reached the driver's side to escort her man, Meeko got out in her new DKNY spandex suit, as well. Her outfit was so tight that it looked like another layer of skin, and everyone could guess she had no underclothes on underneath. As Victoria opened the door, escorting Babyface out, Meeko stood to the side holding his new four thousand dollar Armani coat as if it was a cape. When he stood, she draped it over his shoulders as he slid both arms into the sleeves simultaneously. Victoria then closed the door behind him.

As they walked past a couple pimps and hoes, you could hear the whispers coming from their mouths, and once they entered Pure Passion, conversations went from loud to low as the customers watched the out-of-town, young-looking pimp. Babyface swiftly moved across the room in an attempt to find a seat, only to see Lonnie B standing at his table and waving for him to come over.

"Whazzup, Babyface? I'm glad you could make it, playa."

"Yeah, Lonnie B, and from looking at this fine-ass bitch dancing on that pole, I'm glad I could make it myself," Babyface said, mesmerized by the sight of the pretty, brown-skinned, Kelly Rowland look-alike.

"Have a seat, Face," Lonnie said, as he made room for him and the girls.

Babyface motioned for Victoria and Meeko to stand on each side of his shoulders, Victoria on the right and Meeko on the left. The club was filled with a lot of ballers, hustlers, pimps, and hoes.

From observing the spot, Babyface could tell the hoes got most of their customers just from hanging around the club. There were more hoes in the club then outside on the stroll.

"Damn, these country bitches is thick," said Babyface as he observed almost every hoe in the spot. On top of that, they were fine, too. Victoria had finally run up on some competition, but for Meeko, the bitches straight outdid her. Although Meeko's face was a flawless dime piece, her body was no match for these country hoes who were raised on fatback and grits. Those bitches were running neck and neck with Victoria, but the only difference is Victoria was a natural dime piece, not artificial like the ones walking around that joint.

As Babyface watched the other hoes mingle with the ballers, he knew this was the place a nigga who's out there getting money comes when he got an extra fifteen hundred for play money. *My bitches gonna turn this muthafucka out,* Babyface thought to himself, *but we gotta do sumthin' wit Meeko and fast.*

"Face, let's have a drink to celebrate a new young playa in town," said Lonnie B as he opened a bottle of Remy XO.

Babyface then turned his head and motioned for Victoria to bring her ear down so he could whisper something to her. "Hey, baby girl, keep an eye on this nigga. These muthafuckas down Memphis got a thang for slipping shit in a nigga's drink."

"Okay, Daddy," Victoria said as she kept watch on Lonnie B out of the corner of her eye.

As Lonnie B poured their drinks, a short, brown-skinned waitress, with thick calf muscles and an ass on her that was so big it looked unreal, came to their table with a bottle of Cristal in a bucket of ice. "Excuse me, sir. This bottle is for you compliments of Lil' Hott. He says he" like to welcome you to his town."

"Well, thank you, Ms. Pretty, and when will a fine woman like yourself welcome a playa personally?" asked Babyface.

The waitress blushed. "You'd have to stick around a while and find out for yourself."

"Don't make me wait too long," said Babyface, as he stared at her with cold eyes, letting her know he was dead serious. "By the way, baby girl, tell the playa that sent this I'm honored by his hospitality."

"I'll let him know, but you can do that yourself. He's right over there," said the waitress, as she pointed to the table where two hoes and the youngest looking pimp Babyface had ever seen sat.

The young pimp nodded his head and held up his drink, which was a compliment sign for pimps recognizing each other's position in the game. Babyface nodded back slowly while halfway closing his eyes, which is a sign to let the young playa know that he wasn't impressed by the champagne, but he respected his style.

The very instant Babyface slightly closed his eyes Lonnie B slipped something in his drink as he looked at Victoria and Meeko, ensuring they would turn their heads when he looked at them. But what Lonnie B didn't know is that while Victoria followed ho rules well, she followed her pimp's rules even better. She still kept him in her peripheral vision as she watched him slip something in her pimp's drink. Victoria was sharp and always on point, and when it came down to Babyface, she was even sharper. Victoria squeezed Babyface on his shoulder, indicating to him not to drink the glass of Remy. Without showing any expression, he smiled and patted her hand as it rested on his shoulder, indicating he got her point.

Babyface made a mental note to reward Victoria later, as well as a mental note to put Lonnie B's head in the dirt first chance he got. For right now, though, he had to play it off. He was outnumbered in a town he hardly knew, and also, he fell for the hospitality pimp shit back in Chicago and vowed never to fall for it again. What puzzled Babyface the most was why Lonnie B would slip something in his drink? As Babyface looked at Lonnie B's eyes, he saw they were glued to his Rolex, and he then knew Lonnie B had been plotting to get his watch ever since he saw it. Lonnie B would never know that he just gave up his life for a stolen watch.

"Hey, Lonnie B, did the waitress say what the young playa's name is?" Babyface asked, while looking over at his table and admiring his style. He could tell he was a boss pimp.

The young pimp had on a grey linen Armani button-up shirt, which was unbuttoned to reveal a cream Armani mock neck silk t-shirt. He also had on a pair of matching grey Armani linen pants with a pair of grey and cream Mauri gators, with a matching gator belt to complete the look. From a distance, Babyface could see the sparkling of his 18-karat Rolex with the diamond bezel and marble grey face. He accessorized with an 18-karat gold chain with a diamond cross and a 2-karat diamond in his earlobe. What fucked Babyface up most was the diamond encrusted gold teeth that were in his mouth.

"That's Lil' Hott; he's the youngest boss playa in Memphis," Lonnie B told him. "Come on. Let's make a toast. You ain't touched your drink yet."

Babyface turned his attention back to Lonnie B, looking him deep in his eyes. As bad as he wanted to crash his skull, he couldn't. He had to wait it out.

"Nah, I forgot to tell you, playa…me and brown liquor don't get along. I'ma pass on the drink."

Lonnie B's face was flushed with disappointment. He was still determined to get his hands on Babyface's Rolex, though. "Since you don't drink brown liquor, how about some champagne?"

Babyface stood and fixed his clothes. "Nah, Lonnie B, I think it's about time for me to leave. Maybe we could do it another time."

"Okay, Face, take it easy, playa, and once again, welcome to Memphis."

"I'm obliged," Babyface replied.

"By the way, you know the playa's ball is in six weeks."

"Oh yeah? Where is it held?" Babyface asked.

"At the Cook Convention Center downtown. And, Face, you gotta be real fly. You can't be bullshitting at no playa's ball. That's a multi affair where a pimp is crowned and hoes choose," said Lonnie B.

"Well, in that case, tell 'em to have my crown," Babyface said as he exited the club right behind Lil' Hott.

Babyface noticed Lil' Hott jump behind the wheel of a pearl white Range Rover, with his two bad-ass hoes taking occupancy in the supple leather seats. Babyface and Lil' Hott locked eyes as they both pulled off in opposite directions.

═══════════

For the next two weeks, Babyface put his game down. He had Victoria working the shake joint. She never danced; she just walked around in her thong and heels and pulled tricks all day and night. Victoria's customers were local drug dealers, and with her charging at least five hundred for the pussy, she was bringing Babyface between two and three thousand every night. The only competition Victoria had was Lil' Hott's hoes, Nana and Tammy. These bitches had half the strip locked down, which was a disadvantage to Victoria mainly because she didn't have a ho sistah to trick with since Meeko was outside working the stroll. Meeko wasn't in good enough shape to work the club. She tried it a few times, but always ended up bringing home gas money, which enraged Babyface. He, therefore, placed her on a strict diet and exercise program of no meat, all vegetables, small portions, and forty-five minutes running on the treadmill everyday.

While Babyface spent most of his time trying to get Meeko in shape, Victoria was down at the shake joint getting money and getting familiar with everyone. She even made friends with Lil' Hott's hoes, Tammy and Nana, something Victoria rarely did. The two were trying to pull her in Lil' Hott's stable. The same thing her and Penny used to do was now being played on her. Consumed with trying to fix Meeko up, Babyface couldn't see Victoria slowly easing away. However, Meeko noticed, but she wanted the bottom ho position so bad that she didn't warn Babyface. Instead, she just sat back and prayed Tammy and Nana's little scheme would work.

Meeko lost a total of twenty-five pounds, but Babyface put the finishing touches on her by sending her to the nearest clinic to get the fatty tissues in her stomach removed. While she was back at the hotel recovering from the liposuction surgery and Victoria was down at the shake joint sucking the life out of Memphis, Babyface was tailing Lil' Hott all over the south side. Babyface wanted to know more about this nigga. He wasn't just a pimp; the nigga had too much clout in his town to be a young pimp with only hoes. Babyface knew this nigga was doing something else. He had a Range Rover worth over a hundred twenty thousand dollars, plus he had a brand new Cadillac DTS worth about fifty thousand. Also, Babyface wondered why every time he saw this nigga in the shake joints, niggas were always coming up to him as if they were asking for something. Babyface made it his business to track this niggas every move, and not wanting to be noticed, he purchased a 1990 Lincoln Continental from Pyramid Auto on Union Avenue in order to do some investigating.

After three days of watching Lil' Hott, Babyface learned the nigga was hustling. But he didn't know how much shit he was moving and what product. At the completion of every transaction, Babyface noticed how Lil' Hott did a funny-looking handshake with the youngsters he was doing business with. Babyface knew this sign, as he had seen it before in Don Diva Magazine when they featured a story on the leader of the G.D.'s.

*Damn, look at this fool,* Babyface thought. *He ain't so smart after all. The whole three days I've been following this nigga, he never once looked back. What if I was the feds? Not only would he get himself locked up, but he'd get his workers hooked up in this case. The next thing you know the whole fucking Southside of Memphis would be on trial for conspiracy. Yeah, he don't need that money. It won't do him no good in jail, so I'ma do him a favor and get it up off him, but the only thing is how?*

Babyface knew he couldn't rob this nigga, and for the size of the work he was passing out, this nigga wasn't moving no light shit. It would be impossible to kidnap him. Babyface scoped that he was always strapped. Also, he learned that Lil' Hott and Lonnie B were partners, and the two often met in 3$^{rd}$ Wall to talk. In fact,

Lil' Hott had been the one to put Lonnie B on the assignment of getting Babyface's Rolex. When Lil' Hott spotted the platinum collector's watch on Babyface's wrist outside of the Shoney Restaurant when Babyface first came to town, he fell in love with it and had to have it.

"For a minute, you country niggas coulda got me. That was a slick move, playing it off like you two niggas ain't partners. But I'm from the Southside of D.C., nigga. Ain't too much you can get pass me. I was born into this shit. Game recognizes game," said Babyface as he talked to himself. It enraged him that he almost fell for the oldest trick in the book. This in itself made him want to kill them even more, but he couldn't. It would fuck things up. Babyface's plan was way more valuable.

———————

While Babyface was putting his move together and Meeko was recovering from surgery, Tammy and Nana were down at the shake joint working on Victoria.

"Hey, Vic, why your pimp don't come down that much?" asked Tammy.

"Yeah, Vic, he never comes to check up on you," said Nana. "He probably tryna make that other bitch his bottom ho."

"Nah, my man loves me. We been through too much. That'll never happen," Victoria replied, although she had started feeling neglected by Babyface lately.

"Yeah, you *think* it won't happen," replied Nana.

"Why don't you come over and meet Lil' Hott? He a pimp for real. I know you unhappy. You been wit that nigga since you started, girl. Why don't you try something new, change the flava?" coaxed Tammy.

Victoria knew they were right. Babyface had been neglecting her. At one time, he was always around to watch her back, but lately he had been spending all his time with that bitch Meeko. Every time she tried to sit down and talk to him, he always brushed her off, yet gave Meeko all his attention. Victoria was secretly beginning to hate Meeko, and Meeko secretly already hated Victoria. Even though Victoria knew Meeko was trying to steal her spot, she also knew she had something that Meeko didn't...a history with Babyface that could never be forgotten or replaced.

"Nah, Tammy, I love my man and I'm loyal," Victoria said, ending the discussion.

═══════════

When Babyface got back to the hotel, Meeko was in the shower.

"Hey, Meeko, you in there?"

"Yeah, Daddy, I'll be out in a minute. I took my bandages off. Wait till you see me."

"Hurry your ass up then," said Babyface, anxious to see his newest invention.

He sat back on the bed and fired up a blunt he'd gotten from a pimp named Preston. As he inhaled, the smoke of some of the best weed he'd ever smoked filled his lungs. He thought about the fortune he was soon to get, his last move that would get him out the game for sure.

"Okay, Daddy, I'm 'bout to come out. You ready?"

"Yeah, come on, baby girl. Let me see what you working with."

As Meeko emerged from the bathroom butt naked with a pair of red pumps on, Babyface couldn't believe his eyes. Meeko had been transformed into a dime piece. She closely resembled a young Janet Jackson from back in her "Pleasure Principle" days. Babyface smiled, but he wasn't just smiling at Meeko. He smiled at the fact of how he turned a tramp into a champ in less than thirty days. Babyface wasn't just a pimp; he was also a magician, 'cause what he was looking at had to be magic.

"Why you ain't saying nothing, Daddy? You don't like it?" asked Meeko, as she turned around modeling her new reformed body.

"Fuck yeah, I like it! Matter of fact, I love it. Damn, girl, you look good."

In all actuality, Meeko looked just as good as Victoria and she knew it. And for that, she loved Babyface even more. To Meeko, he was her savior, her god.

"Come over here," he said, as he ran his hands all over her body as if it was a fine piece of art. Instantly, his dick hardened, and he proceeded to both aggressively fuck and softly make love to her.

After he laid the pipe like a true plumber, Meeko laid back on his chest with tears running down her face. "Daddy, I'ma get you rich. I'ma make you so much money. Ain't a ho in the game can fuck wit me now."

Babyface knew Meeko was not just referring to any ho in the game; she was indirectly talking about Victoria. "Yeah, Meeko, I hope that's true, 'cause you got a whole lotta trickin' to do to get back that money I spent getting you ready."

"Daddy, I'ma get that back and multiply it a thousand times more."

While Meeko and Babyface were lying in bed talking, Victoria came in. As she entered the bedroom, she couldn't believe Meeko looked just as good as she. Victoria stood there in shock with her hand over her mouth.

"Oh my god, Meeko, you look good," Victoria exclaimed.

"Thanks, Vic, but what are you doing back so early?" asked Meeko as looked toward Babyface for him to check Victoria.

Victoria quickly lost her excitement. "None of your business, bitch! You don't question me! I'm a bottom ho. You outta pocket. Anyway, get the fuck up. I gotta talk to Face in private."

Meeko didn't move; instead, she looked at Babyface while rubbing his dick.

"Bitch, leave! Can I get some dick sometimes," Victoria angrily said.

"You ain't getting enough down at the shake joint? I hear you got all the clientele,"

That did it. Meeko had just disrespected her right in front of Babyface. "Bitch, I'll break your fucking jaw in here," shouted Victoria as she lunged at Meeko.

"Hold the fuck up! Now you bitches is tripping again. Meeko your ass is way outta pocket. Don't ever in your fuckin' life disrespect her or my pimpin' like that again," he said, as he coldly looked into her eyes.

"I'm sorry, Daddy. It won't happen again," Meeko said, as she got up and exited the room.

As Victoria closed the door behind Meeko, Babyface could tell she was still mad. "Vic, don't trip off that shit. Now what is so important you wanna talk to me about?"

Victoria sat down on the bed next to him. "Look, Face, I know you love me and you know I love you, but you're lettin' this bitch come between us. It was never like that when Penny was around. This bitch tryna steal my spot, and I can't let her do that."

Tears started to form in her eyes as she spoke.

"Vic, you better not cry. What the fuck is wrong wit you? You know can't nobody come between us; we connected for life. How the fuck I'ma let a bitch who ain't got no history wit me come between us, huh, Vic? From what you saying, you make me sound like some weak nigga. That's total disrespect. How you gonna think like that? What, you lettin' them bitches down at the shake joint get in your head? Come on, Vic, I taught you better than that," he scolded her. "You're a diamond; don't turn into a stone. I can't believe you would question my love. What the fuck drug you taking, huh, Vic?"

Victoria evaluated Babyface's sincerity, and realized she had been wrong for even doing such a thing as questioning his love for her. While letting his words sink in, Victoria felt ashamed at letting Tammy and Nana get in her head.

"You're right, Face. I'm trippin'. I don't know why my stupid ass would think like that. Nigga, you ain't going nowhere without me," she said, regaining her confidence. "I'm your bitch for life, and besides, ain't a human being in this world that can fill my shoes. I'm sorry, Face. I really am sorry."

He was happy to see Victoria snap back, 'cause for a minute, he thought his best ho was contemplating on leaving him.

"Damn, baby girl, don't ever scare me like that again. For a second, I thought I was gonna have to peel your cap. You know I can't have you leave me like that. It's to the death with us." Babyface smiled.

"Shut up! You know you ain't gonna kill me," she said, while playfully hitting him on the arm. Playful hits soon turned to wrestling, which in turn led to fucking. This was the old Babyface that she knew and missed.

Afterwards, Babyface and Victoria lay in bed talking.

"Hey, Daddy, you know a lot of pimps and hoes in town are getting ready for that playa's ball."

"Yeah, I know, Vic. We gonna turn that muthafucka out," he replied.

"You know that nigga Lil' Hott is giving a pre-playa's ball party down at the Premier Club."

"Yeah, I know that, too, Vic, but I got plans for that."

"What's up? Lay it down to me, Daddy."

"Vic, we 'bout to make the biggest move and then we out. We going back home to fulfill our dream."

"What's up then? Tell me what I gotta do," said Victoria.

He then told her about his plans and what he was gonna do with Meeko. He told her how he was gonna get Lonnie B out of the picture first, but that she and Meeko couldn't join him at the pre-party.

"Daddy, why we can't come?"

"'Cause, Vic, it's part of my plan. You see, every playa from outta town gonna be there flossin' they hoes. By the time the playa's ball comes up, niggas ain't gonna be that thrilled no more 'cause they already seen a nigga's hoes. You see, Vic, a pimp's ho is his secret weapon. I can't let these niggas see my bitches, so when it's time for the playa's ball they can go try to fix they bitches up better," Babyface explained.

"You right, Face, and I got the perfect outfits for me and Meeko."

"Yeah, well, I'ma leave that up to you, but I can guarantee you they gonna crown me Pimp of the Year, 'cause you know why?"

"Why," Victoria asked, playing along.

"'Cause I'm Babyface, and can't a pimp in the game take my place."

"You got that right," Victoria said as she kissed the love of her life.

# CHAPTER 16

## PIMP OF THE YEAR

Tonight was the night, the start of Babyface's plan. He'd talked to Victoria earlier and laid out the whole format. Although he knew she was with it, he thought Meeko should be the one to carry it out. Babyface got his self together for Lil' Hott's party premier, but before he went there, he stopped at the massage parlor on Winchester Street to holla at Dollbaby, one of the last old school pimps Memphis had left. He was an old timer, but still in the game. In fact, out of all the pimps Babyface ever met besides Bone, Dollbaby kept it real. He liked Babyface and saw his potential. Therefore, when Babyface came to ask for a favor, Dollbaby obliged.

As Babyface pulled in front of the Premier Nightclub, he could tell by all the different license plates on the luxury cars that pimps came from all over ready for the playa's ball. From all the Benz's, Jags, etc., parked outside, he was no longer the only one with a tight whip. And the fact he didn't have any hoes with him didn't help either. Therefore, his arrival didn't cause many heads to turn. However, Babyface was pleased because he didn't want to draw too much attention. He came for one purpose, to start his mission and prepare for his long-lasting future.

Once inside, Babyface observed all the potential pimps who thought they were worthy of the Pimp of the Year crown. Most were straight up bammas to Babyface, but some were smooth-ass, wealthy niggas with jewelry pieces that looked like they belonged in a museum. Babyface was amused at their pimp cups as he saw those popping bottles and showing each other hospitality. The atmosphere was cool, with everybody introducing themselves and telling their pimp stories. It reminded him of a family reunion.

As he walked briskly through the crowd of pretty hoes and fly ass pimps, Babyface could have sworn he saw Tookie. *Nah, that can't be him. I know them niggas had to kill him about them pound cakes.* When he turned back around from looking to make sure it wasn't Tookie, he found himself face to face with Lonnie B.

"Whazzup, young Babyface. What the pimp life like?" said Lonnie B.

"It's cool," replied Babyface. "Having a lil' trouble in the stable, but it's nothing I can't handle."

"I hear ya. Pimpin' ain't easy. Come on over and have a seat," Lonnie B offered. Shit, why not? Might as well sit down and check out some potential hoes. Never know who you gonna knock"

"Yeah, you right, Lonnie B. 'Cause I damn sure need more bitches in my stable."

While Lonnie B was talking, Babyface observed Lil' Hott, his two hoes, and an entourage of pimps and hustlers. He was busy playing host to these muthafuckas, while his partner was busy trying to work Babyface for his Rolex.

"Hey, Face, you still coming to the playa's ball?"

"Yeah, I'll be there, but I know somebody who ain't."

"Damn, Face, you having that much trouble in your stable that you gonna leave your hoes behind?"

"I'ma leaving one of 'em. The bitch can't be trusted," Babyface replied.

"Well, Face, you know what they say. If a bitch can't be trusted, then that bitch must be busted; if a bitch ain't about your doe, then that no good ho gots to go."

"Oh, believe me, Lonnie B, this bitch sure 'nuff bout to go."

"How 'bout a drink, Face? You look like you need one. And I know you don't fuck with that brown liquor, so how 'bout some champagne?"

*This nigga must really think I'm stupid. I got something for his ass, though,* Babyface thought. "Sure, Lonnie B, I'll have a drink wit you. Besides, we never got the chance to properly celebrate my pimpin' in Memphis."

Lonnie B was all smiles. He knew for sure he had Babyface now. After pouring Babyface's drink, he began to pour himself one in his gold pimp cup with the initials L.B. in rhinestones. As Lonnie B was pouring, Babyface hit him with the oldest trick in the book, and like a dummy Lonnie B fell for it.

"Damn, that's a fine-ass ho over there staring at you, Lonnie B. You must be boss pimpin' to have a ho check you out from the back."

When Lonnie B turned around to see who Babyface was talking about, Babyface easily and swiftly dropped the small, laced white pill he had gotten from Dollbaby into Lonnie B's drink. Babyface didn't know how it worked, or better yet, if it did work. All he knew was that Dollbaby said a nigga had less than eight hours to live after it dissolved in his body.

*I hope this shit works. If not, this is gonna put a dent in my plans, but if it do work, then a nigga's on his way to the big leagues.*

Lonnie B turned back around to Babyface. "Nah, Face, you seeing thangs, playa. That bitch ain't looking at me. She's more like looking at Lil' Hott. But while we sittin' here talking, there's a ho over there in the cut watching you."

Babyface knew this was Lonnie B's moment to drop his pill. Therefore, he gave him more than enough time to work. As Babyface slowly turned around, Lonnie B quickly made his move. When he turned back around, Lonnie B was all smiles. He just knew he had Babyface this time.

"Come on, Face, let's make a toast."

"Okay."

As they put their cups in the air to touch, Lonnie B did the honors. "To the pimp of the year…whoever that may be. May you have a long lastin' pimp career." Then Lonnie B gulped down his champagne like water and watched Babyface at the same time. "Why ain't you drinking? We just made a toast, playa."

"Hold up, Lonnie B. Let me see that bottle," Babyface said,

while lifting the bottle to eye level. "Man, what the fuck you 'bout to make me drink? Look, playa, I'ma boss pimp. I don't drink no cheap ass Moet."

"Ah, come on, Face. It ain't nuthin' but some Moet. Go 'head and drink the shit."

"Nah, Lonnie B, I'm a pimp and I pimps too fucking hard to be drinking that cheap shit. Man, you should be ashamed of yourself. Look at your surroundings. You gonna let muthafuckas see you drink this bullshit? Nigga, when I met you, you said you were Memphis' finest. You can't be drinking some thirty dollar champagne. Man, you just disrespected my pimpin', Lonnie B. Never should you treat a real playa like that. Man, I'm gone. You just ruined my night, and besides, I gotta go check on my trap. My bitches is out there getting that paper while all you nigga's bitches is in here spending y'all's money. I'll holla at you, Lonnie B."

"Hold up, Face. Look here, playa, I can order some Cristal. I ain't nowhere near cheap. My pockets run deep like the James River creek," said Lonnie B.

"Oh yeah? Well, in that case, my pockets are overflowin' like the muthafuckin' Atlantic ocean," Babyface replied as he got up to leave. "No thanks, Lonnie B. I'll drink wit my hoes tonight. See you at the playa's ball, if you can make it."

---

The next morning while Lonnie B was being pronounced dead, Babyface was pulling out of Smith's Imports car dealership in his brand new pearl white 600 AMG Mercedes Benz with butter biscuit leather interior and bamboo wood grain. Babyface's Benz was like a living room on the inside. He had a navigation/DVD player up front with a flip down TV in the back, and the back was equipped with a pull-out cocktail bar. This was Babyface's dream car, which he finally got, and there was no better time than getting it right before the playa's ball. Next, he went down to Jack's Jewelers on Popular Street. He already had a diamond bezel, so he got his watchband iced out in all diamonds the same exact size as the diamonds in his bezel. He paid eleven thousand to have them set in. Although they weren't official Rolex diamonds certified by Rolex, they were the best quality VVS diamonds and glossed just as well. He didn't have to go shopping for clothes since he had prepared for this moment early while in Chicago. Therefore, Babyface was all set and ready to go, but he had to do one thing... prepare Victoria for her most effective and dangerous move.

When he arrived back at the hotel, he pulled Victoria into the bedroom away from Meeko so they could speak in private. Victoria knew something was about to go down from the serious expression on his face, not to mention he had poured her a glass of Hennessey.

"Sit down, baby girl. I gotta talk to you. Now I want you to listen closely 'cause I'ma need your undivided attention."

"Whazzup, Face?"

"Look, I've been planning this move ever since the day we got here, and it's what's gonna get us out the game."

"What's that, Face?" Victoria asked, anxious for him to get to the point.

"Well, baby girl, this is your most dangerous task, and I need to know now if you're game enough for it."

"Face, you know I'll do anything for you. Now tell me what I gotta do and what position to play."

Babyface looked Victoria deep in her eyes. As bad as he didn't want to, he had to. It was their only way out, and Victoria was the only person capable enough to pull it off.

"Vic, you gotta choose Lil' Hott," Babyface said.

"What! You know I can't do that. I can't leave you. How you gonna make me do this," she said as she began to cry. She knew he didn't approve of crying, but she didn't care. His words coerced the tears out of her eyes. She couldn't believe he'd throw her away like this. "Why can't Meeko do it?"

"'Cause, Vic, she ain't built like you. She ain't cut from that cloth. She is too dependant on me. She'll break and most likely end up dead."

"What if I break?" Victoria cried.

"I know you won't, Vic, and you know why? 'Cause I trained you not to break under pressure. Look, baby, It's only gonna be for a little while. We gotta do this."

"Well, what you want me to do, Face?"

"Baby girl, I've been tailing this nigga ever since we got here. This nigga is paid. He movin' bricks like welfare cheese, and since them bitches tryna get you in his stable, it'll be real easy for you to slide in and get up under him to get to that money."

"How am I gonna get that close? He already got a bottom ho," said Victoria.

"Yeah, he got a bottom ho, but nobody is loyal to ho rules like you. And to top it off, you look better. Now, baby girl, it's gonna be real easy for you to get in that position. Reason why is because when you choose him, you gonna give him my watch. He's fiendin' for this shit. Plus, I'ma leave you ten thousand in a hotel, so every time you give him a bankroll, you can come chip off the ten and give him at least a thousand more than them other bitches. I guarantee within two weeks you'll know where that bank at."

"And while I'm doing all this, what you gonna be doing?" Victoria asked.

"Baby girl, this the real twist. You know how Meeko wants your bottom ho position so bad. By you crossing me, it's gonna make her even more loyal. She gonna hate you; she gonna think I'm fucked up about it, and she gonna try to do whatever you did for me and more. So, I'ma take her back to D.C. wit me, and while she out on the stroll, I'ma finding us a house and prepare to look for a spot to pen up the strip club. When I come back to get you, I'ma give her the option to leave or either work for you at the club. Vic, it's the perfect move. We're killing two birds wit one stone. Baby girl, I know how you feel about it, but I really need you on this."

"What if he got partner, Face?" She worried something would go wrong with his well-thought-out plan. "What if he catches on?"

"Baby girl, I killed his partner last night. I know you heard about the dude Lonnie B dying in his sleep. That's my work, and another thing, Vic, how can a nigga catch on to a bitch that stole a sixty thousand dollar watch from her pimp and gave it to him. Baby girl, the nigga ain't that smart. I'm telling you, I know. I studied his every move," he assured her.

"Babyface, are you positive this is gonna work?" asked Victoria as she wiped away her tears.

"Vic, do you think I'd risk losing you if I wasn't sure? Baby, I'm absolutely positive it'll work. And after all this shit is done, we outta the game for good. Baby girl, I love you too much to put you in this position. You think I wasn't scared to place you there? Of course, I was, but after evaluating the circumstances, you're our only hope."

"Babyface, I love you and you know I'ma do my best, but if I fail, please don't leave me down here."

"Vic, you ain't gonna fail me. You never have and never will. Know why? 'Cause I ain't gonna fail you. And when all this shit is done, we gonna take us a vacation. Now come here and stop that crying."

Victoria got up to hug him, and he held her tightly in his arms. He then kissed her passionately and made love to her like he never did before.

═══════════════════

The next day, Victoria went down to Pure Passion to give Tammy and Nana the hint that she's getting tried of Babyface. She made them think she was unhappy with her pimp by lying about him giving her bottom ho position to Meeko. She knew this was dangerous job, but she also knew this was something she had to do, and she planned to do it well. Of course, Tammy and Nana took the bait, and did not hesitate suggesting that Victoria join Lil' Hott's stable. Before departing, she told them she would give it much consideration.

*Babyface's lil' plan is starting to blossom already,* Victoria said to herself.

While Victoria was down at Pure Passion working her shit on Tammy and Nana, Babyface was at the hotel gassing Meeko's head.

"Meeko let me ask you something, and I want you to tell me the truth," said Babyface.

"What's up, Daddy?"

"Tell me what the fuck is up with Vic. Is she getting tired of shit? Is she trustworthy?"

Meeko saw this as her opportunity to steal Victoria's position, so she worked fast. "That bitch can't be trusted, Babyface. I'm telling you, she be hanging with them bitches Nana and Tammy too much. Plus, she always be crackin' slick behind your back." Meeko knew she was lying, but she had to give it her best shot. "I'm telling you, Daddy, you need to cut that bitch. She gonna be our downfall."

"If I cut her loose, though, that only leaves me and you. Now, Vic done made me a lot of money, Meeko. How you gonna top that?"

"Daddy, I swear on my life. I'ma make you rich. I'll fuck a dog if he got money. Face, please, I know I can be that bottom ho. I know I can do it. Just gimme a chance, Daddy. I'll prove it to you," she pleaded. "I'll put my ho game down day and night till my heels break. Look at all you done for me. Please gimme that chance to show you I'm worthy."

At the sound of her sincerity, Babyface knew he had accomplished his second goal. "Okay then, Meeko. I'ma drop that bitch like a hot potato, but only after the playa's ball tomorrow."

"Why can't you drop her now?"

"'Cause I at least have to have two hoes at the ball," he replied.

"Oh, I see, and after that I'm bottom ho, right?"

"You already bottom ho, but Vic won't know till after the ball."

Meeko jumped all over him. "I love you, Daddy. I love you. I love you. I swear you won't regret it. I swear ain't a ho in this world gonna love you like I do."

"I know, baby girl. Now what you still got them clothes on for? I gotta break you *all* the way in."

That night, he gave Meeko what she had wanted for a long while: a good fuck and the bottom ho position, or at least that's what she thought.

# CHAPTER 17

## THE RED CARPET

I t was few hours before the playa's ball and the excitement was building as Babyface, Victoria, and Meeko prepared to shine like no other. Victoria and Meeko kept their outfits a mystery, wanting to surprise their pimp with their selection for the night. Therefore, after dressing, they stayed covered in their furs, with only their knee-high gator boots showing. Babyface couldn't wait to see how they were going to represent him; he knew they wouldn't let him down.

Before they walked out the door, Victoria looked him in the eyes and said, "I have something for you," as she handed him a small gift-wrapped box.

"What's this," he asked, while tearing away the wrapping.

"We've been saving up ever since we got here to get you this," Victoria replied.

When he opened the box, Babyface couldn't believe his eyes. "How the fuck you save up for this you? You bitches were making that much money?"

"Well, Daddy, it was really Victoria. She put in the most," said Meeko.

Babyface looked into her eyes. It was enough to make a grown man cry; yet more than enough to make a real pimp proud. He examined the platinum Rolex bracelet with diamonds flowing through the middle. He then put it on his wrist; it matched his watch perfectly.

"Thank you," he said, as he turned his wrist so the diamonds could reflect off the light.

Meeko could feel the tension in the room. She knew Babyface

was touched by Victoria's gift, so she attempted to outdo her with her gift.

"Open my gift, Daddy," said Meeko as she smiled like a child giving her father his first gift.

Babyface opened the second box, revealing the biggest diamond earring with no flaws. "Damn this is a pretty muthafucka. How many karats is this?"

"Five, Daddy. I had that shit on layaway since the first day at the mall."

"Thanks, Meeko," he said, while taking out his 3-karat earring and replacing it with the new 5-karat. "Damn, y'all sure know how to make a nigga look like a star," said Babyface.

"You are a star, Daddy. You are," Meeko replied, as she looked him up and down with praise.

═══════════

As Babyface pulled up at the Cook Convention Center in downtown Memphis, he saw all types of luxury cars, bright suits, furs, and excessive jewelry. This indeed was the family reunion for all pimps and hoes. He saw old pimps, middle-age pimps, and young pimps, which weren't many. Also, he saw a variety of hoes from all over the globe: fat, old, short, tall, pretty, too pretty, young, ugly, too ugly…all kinds from all over representing their pimps. This was a pimp's dream…the playa's ball….to be a part of something that represented his lifestyle in the fullest degree.

When he pulled into the front center of the lobby, everybody turned their heads and focused on the pearl white 600 AMG Benz sitting on 20-inch chrome rims. Babyface brought something new to the pimp game, but nobody could figure it out until he opened his door to get out. Most of the other pimps that pulled up were cranking some old-school pimp shit in their systems, but not Babyface; he was different. This was his moment to really shine and show muthafuckas the pimp he really was. This in itself was the red carpet for pimps; some even posed to take snapshots as if they were true stars.

As Victoria opened her door, the crisp flow that came out of Babyface's speakers fit the mood. There couldn't have been a better song. Jay-Z's flow made it seem as though he made the song just for the playa's ball. *If you a pimp/go on brush your shoulders off/ladies is pimps too/go on brush your shoulders off.*

Everybody stood on the side bobbing their heads to Jay's poetic flow while Victoria got out. When she emerged from within the car, a series of oohhs and ahhhs filled the air. She had on pear-shaped Tiffany diamond earrings and a full-length white mink with knee-high white gator boots. As everybody stood around wondering what she was wearing underneath, Victoria gracefully walked around to Babyface's side and struck a pose. She looked so good that a few muthafuckas even took snapshots of her.

Next, it was Meeko's time to shine, as she stepped out of the back seat in some pink knee-high gator boots and a pink full-length fur. The pink set off her dark-skinned complexion, and she got just as much attention from the crowd of spectators as Victoria. Meeko walked over opposite of Victoria and they faced each other. Then, Victoria opened his door to escort him out, while Meeko held his fur coat like she was about to drape a king with his cape.

Babyface stepped out in a pair of black Gucci print slip-ons, perfectly tailored black Gucci slacks, and a matching Gucci print belt. To top it off, he had on a black Gucci print dress shirt, but it wasn't a regular Gucci shirt. It had French cuffs with diamond Gucci emblem cuff links. Finishing the look, he wore a Gucci print brim hat. Babyface put a lil' thug in his outfits just to let these niggas know he didn't value this expensive shit. So, with that, he had his shirt halfway tucked in, just enough so you could see the Gucci emblem on his belt buckle. Also, he had his hat cocked slightly to the right, just to give his 5-karat earring in his left earlobe enough room to breath. Babyface was Gucci'd out, but what really made the show was when Meeko draped his fur coat on his back. He had the thickest chinchilla a nigga had ever seen.

The pimps and hoes loved his show so much that they clapped.

Babyface did it again, just like he did on 14th Street in Chi-town; and now his biggest show ever would be his graceful bow out of the game, 'cause this was the first and last playa's ball he'd ever see. Face wanted a future. Like itself was better than this. This game didn't breed anything but prison and death.

As they walked into the convention center, hoes stole stares at Babyface and some were even bold enough to look him straight in the face. Victoria and Meeko were on their best behavior, though, as they walked with their arms hooked onto each side of Babyface's arms. Their eyes immediately hit the floor every time a pimp tried to make eye contact. *Who the fuck is this young nigga, Babyface* was the biggest question at the playa's ball.

As Babyface walked through the crowds of pimps and hoes, some made small conversation while others tried their hardest not to show their hate; yet, it was written all over their faces. While he was about to shoot game at this bitch who kept eyeing him, he was interrupted by loud clapping. When he looked down in the lobby, he noticed Lil' Hott and a bunch of muthafuckas standing around him, rooting for him like he just won a basketball game or something. Babyface knew what it was; he made such a big impression that these muthafuckas were hating on him...hating so much that when Lil' Hott stepped in, they damn near broke their necks to give their homey some props.

Babyface had to give the lil' bamma his props, though, because he was kinda fly in his cream Armani tuxedo jacket, with cream slacks, cream Mauri gators, and full-length white chinchilla with the matching fur brim hat. His hoes looked good, too, but they couldn't fuck with Victoria and Meeko. One ho had on a lime green mink with a lime green Versace dress, the same dress that Jennifer Lopez wore at the Grammy's, except his ho had it cut into a short skirt. She also had on a pair of velour Versace knee-high boots. Lil' Hott's other ho looked even better in her blue and white mixed fur coat, midnight blue see-through Chanel dress, and matching boots. The ho didn't even have on a bra or underwear, so one could see she was straight naked underneath the sheer material.

While everyone conversed and shot game with each other, Victoria whispered in Babyface's ear, "Daddy, we're ready to take our coats off now. Come on, let's go take a picture."

As the crowd of pimps and hoes stood around waiting to see Babyface and his hoes take their flicks, Meeko whispered, "Daddy, we 'bout to fuck this party up."

Babyface stood in the middle, while Victoria was to his right and Meeko to the left. Just as the picture man was about to snap, Babyface stuck out his hand. "Hold up." Babyface then gave his hoes permission to remove their coats.

As Victoria and Meeko did as instructed by their pimp, everybody stood in shock, as this was their first time ever to see some shit like this at a playa's ball. Victoria had on a white gator, diamond studded thong and bikini top with her matching gator knee-high Mauri boots. Meeko had on a pink gator, diamond studded thong and bikini top with matching gator knee-high Mauri boots. To top it off, they both had in big-ass, 5-karat diamond navel rings.

Babyface could hear the whispers that spoke of his victory as the picture man continued to take shots. Lil' Hott's hoes even gave their props.

"Damn, Tammy, you see, Vic?"

"Yeah, Nana, that bitch killin' 'em. Hey, Daddy, that bitch gonna be in your stable by tomorrow. Me and Nana worked on her good," said Tammy, while looking at Lil' Hott.

Lil' Hott was an undercover gorilla pimp. He didn't hit his hoes in public, but behind closed doors he had a signature chokehold that his hoes feared.

"Yeah, well, if she ain't in my stable by tomorrow, I'm fuckin' both you bitches up," said Lil' Hott, as he secretly adored Victoria.

He wanted Victoria just as bad as he wanted Babyface's watch. He didn't have proof, but he knew Babyface had something to do with Lonnie B not waking up out of his sleep. As Lil' Hott locked eyes with Babyface, neither one of them gave the other his props; they just stared at each other with that killer look in their eyes. The only thing going through Babyface's mind was, "Nigga, I'ma take your whole stash," and the only thing going through Lil' Hott's mind was, "Nigga, I'ma knock your ho and you don't even know it.'

"Hey, Tammy go tell that bitch don't come to my stable empty handed. I want that nigga's shit," said Lil' Hott.

"Okay, Daddy," Tammy said.

"Well, bitch, what the fuck you waiting for? Get your ass up."

Tammy quickly went over to Victoria's table, and without looking at Babyface, she whispered in Victoria's ear. "Hey, Vic, Lil' Hott said don't come in his stable empty handed. I'm telling you, once you get on this team, you'll love it. Make your new pimp happy and take this nigga's shit," said Tammy as she flashed a fake smile and left.

"What that bitch just say to you, Vic," Meeko asked once Tammy was out of earshot.

"Oh, she just complimented us on our outfits," Victoria replied.

"She ain't have to whisper that in your ear," Meeko said.

Victoria looked at her with a stern look. "So what you tryna say, Meeko?"

Meeko couldn't take it no more. She couldn't hide the fact that Victoria was going to get dropped and didn't know it. She hated that Victoria was a traitor, so she just let it out.

"Bitch, if you wanna go with them bitches, you can leave wit 'em, 'cause tomorrow your ass is out anyway. Bitch, you're through. I'm bottom ho now. Babyface, don't need no untrustworthy bitch like you. I don't see how he kept your tramp ass this long. Ain't that right, Daddy?"

"Yeah, Meeko, that's right. Hey, Vic, you're out, bitch. You can leave wit that nigga now if you want," said Babyface as he looked at Victoria, not wanting to do it like this but the opportunity presented itself. Their lil' scheme was working perfect.

Victoria appeared to be heartbroken by his words. "Well, can I go back to the hotel and get my things? At least you could let me have my stuff," said Victoria, as tears formed in her eyes. Even though they were playing a game on Meeko, her tears were real. As bad as she didn't want to do this, she felt she had to. She couldn't let Babyface down.

"Yeah, bitch, you can have your shit, but you getting the fuck out tonight," Babyface replied. "Hey, Meeko, go get me a drink." As soon as Meeko left the table, Babyface leaned over to Victoria. "I love you and don't ever forget it. I'll be back to get you when you call. If at anytime you wanna pull out, I'm coming to get you. I hate to do it like this, but this is the only way."

"I know, Face, and I'ma do my best. I'll have that money for you."

"So what did that bitch say to you?" he asked.

"She told me Lil' Hott said don't come empty handed."

Babyface smiled. He knew he had put the perfect plan together. "Okay, Vic, when we get back to the hotel, I'ma give you my jewelry."

"Okay, but keep the bracelet. I don't think I can stand seeing him wear it. That bracelet is sentimental, and every time you put it on think of me," said Victoria. "I love you, Face, more than you'll ever know."

"I already know that, Vic, and I love you just as much, if not more."

As Meeko approached, Babyface started to put on a bigger scene. "Now, bitch, the sight of you is makin' me sick," he said to Victoria as Meeko sat the drinks on the table. "Matter of fact, fuck this playa's ball shit. The way I see it I'm the only real playa here anyway. Now go over there and tell your new pimp you're going back to pick your shit up and that you'll be in the hotel lobby waiting on him."

With her head lowered, Victoria rose and walked over to Lil' Hott's table.

"What's up, ho? You ready to get wit a real pimp or what?" said Lil' Hott.

"I'm 'bout to go back to my room and get my shit. I'll call for you to pick me up."

"A'ight, ho, but like I said, don't come to my stable empty handed."

"I won't, Lil' Hott," Victoria replied.

"And from now on you call me Daddy," he said, while coldly looking her in the eyes."

"Yes, Daddy."

"Vic, call me. As soon as you pack, we coming straight to get you," Tammy said.

"Welcome to the family, Vic. You won't regret it," said Nana.

"Thank you, Nana."

As Babyface got up to leave, Lil' Hott looked him coldly in the eyes. This was the first time they'd spoke a word to each other.

"Why you leaving so early, Face? What's wrong? Can't stand to see a real pimp get crowned?"

"Nah, playa, I look at myself in the mirror everyday. I came out the pussy wit the crown. Nigga, I was born to pimp," Babyface replied.

"Well, I suggest you go back to where you was born, 'cause in Memphis, you ain't pimpin' shit, nigga."

"Yeah, whatever, Lil' Hott. From the way you speakin' to me, it's obvious that you're headed for self destruction. I would like to advise you that it would be wise to reconsider your actions toward me and keep it on a playa's level. After all, in a few, you'll be pimp of the year. Now act like one, baby," said Babyface as he quickly rolled out, not giving Lil' Hott the chance to pop back.

# CHAPTER 18

## BOTTOM HO

While Victoria was back at the hotel packing, Lil' Hott was on stage at the playa's ball getting his crown. Babyface came into the room and grabbed her tight, he held her in his arms as if it was the last time he'd see her.

"Vic, I love you. Now, it's ten thousand in the mattress for you. Just make sure you come and pay for the room everyday. Here, take this." He pulled off his Rolex and handed it to Victoria, remembering the history of it. The watch caused so much fucking trouble; yet it also saved lives. He thought back to when and how they first got it, how it got him locked up, how it made Victoria a ho, how it got Lonnie B killed, and how it was now going to get him out of the game and fulfill his dream. Although he loved his watch, it didn't matter. It was worth the risk.

"Face, you sure you wanna give this to him? What if he tries to sell it?"

"Then we'll get another one wit his money, courtesy of Lil' Hott."

Victoria couldn't stand looking at him; every time she looked in his eyes she wanted to cry. It was painful, and this was the hardest part of the plan, the moment she left his side.

Babyface grabbed her face and kissed her long and hard. "Vic, promise you won't cry."

"I promise, Face," said Victoria, while looking at the ground.

"Now go 'head and call this sucker. He got our money waiting on us."

As Lil' Hott pulled up in front of the motel in his Range Rover, the perfect song played from inside as Tammy opened the door to give Victoria the front seat. He was playing "I Choose You" by Willie Hutch, some old-school pimp shit.

As Victoria got inside, he looked over at her and said, "Lil' mama, you made the right decision. I just wanna know what took you so long."

"Daddy, I peeped you the first day I got here, but I knew I had to make you happy, so I stayed wit the nigga for a while just to cop you this." Victoria pulled out the Rolex, handed it to him, and kissed his cheek.

"You did good, lil' mama. Come on, I'ma take you to your new home.

After a few days in Lil' Hott's stable, Victoria brought Lil' Hott back his first big bankroll. She knew not to bring him back any bullshit ass money, or else she would feel the wrath of his choke-hold, just as she did when she first came into his stable. Lil' Hott had to make it know to her to take him serious at all times, so before fucking her, he took her to his penthouse and laid down his gorilla pimping. He grabbed Victoria by the throat with one hand and told her if she was to ever cross him like she did Babyface, he would kill her and throw her ass in the Mississippi river, like he did a few others who weren't to be trusted. Victoria knew the nigga was serious, and as bad as she wanted to call Babyface to come get her, she couldn't. This was the first stage, and she had to go through with it. After shaking Victoria up, Lil' Hott fucked her in every position, and then made Tammy and Nana have their way with her. The very next day, Victoria was down at the shake joint working.

Lil' Hott liked Victoria. Therefore, after laying his gorilla game down, he changed his game back to good pimp. He took her to the finest restaurants, to movies, plays, and all that other good shit that got a bitch wide open. Although she liked the treatment, she still knew she had a mission. Victoria knew she had to get that bottom ho spot from Nana, but how long would it take was the question. She had already earned his respect. He loved the way she had sex, he fell in love with her ho manners, which was something Nana and Tammy needed help with, and now was the time to show him she was a money-getter.

───────────

As soon as Babyface and Meeko hit D.C., they got a room at the Ramada Inn on Indianhead highway. He had big plans for Meeko, but first he had to take care of a few things. The next morning, he went to the Brentwood post office to check on his money. Pleased to see his $225,000, he took out $25,000 and left the rest. His mission was to find a place to stay and then show Meeko the city before he did anything else. Also, he planned to visit Candy at the D.C. jail and get her a lawyer.

He got an apartment at Riverside Towers in Alexandria, Virginia. His apartment was on the 12th floor, and often times he would stand on his balcony, which overlooked D.C., and think about Victoria. The first week at home, Babyface went straight to work. After showing Meeko around and taking her shopping, he went to visit Candy.

Candy was shocked to see Babyface. She thought she'd never see him again, but then again, she also knew he was loyal to Bone.

"Hey, whazzup, baby girl?"

Candy immediately became concerned with his appearance. "Babyface, you don't look like yourself. You look like you just lost your best friend."

"Candy, so much shit's been going on that I don't know where to begin."

"Well, we only got one hour, but you can start now, Daddy."

"First, tell me what's up with your case."

"Face, these people tryna smash my head in the dirt for some old shit," Candy replied.

"How much time you facing?"

"Ten years, Daddy, and this punk-ass defender keeps telling me to take a plea for eight and a half."

"Don't worry 'bout that. As soon as I leave here, I'ma go and get you a lawyer," he told her.

"Why you look so down?" she asked.

"What am I supposed to look like, Candy? One of my hoes is facing ten years."

Candy knew that wasn't the only reason Babyface looked confused, so she pressed on. "What happened in Chi-town, Face? Where is Penny and Vic? Why didn't they come wit you?"

Babyface found it hard to look Candy in the face as he told her everything that had happened from the time she was arrested up until the present, but leaving out the murder Victoria committed and Lonnie B. Candy's eyes became watery as she thought of Penny, who had been like her daughter. Now, she was dead. Another thing that saddened Candy was the fact that Babyface left Victoria behind. One of the happiest moments she ever had since she'd been in jail turned into her worst in less than thirty minutes.

"Face, I can't take all this bad news. I gotta go back to my cell. I can't let these muthafuckas see me cry."

Babyface understood, and as Candy left the visit, he assured her that he would do whatever to get her out. After leaving the jail, he went to the office of one of the best lawyers in D.C., Nikki Locks. For Candy's case, she wanted $30,000, with $7,500 up front and the rest under the table. She assured him that Candy would not get over one year in jail, and after that, she would put in reconsideration to have her time cut in half. Therefore, Candy would be looking at only doing six months, plus the time she already served.

Going into the second week of being in Lil' Hott's stable,

Victoria earned her keep. Today was her first time to finally get inside. Lil' Hott's connect had called and told him he was ready. Usually, Nana who rode with Lil' Hott, but since she was sick and the fact that Victoria played her position well, Lil' Hott had her do what Nana always did: pick up the drop and follow him to his stash house on the Southside of Memphis. Whenever he picked his shit up, he'd always have Nana follow behind him with the bricks in the trunk of the Caddy.

After he loaded the twenty bricks of coke into the trunk of the Caddy, Lil' Hott followed her in his Range Rover. Once they reached the stash house and were inside the garage, he popped the trunk and Victoria helped him carry the bricks inside. This was the first time she saw what he was really getting.

*Damn, Face was right. This nigga is paid. But where do he keep the money? I know he ain't that stupid to have his bankroll here with the product.*

As Victoria watched his every move, she made sure not to look suspicious. She acted like she wasn't interested in what he was doing, just being a good ho. She got the first mission accomplished, knowing about the stash after only two weeks. Now, she just needed to know where the bank was.

---

Meeko's first two weeks in D.C. went well. Babyface didn't put her straight out on the stroll, though. He had to check it out first. So, instead, he placed a dating service ad in the yellow pages for a sexy black woman available twenty-four hours a day. This is what they called new age pimping. Everybody was doing the call girl thing. It was good money, but his main reason for placing the ad was to burn Meeko out before Victoria made her move and came back home. He planned to have her work the stroll and call service at the same time. Meeko didn't care; she just wanted to make him happy.

"When I'm going down to the strip, Daddy?" she asked one

day.

"I gotta go check it out first, Meeko, and make sure shit still the same." But what he really was going to do was see if shit died down after he'd been gone. He also wanted to see King's bitch-ass. He heard King had gotten locked up while they were in Memphis, but he could have gotten out by now, and before Babyface put Meeko on the track, he wanted to make sure he was still locked down. He didn't care about Liddia and Precious. Hell, a ho gonna be a ho. His focus was to get back at King's bitch ass. It was King who told Royal's twin brothers, Mickey and Mousey, that Babyface killed their brother. In all actuality, Babyface wanted so bad to avenge Penny's death; he held King responsible.

As Babyface pulled up in Ho Valley in his 600 AMG Benz, all hoes turned their heads, except for Tina, who was a renegade ho. She was the only ho on 14th Street without a pimp. At one point in her ho life, the only nigga she considered having as her pimp was Babyface, but after hearing all the rumors of him breaking the pimp rules and leaving Victoria in Memphis, she knew something wasn't right with him. Victoria was his bottom ho, straight loyal, and if kicked her off the team, it had to be for something he did. At one time, hoes couldn't wait for him to come back to D.C. so they could choose him. He was looked at as a savior. But now, almost every ho on 14th Street despised him and he knew it. This was what he wanted. He planned it this way, so when it came time for him to finally check out of the game, he wouldn't be pressured for the streets to call him back.

"Hey, Tina, come here. I need to talk to you for a minute."

"Look, Face, if you looking to knock a ho, this ain't the place to be, and besides, I ain't looking for no pimp."

"Nah, Tina, that ain't my mission. I just wanna ask about an old friend I haven't seen since I've been back."

"Who, Face?" Tina asked.

"King…where the fuck he at?"

"You haven't heard?"

"Heard what, Tina?"

"King's ass is in jail for attempted murder," she told him.

"What! Attempted murder?"

"Yeah, Face, he damn near killed Liddia after he found out she was strung out on that shit."

"What! Hold up, Tina. Run that by me again."

"Yeah, Face, ever since Liddia returned she been on that heroine. That bitch been putting that spike in her arm. They say she was handling it for a while, because she was pretty and able to turn a lot of tricks, but as soon as election time came around, the feds did a clean sweep and the whole strip was dry. Since the bitch couldn't get no money, she stole King's."

"Damn, that's fucked up," Babyface replied. "What about Precious?"

"Oh, that bitch is still the reigning queen. Me and her are the only hoes out here without a pimp. She straight loyal to that nigga King."

"Damn, Liddia and King is gone, but Precious is still that bitch." Face thought about taking his frustration he had for King out on Precious, but he knew that wouldn't soothe his problem. Precious was just being a good ho, the same thing Victoria was doing now. Besides what did he look like doing something to a bitch? That was against his morals and principles. However, he did make a mental note to tell Precious to stay the fuck away from Meeko.

Everything was set up perfect. His enemy was in jail and the coast was clear to finally bring the baddest ho onto 14th Street since Victoria. That night would be Meeko's debut on the stroll.

Meeko's first night on the stroll was a memorable one. As she stepped out of the pearl white Benz, pimps and hoes couldn't believe Babyface had knocked a ho while out of town that looked just as good as Victoria, or to some even better. When Meeko stepped off the sidewalk and placed her Gucci heels on the concrete of 14th Street, she didn't take more than three steps before a trick rolled up beside her in his car.

Just as Meeko was about to get in, she looked in the trick's window reflection and saw another ho quickly walking up to steal her trick. After hopping in the car, Meeko rolled down her window, and while looking Precious directly in her eyes, she said, "Ho, you could never steal my trick. I was taught by the best. I'm Babyface's ho…top-flight Boss Bitch…and by the way, my name's Meeko. Pleased to meet you."

As the trick drove off, Precious stood there heated. The same move she had put down for years on hoes' first nights just blew up in her face. Precious was getting old and she saw there was another ho trying to take her crown, just like Victoria did.

While Meeko was sucking the life out of D.C. and Victoria was putting the finishing touches on Lil' Hott, Babyface was out searching for a spot to open up his strip club while house hunting. While driving down Indianhead Highway, approaching the southeast Maryland borderline, Babyface noticed a "For Sale" sign on an old restaurant right off the highway. As he turned his car around, he thought to himself it would be the perfect spot for his club, right smack in the middle of southeast D.C. and Glass Manor. It was a busy ass district, with Eastover Shopping Center across the street as well as other retail and liquor stores. Babyface also noticed it was a high crime area which attracted all types of hustlers with major bank. With a strip joint nowhere within a ten mile radius, this was the perfect spot indeed. After pulling into the Seashell parking lot, Babyface went in to talk to the owner, a Chinese guy with an American name. As soon as he stepped inside, Babyface fell in love with the place.

"I want to buy this place," Babyface said, not beating around the bush.

"Well, do you have the money?" asked Mike.

"What you want for it?"

"Two hundred thousand," Mike replied.

"What if I told you I had cash?"

"Then I'd say bring the money, proper I.D., and proof of income."

"What if I say it just fell outta the sky and put another $50,000 wit it just because you're a nice guy?"

At the sound of getting an extra $50,000, Mike knew Babyface was serious. Although he knew it might be drug money, he was willing to take the risk. Also, if anything fell back on him, he could always deny taking cash. There wouldn't be a trace.

"Okay, let's stop the bullshit. Do you really want this place?"

"Hell, yeah, I want it," said Babyface.

"Okay, let me see some I.D."    When Babyface handed it to him, the owner found it hard to believe that Babyface was his real name. "Come on, show me some real I.D."

"That is real," said Babyface.

"I tell you what. Bring me your birth certificate and social security card, and then you got yourself a store."

Babyface wanted this place bad, and although he was mad, he kinda understood. Nobody believed him when he showed his I.D. All his life he'd been ridiculed by his name.

"Okay, Mike, I'ma do that, but in the meantime, take this thousand dollars as a down payment

The next day, Babyface went down to Social Services in downtown Washington D.C. and picked up his credentials. He looked them over and laughed before placing them in his glove compartment. He was on his way to retirement, and as soon as Victoria pulled her move, he planned for them to take a vacation and then comeback and start their new life. While daydreaming about his future, he also thought of Victoria. She'd been down there for almost a month now, but she never called, not even to say that she was alright. He wondered what was taking her so long, and for a second, many negative thoughts raced through his mind.

*Damn, I hope Vic ain't blown her cover. Did this nigga do something to her? Did he know about Lonnie B? Was he smart enough after all to be able to pick up on the move? Did Vic fuck*

*around and fall in love wit the nigga?*

After thinking the worst, Babyface snapped out of it. "Fuck nah, Vic's a warrior. Vic loves me. That's my bitch for life, and ain't no way in the world Vic would fail me. It's just taking her a little more time than I thought."

# CHAPTER 19

## GOES AROUND COMES AROUND

**W**hile Babyface was in D.C. getting everything ready for his and Victoria's future, Victoria was down in Memphis putting on a real show.

Lil' Hott served his last three bricks, and was almost at the half a mill mark he needed for his connect, Paco. He knew he couldn't come to his connect short, especially since Paco had dropped the number for him twice. Also, Paco was doing him a big favor. He was gonna give Lil' Hott his biggest stash, a deal of the century, fifty bricks straight off the Gulf of Mexico for $800,000. All he wanted was for Lil' Hott to put up a half a million as a deposit. They both were loyal to each other.

Ever since his partner Lonnie B died, Lil' Hott took over the business. At first, he was only coping ten bricks, but whoever slipped something in Lonnie B's drink did Lil' Hott a favor. He took Lonnie B's stash and added it to his, along with what his hoes were bringing in. Lil' Hott was moving up. It got to a point where his pimp money didn't even really count. It was enough to pay the mortgage on his house in south Memphis and his new penthouse, insurance, clothes, food, and a few expensive gifts. He practically lived lavishly off his hoes' money, while he built his drug empire. Lil' Hott was only ten thousand short from half a mill, and that included every nickel, dime, and penny his hoes had. He couldn't pass up the deal, though. He wanted it bad, and the fact that Paco wanted to give it to him before he left the country made him want it even more.

While Lil' Hott talked on the phone to Paco, Victoria eavesdropped as she walked around the bedroom naked, faking like she was looking for something.

"Hey, Paco, look I'm just a lil bit short...C-mon, Paco, how long we been doing business...It's only ten thousand...I'll have it to you before you leave...What!...You leaving in the morning...Yeah, yeah, I understand, Paco...Look I'ma try and get that for you before tomorrow...Yeah, I understand...Okay. Fuck!" Lil' Hott screamed as he hung up the phone. "Damn!"

"What's wrong, Daddy?" asked Victoria.

"You, bitch! Why the fuck you ain't out there getting my money?" said Lil' Hott, as he grabbed Victoria's throat with one hand, causing her to choke.

As he held her against the wall by her throat, he called for Tammy and Nana to come upstairs. When they entered the room and saw Victoria pinned up against the wall, they instantly got scared, fearing they would be next.

"Yes, Daddy?"

"Bitch, come here!" He then smacked Tammy. "You lazy ass bitch, you been in here all day eating up shit and doing nuthin'. You ain't brought a nigga bankroll ever since Vic been on the set. I swear to God, bitch, I need ten thousand by nine o'clock tomorrow morning, and if none of you bitches can't get it, don't come back, 'cause if you do, you'll be food for the fucking fish. Now get the fuck out, all you lazy ass bitches!" He then kicked Nana in the ass hard as he could.

═══════════════

While Vic was getting the life choked out of her, Meeko was on her way to new client who saw the dating service ad.

"Daddy, I'm going to the Days Inn on New York Avenue. I got a client tryna spend some money. He sounds like one of them white, political muthufuckas, so I'ma work his old ass."

"How long you stayin'?" Babyface asked.

"Oh, this ain't gonna take but a good fifteen minutes."

"Well, I can take you and drop you off."

"Daddy, do you think you could wait outside for me and then drop me off on the stroll. I ain't gonna be but fifteen minutes. Please, Daddy. I've been working so hard, I hardly see you. At least, give me that much. I can make the ride real comfortable," she said, while licking her lips.

She hadn't had sex with Babyface but a few times since they been back in D.C. She needed him so bad, she settled for sucking his dick every chance she got.

"Okay, baby girl, and since we haven't spent that much time together, after you finish working this cracker, I'ma give you the night off, run you a hot bath, and punish that pussy all night long.

As soon as Meeko heard that, she grabbed her things before he changed his mind. "Okay, Daddy. Let's go," she said quickly.

Babyface parked in the lot right across from the hotel room. As Meeko entered the room, Babyface reclined his seat and closed his eyes. After about five minutes, Babyface looked up, wondering why there were two detective cars pulling up in front of the room Meeko had just went into. Five seconds later, he saw Meeko being escorted from the room in handcuffs.

*Damn! Fuck! This shit always happens to me.* He watched as they placed her in the car and took off. *Damn, Meeko, how the fuck you let 'em trick you like that? Damn! Fuck! These muthafuckas are fucking up my plans.*

Babyface went back to his apartment and waited for Meeko to call. When she hadn't called by nine o'clock that night, he grew impatient and called down to the police station.

"Hello, 6th District Police...May I help you?"

"Ah, yes, I'm calling to check on my niece Tameeka Clark. She was arrested earlier and I think she may be there."

"Hold on, sir." After a couple minutes, the officer returned to the line. "Excuse me, sir, did you say the two of you were related?"

"Yes, ma'am."

"Well, that's a surprise. Why don't you come down the station and have a talk with the detectives."

"Detectives? For what?"

# VICTORIA'S SECRET

"Well, sir, if that's your niece, maybe you could explain why the juvenile has been missing for the last three years."

"What!"

"Sir, you sound surprised. Are you really her..."

Before she could finish, Babyface hung up the phone.

*Damn! What the fuck is wrong wit that bitch? She been lying ever since the day we met. She knew I wouldn't pimp her if I knew she was underage. Damn, the whole time I'm fuckin' this bitch she a kid. I could get thirty years for that shit. I should've listened to Vic and left that bitch back in Chicago.*

Babyface fixed a drink, went out on the balcony, and looked out over the city, thinking about how D.C. turned him into what he was today. As he looked into the night, he saw the bright lights of the Capitol and the Washington Monument. *Damn, that shit looks pretty. How can a city look so beautiful and be so fucked up? From the outside, a muthafucka would think he was in heaven until he got inside and found out that D.C. was the devil's permanent residence. Vic, where the fuck are you, and why haven't you called?* he said to himself as he looked into the night. *I need you, baby girl. Pick up the phone and call.*

═══════════

Victoria, Tammy, and Nana were down the shake joint hoeing their asses off, but weren't getting any money. It seemed like the ballers were getting tired of fucking the same ol' bitches all the time. They knew if they didn't brig Lil' Hott ten thousand by tomorrow that somebody was gonna get fucked up or maybe really end up in the Mississippi River. It was almost ten o'clock at night, and all their money put together wouldn't amount to a thousand dollars.

*Damn, I gotta do sumthin',* thought Victoria, as she walked over to one of her old tricks and told him she would give him some head for a ride. She instructed him to go out front and wait for her.

"Hey, Nana, look, I got this nigga outside flashin' a big-ass bankroll. I'ma take him to the hotel, fuck his brains out, and try to get all that money for Daddy. Okay?"

"Go head, Vic, do whatever you gotta do. Hell, if that nigga want you to lick his ass, do it, girl. And better still, if you can get him to call some of his friends, tell 'em you got two bad-ass freak bitches down at the shake joint ready to do whatever," Nana replied.

"Okay, ya'll, I'ma do my best."

Victoria did what she had to do for the ride to the Hampton Inn. She gave the guy a hundred dollars not to go back to Pure Passion, and she told him if he ran into her hoe sistahs to tell 'em she's on the Southside of Memphis with his friends. As soon as she got in the room, she went straight to the phone and dialed Babyface's number.

"Hey, Daddy."

"Vic! Whazzup, baby girl? You alright? Why haven't you called?"

"'Cause I told myself I wasn't gonna call until I was ready," she replied.

"Vic, I miss you so much."

"I know, Daddy. I miss you, too, but now ain't the time for all that, so get your butt on the next plane smokin' and call my cell phone as soon as you get to Memphis."

"Give me your address, Vic."

Victoria gave Babyface the address to the penthouse. "Now, Daddy, hurry up."

"I'm walking out the door as we speak, Vic."

"Hey, Babyface."

"Yeah, Vic?"

"I told you I was your bitch for life."

"You proved that a long time ago, baby girl. Now, go 'head and do your thang."

"I love you, Daddy."

"I love you, too, Vic. Now get the hell off the phone."

After hanging up, Victoria dug into the mattress and pulled out the remainder of the money Babyface had left for her, which was seventy-five hundred. After thirty days, she only had to chip off twenty-five hundred. Victoria made more money than Tammy and Nana all the time without having to hit the stash, and she only hit the stash when she wanted to outdo their bank put together. She added her other five hundred to it, and then went to the mirror, fuzzed her hair, and rubbed some soap in her eyes to get them bloodshot red. As she looked at herself in the mirror, Victoria looked like she was working five ho strolls at one time. Once satisfied with her appearance, she called a cab to take her back to the penthouse. It was eleven o'clock when Victoria walked through the door.

Lil' Hott was sitting in the living room counting his money, not expecting the any of the girls to be back so soon.

"Bitch, what are you doing back?" asked Lil' Hott as he examined Victoria, who appeared worn out. "Bitch, I swear to God if you ain't got no money, I'ma kill your ass right here in this living room."

Victoria dropped to her knees and started her Oscar-winning performance, with fake tears and all. "Daddy, please…I been out there all night fucking, sucking, and I've even been gang banged by ten ballers at once. Daddy, I tried my best, but please don't send me back out. I'm worn out. I swear I did my best," she pleaded as she handed him the eight thousand dollars. "Daddy, please…"

Before she could finish, he cut her off with a hug, holding her tight in his arms. Out of all his days of pimping he had never seen a ho like Victoria; she was one of a kind and deserved to be treated like royalty.

"It's okay, lil' mama. You did good. You did so good that it's a must I make you bottom ho. Now, come on upstairs so I can run your bath water."

Lil' Hott grabbed his gym bag of money, put the eight thousand in it, took it to the room, and placed it under the bed. He then proceeded to treat her like a queen. As she took off her clothes, he ran her a nice hot bubble bath. While looking her over, he couldn't believe what Victoria had just done. She brought him the biggest bankroll ever, and from the way she looked, he could imagine the hell she went through getting him that money. He made a mental note to reward her with something real nice after he finished moving his next shipment.

"Hey, Vic."

"Yes, Daddy?"

Lil' Hott couldn't believe what was about to come out of his mouth, but he had to say it because it is what he felt. He couldn't hold it back. Victoria did the ultimate for him in only a few hours.

"I love you, Vic."

"I love you, too, Daddy."

After Lil' Hott finished washing her body, he left her soaking and went downstairs to get some champagne to celebrate him meeting his goal and her becoming bottom ho. Once he left the bathroom, Victoria pulled her pocketbook open and frantically searched for the sleeping pills she bought the other day. When she heard Lil' Hott coming back up the stairs, she quickly put her pocketbook back down on the bathroom floor beside her clothes and smiled as he walked in with a bottle of Cristal and two glasses. As he was pouring both glasses, the phone in the bedroom started ringing. Instantly, Victoria feared it was Tammy and Nana calling to tell him that she never came back. Just as he was about to get up to answer, she tried to stop him.

"Where you goin', Daddy?"

"The phone's ringin', lil' mama."

"Let it ring then. We suppose to be chillin'," she said in her childish voice.

"I can't, Vic. It might be my connect calling back. I just paged him."

"Okay, hurry back, Daddy."

"Alright, lil' mama," he said, as he went to answer the phone.

As soon as he left, Victoria reached back in her pocketbook, found the pills, chewed three up, spit them in Lil' Hott's glass, and stirred. She rinsed her mouth out with her champagne and spit it in the tub. When he returned, she could see from his expression that something was wrong.

"What's wrong, Daddy?"

"Vic, why the fuck you start drinkin' without me? This is suppose to be our celebration."

Victoria smiled childishly, and in her whiney voice she said, "I'm sorry, Daddy. I was thirsty. I didn't drink that much. Come on, let's make our toast. Here's to the realest pimp in the game, Lil' Hott, a ho's dream pimp."

Believing every word she said, he gulped down his champagne like lemonade on a hot Sunday afternoon. For the next three hours, Victoria and Lil' Hott made love like it was the last time they'd ever be together, as the sleeping pills started to take effect.

———————————————

Babyface's plane landed at 1:10 a.m., and by the time he got off the plane and rushed through all the security points, he was in a cab headed for The Carriage House Suites on Main Street by 1:30 a.m. Babyface took out his cell phone, and as soon as the cab turned onto Main Street, he started dialing Victoria's cell phone number.

"C-mon, Vic, pick up the fuckin' phone," he said, as he waited impatiently.

"Where you at?" she answered frantically, without even saying hello.

"My cab is pulling up right in front of the building."

Before he could finish, she hung up the phone and tip-toed back in the room. Victoria was butt naked. She didn't have time to put on her clothes, and also, she couldn't get Babyface's watch back. Lil' Hott still had it on it and it was too risky. Victoria slowly and quietly pulled the gym bag full of money from underneath the bed. As she was leaving, Lil' Hott called out for her in a groggy voice.

"Vic, come back to bed."

"I'll be right back, Daddy. I gotta go pee-pee."

She then hurriedly tip-toed down the steps barefoot and grabbed her fur coat off the couch. She didn't even bother to put it on; she was too anxious to get out the penthouse. As she headed for the elevator, she threw the coat on. Once inside the elevator, an elderly woman looked at her as if she was crazy. Here she was standing in an elevator going down to the lobby in a full-length white chinchilla fur with no shoes on. When the elevator doors opened, Victoria ran out of the lobby as fast as she could without looking too suspicious. As she entered the cab, she could see Tammy and Nana just pulling up in Lil' Hott's Caddy. She quickly laid her head in Babyface's lap as he told the driver to drive away.

Tammy and Nana never saw Victoria. Then again, she was the last thing on their minds. They were more worried at what Lil' Hott was going to do to them for only bringing back fifteen hundred.

As the cab turned off Main Street, Babyface pulled Victoria up and held her tight. "It's okay, baby girl. You did it. You did it, Vic." He then kissed her hard, as she held on to him for dear life. "I missed you, baby girl," he said between kisses.

"Where you two lovebirds wanna go?" asked the cab driver in his African accent.

"Take us to Little Rock Arkansas Airport," Babyface replied. He knew Little Rock was at least an hour away, but he didn't want to risk Lil' Hott catching them at the Memphis Airport.

"Lil Rock? Man, you must be crazy. That's an hour away from here."

Babyface then peeled off five one-hundred-dollar bills. "Will this be enough for your troubles?" he said, as he handed the driver the money.

After inspecting the bills to make sure they weren't counterfeit, the driver turned around, smiled at the loving couple, and asked, "What kind of music do you like?"

Victoria laughed as they rode to their destination.

Once they got to Little Rock Airport, they checked into the airport hotel. The next morning, Babyface cut open Victoria's fur, stuffed $475,000 in its lining, then sewed it back and sent it off to his P.O. Box. Next, he went to the local souvenir shop and bought her some cheap ass outfit.

"Here, baby girl, put that on," he said when he returned to their room.

"Babyface, where did you get this bullshit from?"

"It was the only thing I could find. Besides, you only have to wear it for a lil' while. Now, c-mon, hurry up and put it on. Our plane leaves for Jamaica in a half hour."

"WHAT! Jamaica! Daddy, you're taking me to Jamaica?"

"Yeah, baby girl, and that ain't all. We're heading to Aruba after that."

Victoria jumped off the bed and hopped onto Babyface, wrapping her arms around his neck tight and her legs around his waist, just like she use to do when her father came home with a gift.

"Daddy, I love you. I swear I love you."

"Vic, I'ma make you the happiest woman in the world."

"You already did that when you first met me. There's nuthin' in the world that can explain my love for you...nuthin'!"

---

Babyface put down the diary as Ms. Winters entered the room.

"Hey, honey, you're still here?"

"Yeah, Ms. Winters, I can't leave. I gotta stay with her. She's all I got. I can't go," he replied, looking like he was about to shed a tear for the love of his life, who was now sleeping in a coma.

After all they been through, he couldn't believe he let this happen.

"What are you reading, darling?"

"Oh, I'm just readin' her diary to see if I can come up wit some clues as to what happened."

"Hmmm...she must've had that tucked away real good for the detectives not to find it," said Ms. Winters.

"Yeah, I'm kinda surprised at that, too," said Babyface.

"Well, I'm glad they didn't find it. I'm pretty sure there are some things in there she might not want the police to know."

"Nah, it ain't that bad, Ms. Winters."

"That's good then, darling. But you know if she comes outta her coma and finds out you was reading that, she gonna be mad," Ms. Winters said, with a light chuckle.

"Won't nobody know but me and you, Ms Winters. You ain't gonna tell on me, are you?"

"No, baby, I wouldn't do that. I would never spoil her joy. I just pray she makes it."

"Well, how's she doing?" he asked.

"Her blood pressure is going down, which is good, and she is signaling all her vitals, so that's good. You got a pretty tough cookie on your hands. Yes, she's a fighter."

Babyface looked at Victoria as she laid there helpless. "I know, Ms. Winters, I know."

"Well, I'ma let you go back to your reading. Call me if you need anything."

"Okay, thank you, Ms. Winters."

"Sure, darling," she said.

Before she left the room, Babyface quickly buried his head back in Victoria's diary.

# CHAPTER 20

## BACK HOME

*One month later*

After vacationing in Jamaica and Aruba for the past month, Victoria and Babyface returned to their apartment in Alexandria, Virginia, which overlooked Washington D.C. One morning shortly after their return, Babyface woke up and started putting on his clothes.

"Where you goin', Daddy?"

"I gotta go take care of something."

Victoria wanted to know where, but knew better than to ask. Even though Babyface had given up the pimp life, he still was the man and ran the show. So instead of asking could she go, she put it in different words.

"Do you need me for anything?"

"Nah, Vic, only thing I need for you to do is love me today more than you did yesterday," he said, as he kissed her lips. "Ewww, girl, go brush your teeth. Your breath stick."

"Fuck you, Face."

"Nah, how 'bout I fuck you when I come back."

"Maybe, depending on how I feel," she replied playfully. "Hey, Face, I wanna go visit Candy today. Do you think you can drop me off, and I'll catch a cab back home? Plus, I wanna do a lil' shoppin' later."

"That's good, 'cause I want you to buy yourself something real nice. I'ma take you out to dinner tonight."

"Ohhh, where we going?" asked Victoria, hugging him.

"I don't know yet, but you need to get dressed so I can drop you off."

———

When Candy came out, she damn near cried as she saw Victoria standing on the opposite side of the glass.

"Hey, girl…"

"Bitch, don't 'hey girl' me. Why you just coming to see me?" Candy scolded.

"Shut up wit your mean self."

"I miss you, Vic," she said in a softer tone.

"I miss you, too, Candy, and you better know I'll be down here every weekend to visit you."

"You better," Candy replied, as they both laughed.

Victoria then filled her in on everything, except for the murders.

"Damn, Vic, he ain't tell me it was all a plan. He gave me the impression that he dropped you for real."

"Come on, Candy, picture that. I made the nigga. You know Face would die without me."

"You got that right," she replied. "Well, Babyface put a real lick down and played it all the way out. Now that's what I call real pimpin'. Pimp hard, nigga, pimp hard."

"No, Candy, it's over for us. We retired, and when you get out, you're retiring, too, 'cause you coming wit us."

Candy looked at her with an expression that said she wish she could, but she couldn't. "No, Vic, I gotta do for Bone. I can't stop."

"Don't you worry 'bout all that. Babyface got Bone. He's getting him a real good lawyer, and when he come out, he coming home to a bankroll and ya'll ain't never gotta do this shit again. Besides, I'm 'bout to have every ho in Ho Valley working in my strip club, so we are going to have more than enough money."

Candy and Victoria laughed and talked the whole visit, which seemed more like ten minutes than an hour. As the visit came to an end, Candy stood and placed her hand against the glass.

"I love you, Vic."

Victoria stood and did the same. "I love you, too, Candy."

"Vic, you the best ho that ever did it, and you're only nineteen years old. Bitches will glorify you forever."

"Well, I couldn't have done it without you, Candy. You taught me and Penny everything."

"I know, baby, I know." At the sound of Penny's name, Candy couldn't take it. She would always be fucked up about Penny's death. "Now get your ass outta here before you make me cry."

---

Later that evening, Victoria waited at home for Babyface in her Chanel dress. She was anticipating their night out on the town. As Babyface walked in the door, he stopped dead in his tracks.

"Damn, girl, you're beautiful. I mean, for real, Vic. You're flawless, baby girl."

"Thanks. Now where we going?" she asked with excitement.

"Come on, baby girl. We gonna have a good time tonight."

As they got in the car, Victoria noticed he was wearing a new watch that was blinging so hard it looked like it was illuminating the whole inside of the car.

"Damn, Daddy, where you get that from?"

"What's that? Oh, baby girl, I got this today. This is a Frank Muller platinum jewel. It cost me a fortune, too."

Victoria looked at the watch and thought, *How could he be so selfish? He went out and bought himself a watch, but didn't bring me back nothing, not even a funky-ass bubble gum ring. After all the shit I did for him, how the fuck is he not gonna get me nuthin'? I'm not even gonna ruin my night and ask, but first thing in the morning, I'ma let his ass know a thing or two.*

With that, she pushed it to the back of her mind to deal with the next day.

As he pulled his Benz into the Ruth Chris restaurant valet, there were three hostesses standing out front waiting.

"Damn, Daddy, this some fly shit, but I don't see no cars out here. Are you sure it's open?"

"Oh, I'm sure, Vic."

Once inside, Victoria couldn't believe her eyes. There were ten waiters and waitress in one long, single-file line. As her and Babyface walked by, each one introduced themselves to her by her name. She couldn't believe what Babyface had done for her. When they reached the last waiter, he introduced himself, as well.

"Hello, Victoria. I'm Kevin, the head waiter, and all these tables are open just for you. Please pick whichever one you like."

Victoria looked at Babyface with shock. He had the whole restaurant closed to the public for the day just to have dinner with Victoria alone.

"Go 'head, Vic. Pick whichever table you want," said Babyface as he held her hand.

She squeezed his hand tight and turned around with watery eyes. "I love you, Face."

"I know, baby girl. Now go 'head and pick a table, any table."

Victoria decided they would be seated at the table in the middle of the floor. The dim lighting of the restaurant and the white candle that sat in a crystal hurricane in the middle of the table created a romantic atmosphere.

"Face, this is some fly-ass shit. I can't believe this. Please tell me I ain't dreaming."

"Nah, baby girl, this here is real," he replied, decked out in his blue Armani shirt and pants.

They ordered stuffed bluefish, cream spinach, asparagus, garlic bread, and a few other dishes that made the table elegant. Vic was so excited she couldn't even eat much. After they sipped for a few on the Dom Perignon, the dessert waiter came over with a 19-karat gold dessert dish and sat it in the middle of the table. As Victoria grabbed for the lid, Babyface stopped her by touching her hand.

# VICTORIA'S SECRET

"What, Face?"

"Hold on a sec, baby girl." As Babyface nodded for the waiter, an all-white grand piano appeared out of nowhere and the professional pianist played the tunes of Luther Vandross's "If Anyone Had a Heart".

Victoria couldn't take it no more. The tears gushed from her eyes like water from a facet. "Daddy, no, you didn't. I can't believe this shit. Oh my god, Face, I can't even understand it. What are you doing to me, Daddy?"

Babyface smiled. "Vic, I love you and there's nuthin' in the world, and I mean nuthin', I won't do for you." As the pianist finished, everybody in the room left. "Now, go 'head and eat your dessert, baby girl."

"Face, I can't eat nuthin' after all this. You got my head all fucked up. I don't think I'm living right now."

"Well, Vic, you are. This is all real. This is what you deserve and much, much more. Now, go 'head and eat your dessert. I had it made especially for you. You wouldn't want to disappoint me, would you, Vic?"

"Never, Face, never," she replied.

When she removed the lid, she could have sworn her heart stopped beating for at least thirty seconds. She was both breathless and speechless as her eyes stayed glued to the 10-karat platinum diamond ring.

"Vic, will you marry me?" Babyface asked in his soft, but serious tone as he looked her deep in the eye.

She couldn't even answer. She was stuck in a trance. She couldn't believe this was happening. For a moment, she was a zombie, until he snapped her out of it.

"Vic, what's your answer?"

Victoria jumped up from the table, knocking everything over, but caring less. "Yes! Yes! Hell yeah, nigga!"

JASON POOLE

The next morning, after an intense night of lovemaking, Victoria awoke to find that she hadn't been dreaming after all, as she gazed at the 10-karat stone sitting on her finger. Just as she looked over to see Babyface's side of the bed empty, he emerged fully dressed from the bathroom.

"Where you goin', Face?"

"I'll be right back, baby girl. I gotta go pick something up." He then called a cab.

*Why did he call a cab when he got a Benz sitting out front,* Vic thought. "Hey, Daddy, what's wrong with your car? Why you callin' a cab?"

"Baby girl, I gotta go take care of something. Don't worry. I'll be right back."

The same as the times before, Victoria knew not to ask anymore questions. If he had something to do, and he didn't want her to know, that's just how it was gonna be.

After a few hours, Babyface returned, and she cooked him breakfast to show her appreciation of the wonderful, romantic night. That day, they stayed in and made love aggressively, fucking all over the house, no holds barred. Victoria gave him every ounce of love she had in her body. No one in the world ever made her feel like this, ever, not even her father. Babyface outdid himself last night, and Victoria vowed to thank him for a lifetime. She planned to make him the happiest man in the world. According to Victoria, there would never be another sad day in Babyface's life.

As nightfall came, they stood on the balcony holding each other and looking out over the city.

"Look at that shit. Ain't it pretty?"

"Yeah, Face, downtown looks so bright and peaceful."

"Too bad that once you get there, you find out it's the most evil place in the world," replied Face.

"Yeah, I know, but we gotta look at ourselves. It's not the place that makes it hell; it's the people in it. Heaven and hell is a state of mind. Like right now, I'm in heaven, but when I was down in Memphis, I was in the deepest part of hell. Face, we are creators and we create our own conditions."

"Girl, what the hell have you been reading?"

Victoria laughed. "Nothing, Face, that's just law, and law governs all event. It's just on us to live by it."

"Okay now, Vic, that's enough of the Farrakhan stuff."

"That ain't Farrakhan; that's Nobel Drew Ali."

"Well, whoever or whatever it is you can kick that shit to Candy on your next visit, 'cause right 'bout now I'm 'bout to put this blunt in the air."

"You're crazy, Face," she said, playfully hitting him on the arm.

"Yeah, crazy 'bout you," he replied, as held her close while smoking his weed.

"What time is it?"

Babyface looked at his iced out watch. "It's nine o'clock. Why? You goin' somewhere?

Victoria turned around and looked at Face. "Daddy, I wanna go to the stroll."

"For what, Vic? That shit is over. You ain't never gotta go down there again."

"I know, Face, but them hoes are my friends. I gotta go show 'em it's a better way. I gotta let 'em know that they can work for me at the club and leave them no good pimps. Face, I gotta try to save Liddy. I know how you feel about her, but I do love her and she will always be my sister. Face, she's the only one I got left in this world besides you."

Babyface looked at Victoria. He knew Victoria was hurt, and he knew she felt if she saved Liddia, then it would take away some of the pain for not saving Penny. This would be her grand finale out of the game. She had to do it. She had to go show these bitches that a ho can be turned into a housewife, but only if she really wants to. Also, he knew deep down inside that Victoria wanted to floss on Precious. She admired Precious all her young life, and Precious took that away from her when she stole Liddia.

"Okay, Vic, you can go, but I ain't taking you. I'd rather you go by yourself. Personally, I don't think I can stand to see Liddia and Precious, and besides, this is your time to shine. I want you to show your ass off, represent me the fullest."

"Oh, you gonna let me push the Benz, Daddy?"

"Nah, baby girl. Come on downstairs. I wanna show you something."

When they reached the parking lot, Babyface handed Victoria the keys to a pearl white Cadillac Escalade sitting in the middle of the parking lot, with a ribbon wrapped around the hood.

Victoria held both sides of her cheeks. "Face, I know you didn't!"

"Oh, yes, I did, baby girl. This is your engagement present. You like it?"

"Fuck yeah! I love it," she said, as she jumped on him, wrapping her arms and legs around him and kissing all over his face. "I love you. I love you. I love you," Victoria said numerous times.

"I know you love me, Vic. Now, go 'head and do your thing. Let them bitches know you got a king at home. And Vic… don't be out there all night. We got some finishing up to do."

"We can always do it in the back of my truck, if you want, or maybe on top…however or whenever, this pussy will always be yours."

"I know. Now, go 'head wit your silly self before I change my mind and take you back upstairs."

She kissed him once more and jumped in the truck. "I love you, Daddy," she said while pulling off.

He knew when he left to go pick it up that morning she'd love it, but he never knew she'd look so good pushing it.

---

Babyface was angered. He had just read the last page in

Victoria diary, and still, there was no clue as to who could have done this to her. They did so much dirt in their life, it could have been anybody. And what about the person who called and told him something happened to Victoria then hung up. Who was that? Maybe that person had something to do with it. Babyface was confused, but determined to find out what happened.

He leaned over and kissed her bandaged forehead. "Baby girl, I'ma find out who did this. I promise. Just hang in there for me, Vic," he said, as he noticed her monitor beeping a little faster, indicating her heart was getting to its normal rate. "That's right, baby girl. Keep fighting."

While Babyface talked to Victoria, Ms. Winters came rushing through the door. "What's wrong, Ms. Winters?"

"I came back to tell you the detectives are back, and they're out front at my desk," she informed him.

"Ms. Winters, I don't mean to be rude, but right now, I don't wanna talk to no detectives."

"I know. I kinda figured that, and that's why I came to tell you."

Ms. Winters held a folder in her hand, and looked like she wanted to tell him something. Babyface couldn't figure out why this old lady was being so helpful.

"Look, there's a back way out. I can get you past, but you gotta hurry," said Ms. Winters.

Babyface kissed Victoria and quickly followed behind Ms. Winters. As he reached the staircase, he turned around to thank her. "Thank you, Ms. Winters. Please take good care of her."

"I will, son. Now, look, these are her records. She was born in this hospital and the detectives are asking for them. Here, take 'em."

As she handed Babyface Victoria's medical records, he still couldn't understand why this lady was helping him. He looked Ms. Winters in the eyes. He just had to know why.

"Ms. Winters, why are you helping me?"

"Because, son, I read the diary, also, and I know who you are.

Now, take this and go, and be careful," she said as she watched him take flight down the stairs.

As Babyface was leaving the lobby, the lil' chubby receptionist tried to get his attention. "Is she gonna be alright?' she asked, as Babyface briskly walked passed to catch and stop the man trying to tow his Benz.

"Hey, hold up, man. That's my car."

"Yeah, well, it's getting towed. It's been here for over four hours. I was supposed to tow it two hours ago," the tow truck driver replied.

"Now, hold up, slim. Let's do this proper. How much is it gonna cost for me to come pick it up?"

"A hundred for the tow and fifty for storage."

Babyface reached in his pocket and peeled off three hundred dollars. "Here, take this."

"Damn, thanks, man."

"Yeah, no problem," Babyface replied, as he got in his Benz and drove off.

He was confused; he wanted to know what happened, and the only clue he had left was the last place Victoria went...down to the stroll. Therefore, he figured he'd go down to the track and ask Tina if she saw anything. He also wanted to find Liddia. If Liddia had something to do with this, he vowed to give her at least seven shots to the face.

*It's only 7:30. The track won't be open until 8:00.*

Babyface looked at the folder in his passenger seat and wondered what was in it. *Why would Ms. Winters give it to me? What is so important about Vic's medical records?*

He reached over, grabbed the folder, and opened it. The first page contained information regarding her birth. He read her full name and then laughed. All this time, he never knew her middle name was Pricilla. He then looked over at her father's name, Tony Wayne Grey. When he looked at her mother's name, he almost fainted.

"This can't be true! Hell no! Fuck no!"

Babyface was so fucked up that he swerved in traffic and almost crashed. He then pulled over on the side of Pennsylvania Avenue and quickly reached for his glove compartment, damn near breaking its door as he pulled out his birth certificate. He placed both papers side by side, and instantly, his head fell on the steering wheel.

On Victoria's birth record under mother's name, it read Diane Beverly Grey, maiden name Diane Beverly James. He then looked on his, and underneath the place for his mother's name it read Diane Beverly James. He reflected back to Victoria's diary when she talked about her mother's illegitimate child who was born three years before her, and the part where her father wouldn't marry her mother until she gave him up for adoption, and also the part where after birthing him, she never gave him a name.

Babyface always wondered were the rumors he heard about his birth true. While at foster homes, his counselor used to tell him that his mother never named him, and the nurse who delivered him didn't want to, either. So, instead, the nurse thought it would be nice to just put down "Baby" in his name slot. Babyface was ridiculed all his life by his name, and now he knew why. Babyface wasn't called that just because he resembled the singer. Nah, it was realer than that. Babyface's true name was Baby James.

He cried out the loudest and most hurtful pain he had ever experienced. He wanted to kill Ms. Winters for giving him this information. Babyface was literally broken down, fucked up in the head. How the fuck can a nigga pimp his sister and fall in love with her at the same time? He then thought about Pimpin' Ken's article in F.E.D.S. Magazine, when he said no morally sane pimp would ever pimp his own sister. In this case, however, neither knew. Yet, that made it hurt even more.

*Vic can't be my sister; she just can't be. Hell no, she can't be.* As much as he wanted to believe himself, he couldn't. The facts were supported by their records: Victoria and Baby James were brother and sister.

The anger built up heavily as he thought about his life. At that moment, nothing in the world mattered to him more than finding out who did this to her. It would be that person who would be held responsible for the pain he'd now been inflicted with for the rest of his life.

*What if she lives? How can I tell her this?* He pushed the thought to the back of his mind. Right then, he didn't care. His focus was on finding the person or persons responsible for this and ending their lives.

After sitting in silence for almost an hour, Babyface reached under the seat, placed his 9mm Taurus on his lap, and raced down to 14$^{th}$ Street. Somebody was going to answer his questions or die. His mission was to find his prey. He no longer was the hunted; he became the hunter.

As he pulled up in Ho Valley, all the hoes turned to look the other way, except for Tina, who looked him straight in the face. He felt Tina knew something. She had guilt in her eyes.

"Get in, Tina."

"Face, I don't wanna be involved."

Before she could say anything else, he pointed his gun at her, but making sure nobody saw him. "Bitch, get in the car now."

After Tina got in, he drove down the stroll, not bothering to even look in her direction. "Tina, I wanna know everything you know, and if I think you're lying, I'ma blow your brains out."

"Face, I don't..."

"Bitch, if you tell me you don't know nuthin', I swear I'll bash your fucking skull through that window."

"Okay, Face, but please, please keep this between us. I can get myself killed," Tina said.

"Bitch, if you don't hurry up and talk, you gettin" killed now," he threatened.

"Face, all I know is this, Victoria rolled up in Ho Valley looking good in her Escalade. All the hoes loved seeing another ho make it outta the game. She was out there telling everybody about the new club you and her were opening, and that every ho out there could come work for her. Everybody was proud of Vic. She asked a few hoes about Liddy, but nobody had seen her. They told Vic that Liddy was so fucked up that she would suck a dick for free on 14$^{th}$ Street. As Precious came walking by, Vic tried to talk to her, but she kept walking down the stroll. Victoria jogged to catch up with her. From a short distance, I could see that the two of them were exchanging heated words. The next thing I knew, someone smashed Victoria's skull and dragged her in the alley. I didn't even hear her scream. Babyface, I'm telling you the truth. I never saw nobody come outta that alley," said Tina. "I thought Vic was dead, so I called the police. I couldn't call you. I didn't know how I could explain to you what had happened. The next morning, I called the hospital to see if you were there, but the nurse told me nobody had come to claim her and that she was in a coma. That's when I called you anonymously and told you something happened to Vic. I only hung up the phone because I didn't wanna be involved. Face, I was scared. Hell, I'm still scared."

"So you're telling me you ain't see who hit her in the head and dragged her in the alley?" said Face.

"No, Babyface. Whoever it was that hit her, did it so fast it was like a shadow coming out the alley and pulling her back in."

"Tina, I'm telling your ass now, if you don't tell me who pulled her in the alley, they gonna find your body in the next one," Babyface said, as he held his gun tight and clenched his teeth.

He was at the point of no return, the brink of his destruction. His mind was cloudy and his thoughts were misguided.

"I swear I don't know. I was standing in Ho Valley and couldn't see that clear. All I saw was Precious, and I'm not even sure she had anything to do wit it."

"Where's that bitch Precious at now, and who the fuck is her new pimp?" he asked.

"Only thing I know is that she was knocked about three weeks ago by this young pimp from Memphis."

"WHAT!" Babyface shouted.

"Yeah, Face, that shit surprised me, too. I never knew Precious to get knocked by another pimp, and a young one at that. They say she chose him the first day he got here."

"Tina, what's his name?"

Face already knew it was Lil' Hott. He was the only young pimp in Memphis, and plus, he had plenty enough reason to come to D.C.; this nigga was chasing his money.

"I forget his name. It was kinda weird...something like Lil' Shot. Face, the lil' nigga got diamonds in his teeth."

Instantly, Face knew who got Victoria. This nigga came to D.C., knocked Precious, and since she was known to be loyal to her pimp, she set Victoria up for the nigga in order to get brownie points.

"Where is this nigga staying?"

"Last week, I saw 'em at the HO-JO Inn on New York Avenue"

"Okay. Get out, Tina."

"Face, before I go, I wanna tell you that I'm sorry for what happened to Vic. Also, I wanna say that I think you're the best pimp ever in the game. I never in all my hoeing life seen a pimp take his ho off the street and marry her. That's some real shit, and if anytime you or Vic need me, I'll be there."

"Nah, Tina, I don't need another ho," said Face, as the thought of Victoria being his sister damn near made him cry.

---

As Babyface pulled in the parking lot at the HO-JO Inn, he spotted Lil' Hott's Range Rover with the Memphis license plates. Babyface parked in the cut so he could watch for what room they were in, hoping to see somebody come out. As time went by, he got impatient. He then got out the car and started walking past each room, putting his ear to the doors to see if he could hear Lil' Hott's Memphis accent. While walking around the first floor, he stopped at one door when he heard somebody talking. Babyface stood on the side to listen more closely, but was disappointed when two faggots emerged from the room and jumped in their cars. He knew he looked suspicious, but so much shit was running through his mind, he didn't care if somebody saw him or not.

When he looked toward the parking lot, he thought he saw someone firing up a cigarette through the tinted glass of their black Cadillac Eldorado. When he looked again, the orange light went out. *Maybe that's just somebody sitting in their car, smoking and minding their business.* Whoever it was, Babyface didn't care, as long as they minded their own fucking business.

As he ascended the stairs to the second floor, he heard screams coming from down the hall. He swiftly ran to the room and put his ear to the door.

"Oh, Daddy, I'm sorry. Please don't hit me no more."

"Shut up, bitch!"

*Smack...smack*

"No, Daddy, please. Please stop, Lil' Hott."

"Shut the fuck up, bitch!"

*Smack...smack*

"No, Daddy, please."

"Now where my shit at?"

"I don't know nuthin' 'bout no money. Please stop."

"Shut up, bitch!"

Babyface couldn't take it anymore. He grabbed for his 9mm and was ready to kick the door open. Then, he stopped and thought for a second. *If I kick it open, I might cause a big scene, and if I knock he'll look out the peephole and most likely bring his strap to the door with him. Damn, I gotta think of something.*

As Babyface looked around, he noticed a room service cart at the end of the hall. He grabbed the cart and pushed it in front of the room so if Lil' Hott peeped out, he could see it. He then knocked on the door and listened carefully.

*Knock...knock...knock*

"Shhhh...bitch, if you make one sound, I'ma kill your ass," said Lil' Hott. "Who is it?" he yelled.

"Room service," Babyface replied.

"I didn't ask for no room service," said Lil' Hott, talking from behind the door.

"I know, sir, but the motel is having an employee meeting tomorrow and there won't be anyone here to pass out fresh sheets and towels. So, my boss told me to give 'em out tonight," said Babyface, sounding just like a motel worker.

Convinced it was a motel employee at the door, Lil' Hott placed his gun back on the nightstand and said, "Just leave 'em in front of the door. I'll get 'em."

"Okay, sir," said Babyface. He pushed the cart down the hall as hard as he could so Lil' Hott would think he'd left, and then pulled out his 9mm Taurus and held it tight as he stood on the side of the door, praying Lil' Hott would fall for his scheme.

As soon as Lil' Hott cracked open the door, Babyface kicked the door with so much force that the impact caused Lil' Hott to be unbalanced, instantly knocking him to the floor. Before Lil' Hott could even think about getting to the nightstand where he sat his gun, Babyface was standing overtop of him with his gun pointed directly between his eyes.

"Don't even think about it, nigga. I'll empty this clip in your head," said Babyface.

As Babyface observed the room, he looked over in the corner and couldn't believe what he saw...the most gruesome act a pimp could do to a ho. What shocked him even more was the particular ho he had done it to. While holding the gun in Lil' Hott's face while he laid on the floor not moving, scared to death, Babyface couldn't help but to notice Liddia crawled up in the opposite corner, butt-ass naked with all types of welts and wounds on her body. Lil' Hott had beat her with a T.V. antenna and poured salt on the wounds, which were so deep and thick he knew she would die if she didn't get any medical attention. As he took a hard look at her veins, instantly Babyface knew Tina had been a part of this scheme. She lied and said Liddia was a hardcore dope fiend, but from what he saw, besides the brutal scars that the gorilla pimp had just inflicted on her, Liddia was still gorgeous. In fact, she looked even better and was in extremely good shape. Babyface made a mental note to go find Tina and kill her first chance he got. Tina lied about everything, and she'd been lying to him ever since he came back to D.C.

He then started thinking, *It probably was Tina who set Vic up, but why? For all I know, she may have lied about King being locked up or Precious being Lil' Hott's ho. Come to think of it, it did sound kinda odd to hear that Precious would choose a pimp after she'd been with King ever since she was sixteen years old.*

Babyface was confused. He needed answers; he didn't know who to kill first; he didn't know if he should save Liddia or not. And how the fuck did Liddia end up with this nigga in the first place? He had questions that needed to be answered, so in spite of Victoria, he spared Liddia's life, which would be the second time he had saved her from being killed by a gorilla pimp.

"Get up, bitch, and put your clothes on. You're coming wit me," said Babyface as he kept his gun steady on Lil' Hott.

"Man, why the fuck you interferin' wit my pimpin'" asked Lil' Hott. "What! You mad about me taking your ho from you. Come on, you know the rules to the game. Your bitch chose me, and besides that, Face, fuck that ho! She did the same thing to me that she did to you. That bitch ain't worth nuthin'. She a renegade ho, but I took care of all that. You should be congratulating a nigga, not tryna kill a nigga. I took care of both our problems, and the bitch stole way more from me than you," Lil' Hott said, as he tried to convince Babyface to spare his life.

After hearing Lil' Hott's plea for his life, Babyface realized for the first time that the nigga didn't even know he was the one who put that master plan together. Lil' Hott thought Victoria was really a renegade ho, and that she just stole from pimps every chance she got. Most likely, Tammy and Nana told him that Victoria always talked about Penny and Liddia, so he thought he could come up to D.C., find Liddia, and beat Victoria's whereabouts out of her.

"Nah, bitch nigga, this ain't 'bout no ho," said Babyface.

"Then what's it about?" Lil' Hott asked. I know you ain't mad 'cause I got Pimp of the Year. Come on, playa, that's some petty shit. If you want the crown, you can have it. Just let me go back to Memphis where I belong." Lil' Hott then looked at his wrist at the platinum Rolex flooded with diamonds. Now he knew what this was about. "What! Man, here, you can have this Rolex back. The bitch gave it to me; I never asked for it," said Lil' Hott, knowing deep down inside he was lying.

"Nah, nigga, you can keep the watch. This ain't 'bout no muthafuckin' watch. This 'bout my sister," Babyface replied, as he cocked back the hammer.

At the thought of Victoria being his sister, Babyface was so fucked up in the head he wondered for a second if he should turn the gun on himself and blow his own brains out. For the second time in years, tears gushed out of his eyes like a waterfalls.

"Aw, come on, baby, I don't know your fucking sister. Who's your sister? This is my first time in D.C.," said Lil' Hott, while looking Babyface in the eyes.

"And I'ma make it your last nigga," Babyface replied, as he pulled the trigger.

*BOOM!*

While Babyface stood overtop of Lil' Hott's body and watched his brains ooze out of his head onto the motel's carpet, Liddia picked up Lil' Hott's gun off the nightstand. Babyface felt two hard blows take his wind. He never knew what hit him, and while falling to the floor, one more shot hit him in the back of his skull.

*BOOM!*

Liddia was standing over Babyface's body with the gun still smoking as Precious and King walked in the room. They watched the whole ordeal go down while sitting in the parking lot in King's brand-new black Eldorado with tinted windows.

"Give me the gun, boo. You did good. You did good," said Precious as she eased the gun from Liddia's grasp.

For a minute, Liddia was stuck in a trance. She couldn't understand what she'd just done. She killed her best friend's pimp/fiancée, but she didn't care. She had been brainwashed. She did it for her pimp, for her ho sistah and mentor, for her family…Precious and King, the royalty of 14th Street.

When King heard Lil' Hott was in town looking for Victoria and that she stole half a million dollars from him, King instantly started putting his plan together. King was from the old-school, and he worked his shit all the way around the board. His plan was to kill two birds with one stone. Everything he laid out went as planned, except for one major fuck up: he still didn't know where the money was stashed. He prayed that Victoria would live after Lil' Hott slit her throat. She would be the only one to lead him to the money. So, instead of letting her die, he had Precious and Liddia call the ambulance to save her life. He figured he'd get Babyface out of the way, and then prey on Victoria when she recovered. For right now, though, he'd settle for two iced out watches worth more than $120,000, and two dead young up and coming pimps, who were threatening his throne.

As King kneeled down beside the two dead pimps whom he had admired but hated at the same time, while taking off their jewels and emptying their pockets, he gave them a jewel that was so precious, it was obvious they missed out on it when they first entered the pimp game. "Well, boys, let me tell you a lil' something about the pimp game. You must know *all* the rules, and from the way it looks now, it seems as though you two were moving so fast that you missed the very first and most important one. So let me give it to you now, 'cause you'll need it in another lifetime. Lesson one, never trust a ho, 'cause the very moment you do, you become one yourself.

═══════════════════

Simultaneously, as Babyface's soul took flight out of this world, Victoria was waking up from her coma.

## THE END

**Want To Become A Cartel Author?**
**Want To Become A Street Team Member?**
**Want To Learn About New Cartel Titles?**
**Visit:**
**www.thecartelpublications.com**

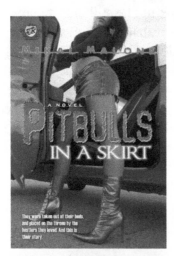

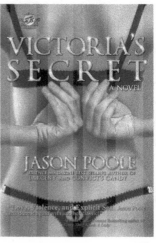

**For ordering contact:**
**Charisse Washington (410) 790-8976**

CPSIA information can be obtained
at www.ICGtesting.com
Printed in the USA
LVHW052104180922
728695LV00001B/30